T0340959

FOR A FEW SOULS MORE

WILE E. YOUNG

Published by Death's Head Press,
an imprint of Dead Sky Publishing, LLC
Miami Beach, Florida
www.deadskypublishing.com

First U.S. Edition

Cover Art: Justin T. Coons

Edited by: Christine Morgan and Anna Kubik

Copyedited by: Kristy Baptist

The "Splatter Western" logo designed
by K. Trap Jones

Book Layout: Lori Michelle
www.TheAuthorsAlley.com

ISBN 9781639511112

For fellow renegade Kristopher Triana.

PROLOGUE

KANSAS, 1880

DEEP WAS THE night as the stagecoach rattled along the trail. A solitary man sat atop it, a pair of horses pulling with all their might to bring him to the place that men spoke of in only fear and fable.

The air was humid; sweat pooled on his brow and he massaged his leg. It hadn't been the same since Lawrence. For nearly fifteen years he'd had to live with it, the changing weather

He focused on the old railroad stretching into the dark beside him. Folks told him it was a fool's errand to head out to these parts, there was nothing to see but scrubland and long-forgotten boomtowns. But that was what he wanted, what had been whispered to him in places that no honest, God-fearing man should have found himself in.

He didn't care anymore; the only thing he worshiped was six feet under Lawrence, lead resting in his head.

The man stared out of his one working eye, instinctively reaching with his right hand before he remembered that it wasn't there.

They must've thought him dead; he would have thought the same. There was just life and pain.

Now he found himself in the deadlands, looking for the place where all paths led in the end, and where the devil had been born. He knew that he was close as the lantern light pooled over the scrap of paper that passed for a map.

The coffin-maker had been specific, had told him how to find his revenge.

A breeze raced down the plains, the lanterns danced and rattled, and a chill raced down his spine. There were noises out in the night, groans that sounded like a great ship sinking into a dark sea.

Then he saw the sign, hanging at the edge of a town.

TRAIL'S END, POPULATION: 1

There had been a higher number, but it had been scratched out and replaced by the dark numeral.

Wrapping the reins around the stump of his arm, he reached down and unsheathed his piece, making sure that it was ready to spit death should the need call for it. But Trail's End was a dead place, wiped clean by the devil's own.

The church at the end of the street was silent and dilapidated; the cross at the top had been inverted, a long-decayed corpse hanging from the nails in its wrist. The General Store and the bank on Main Street were just as empty.

He could see the travel office and the stagecoach rotting in front of it. It was missing its wall, the corpses inside trying to shield themselves from what had come here.

The only light came from the saloon; it flickered from the doorway but did not beckon with warmth or the promise of rest. It was nothing but an invitation.

He brought the stage to a stop, dismounting slowly, groaning as his leg hit the ground. He aimed his gun, trying to blink to clear the sweat from his sight only for his left lid to catch on the lead where it used to be.

Cobwebs dangled from the ceiling, a few decayed corpses still sat around the tables, but the man who kept the bar watched him with hard eyes that showed no fear of the gun pointed directly at him.

"Put it away, sir. You won't need it here." The bartender's words didn't set him at ease. He didn't holster his weapon, but he did lower it, taking a deep breath before sidling up to the bar.

"Have a name, stranger?" the bartender asked, wiping down a glass and turning to retrieve something that looked like it had been distilled back before the country had been founded.

He accepted the shot the bartender poured for him before he answered. "Granger Hyde."

The bartender nodded his head and poured him another. "I'd say it was a pleasure to meet you, but I think we both know why you're here."

Granger downed the second glass and placed his gun before him. "If you're going to try to stop me, Mister, I won't hesitate."

The bartender chuckled darkly, pulling a cigarette from the pocket of his vest and flicking a match against the counter. "You've got the nerve, Mr. Hyde, but threaten me again and I'll be happy to air your insides." He blew a stream of smoke into the air. "The law ain't gonna come looking, I expect."

Granger stared at the man with undisguised loathing. After all, he had been partially responsible for taking everything from him.

"What you want is up there." The bartender pointed out of the broken window toward the church. "Just go on up there with what you brought. I won't stop you, long as you answer one question." He reached over and tapped what had been Granger's left eye, the shell of lead encasing it. The clinking echoed off the walls like a nail being driven into flesh. "Did my boy do that to you?"

Granger stood, showing the misshapen flesh where his hand used to be. "Yes."

The bartender nodded and pulled a knife from the underside of the bar. "You might be needing this."

Granger stared at the weapon, barely big enough to fit

3

in his hand, the blade made of black stone. He took it and tipped his hat to the bartender who nodded in return.

"Best of luck, friend."

He breathed hard as he returned to the stage, sweat running down his back. This next part was hard, but it had to be done, he had to bring justice. Nothing and no one else could do it. The man he had to put under couldn't be killed by a gun.

He threw open the door and the whore he had taken back in Buzzard Creek screamed. He'd bound her hands and feet, making sure that she couldn't use either to free herself.

She was pretty; dark brown hair the color of chestnuts with freckles across her cheeks, her wide eyes staring at him with fear. He felt guilty as he cut through the gag he had shoved in her mouth.

He'd paid her well over the days of their companionship, enough for her to believe that he would take care of her, and more importantly her unborn child. He played the part of an injured veteran, and when the time was right, he had taken her away.

"I'm truly sorry, Lizzie, you deserve better. But so did my boy."

He pulled the knife and began to cut the dress from across her stomach, smiling as the swollen belly emerged. She begged him not to hurt her or her unborn child.

Granger plunged the knife into her belly pulling sideways and feeling the heavy skin struggle to keep itself together, the dark blood pouring over his hands and into the dust of Trail's End.

Lizzie gurgled and her pleading cries of agony trailed off into nothing. Granger said a quick prayer for her before he dug his hand into her insides, feeling the warmth as he shifted aside her intestines until he found her womb.

His hand gripped the head of the unborn child. "There you are."

The bartender's knife did good work, and it did not

take much for it to open her womb, a musky scent wafting through the air.

Her flesh gave way, his regrets completely forgotten. The dead fetus in his hand was all that he needed, and he clutched it tight against his chest.

It was a long hill to the church and Granger took his time, careful to find his footing. When he reached the top there was nothing waiting for him but an open doorway.

He could feel it calling to him, and for a moment, barely a blink of an eye, instinct screamed at him to turn back. Then he strode inside.

There were few furnishings: rotten pews, the pulpit, and old moth-eaten drapes that hung over broken stained-glass windows. Something white lay on the altar at the center, a pale mass that filled him with dread but was the entire reason he had come.

It was shaped like a woman, this pile of salt. He could see her face, the defined eyes that were closed in grief, the mouth that was open in one last sob; even the fabric and designs of her dress were etched in extraordinary detail.

Granger approached her slowly, reverently, and placed the dead fetus on the altar, then turned to dig into the salt woman's belly, hollowing it out until there was an area big enough to fit the red corpse.

He placed it inside and replaced the salt until the small, undeveloped flesh was completely covered. Then he collapsed to the floor, feeling the pain in his leg, the unmerciful metal that covered his eye, and the ache of his missing hand.

"I don't know if you can hear me if this is how this is supposed to work, but I'm at the end of my rope and I was told this could bring an end to it."

He looked at the salt woman. "You were his mother, and he took my boy from me. I'm giving up my chance to see my son ever again, following the devil's trail just to see you, to settle the scores of folks he's hurt."

The wind blew in from the open door, but nothing

moved. Granger leaned forward and wrapped his hand around his stump in supplication, watching the lady's face for any sort of sign.

"You gave birth to monsters; all I'm asking for is that you do it one more time."

Granger had brought what was required, just like the coffin-maker had said. He had committed murder and now all he could do was plead.

"Please, I beg of you, send me her that can kill Salem Covington."

The salt woman's belly began to move.

CHAPTER ONE

LOUISIANA, 1881

MY STAGE MADE its way down the trail, endless cypress trees lining both sides of the muddy road, Spanish moss dangling down to rake their grey touch across my coat.

In the distance were the smokestacks of New Orleans and my dying teacher. It was the way of things; time marched on for every man and woman in this world, and for the great Voodoo Queen it was no different.

I mentally counted how many were left, that breed who knew the secret rites and words to track with the powers and principalities that blew in the wind, lurked in the murky water and nested deep in the earth. Not many, just stories of their times and lives.

And I knew them all.

I would have to be careful approaching the city. It had been a long time since I had been this far east, but there were still many men in this city who would love to see the Black Magpie swing.

I took a deep breath, drinking in the humidity, urging Soldier and Maestro onward, the twin horses pulling the stage faithfully, their many years beginning to weigh on them. They weren't the only ones.

My hand reached down and stroked the Gun's grip while it whispered sweet death into my mind. A bank robber at Silver Cliff had gotten away with his score only to find me waiting for him at his camp. I asked him how it felt to sell his soul for something so immaterial. Then I killed him.

That was the curse and blessing of the Gun, the bargain that had been struck: ten thousand guilty lives and my soul to keep. At least, that was what I'd been told.

Didn't have to be some scholar to know that I was bound down south. If any god took me in after this life, I'd have thought him a fool. Of course, I had plenty of track left and Trail's End was still a long way off.

A pained yipping drew me from my thoughts, and I pulled back on the reins, bringing the stage to a stop. My horses stamped the ground impatiently. A grey mist seemed to hang over the morning, drifting across the path and making it seem like the sky had come down to mix with the earth.

Someone was torturing an animal.

It sounded like a dog, and each yelp of pain was interspersed with the sound of multiple people laughing. I had run into enough torturers, sadists, and other sorry excuses for men that I knew what they were doing.

The Gun spoke to me, practically laughing in my mind as if there was another choice I would make.

I descended from my stage, drawing the Gun, and adjusting my coat and hat, plunging into the thick gloom in the trees.

It had been two days since I had engaged in my own cruelty.

And my weapon was ever-hungry.

"Get him again, Frankie!"

Frankie, a man with no shirt and three teeth, stood up carrying a glowing hot iron rod. He leered at his two compatriots who sat around the fire, brewing stew in a pot.

FOR A FEW SOULS MORE

A red wolf had found itself in a snare and these three men were busy making it suffer. It snarled and whined, teeth bared, as Frankie approached, its eyes reflecting the glowing light. Then the metal touched the beast's flesh and it howled, whining and trying to escape as its fur seared off, flesh peeling, leaving a melted ruin behind.

The wolf fell to the ground while Frankie held the cooling metal high and howled in triumph. I thought it sounded similar to the wolf itself.

"How long we going to do this? Stew is almost ready."

Frankie turned. I thought his long blond hair looked like dirty sunlight. He sneered, "Shut the hell up, Bennie. We aren't in a rush, plenty of trappers paying good money for a red wolf pelt . . . "

He glanced down at the whimpering animal. "Even if it is missing a few bits."

I regarded it all with a cold gaze, the flesh beneath my left eye itching, the old brand scar acting up, phantom memories of when something burning hot pressed into my own flesh.

Normally, I would sit and listen to them gab, scooping up their lives and stories. Let them spill out their secrets, who they were when no one was watching. These were the things that I lived for, the stories I could tell. But I wasn't some kind of hero. I just didn't believe in causing pain to something that didn't understand why you were doing it.

The brush pulled away as I stepped into the clearing, the Gun held tight in my hand. Frankie had a moment to look bewildered before the shot, the one that pulped his tongue and sent his teeth spiraling to the ground. He made a gurgling noise like he was trying to ask who I was, each movement of what was left of his jaw causing blood to bubble up and run like a waterfall from the hole in the back of his neck and from the gap where his teeth had been. Then his eyes rolled up and he toppled to the ground.

Bennie came up screaming and I put a bullet in his kneecap, making him scream louder. The last one went for the piece strapped to his hip and I turned, placing my Gun to his forehead.

This one was portly, and he tried to stammer out some plea that I barely listened to, leaning forward to take in his scent, a mixture of salt and an animal-like musk. A familiar scent.

"Pig farmer, are you? The other two as well?"

The man looked confused by my question. Most folks did when I began my inquiries if only to satisfy my never-ending hunger for stories, but he nodded.

"YOU SON OF A BITCH!"

I glanced at Bennie, who had finally decided that the meaty hole where his kneecap used to be was less important than the man who had made it disappear. He pulled iron and fired, but the shot went wild, catching his friend in the head.

The portly man's nose and lip exploded, splattering me with blood and teeth. The corpse fell straight into the campfire, the sizzle and pop of melting skin, complementing the sweet scent of cooking meat.

I sighed and wiped my face, smearing the man's blood into my stubble and across my cheek, drawing old Comanche war symbols.

Then I stepped over to the last living man, Bennie.

He pointed his piece directly at my forehead and pulled the trigger, but the gun misfired. He whimpered and thumbed the hammer, another misfire. Fresh tears came to his eyes as I gently reached out and wrapped my hands around the revolver's barrel. Try as he might, he would fail. I could not be killed by a gun.

I gently tossed it into the night and stared at Bennie silently, taking in the way that his lips quivered.

He stared back at me, but he only spoke when his eyes fell on the brand under my left eye. His mouth dropped open and he immediately began to plead for his life, calling out to Christ and anyone else that he thought could help him.

FOR A FEW SOULS MORE

"Shhhh, Bennie. I have questions for you," I said, putting a finger to my lip and pulling out the large Bowie knife sheathed to my hip.

"Please, Mr. Covington, please!" His voice became shrill as I reached for his scalp.

"No need to beg, that's a waste of breath. And don't spare the details of your friends or yourself. When I'm finished, that's all that will be left of you in this world."

Bennie screamed as I made the first cut above his brow.

The portly one had been named Angus. The three of them had been farming pigs for a few years together. Bennie had been married to Frankie's sister and Angus had been Bennie's cousin. When I had asked about the wolf, he said it had been killing their piglets, that they'd lost money, that it was just revenge and mindless cruelty.

I wondered how long it would be before their wives and the local law found what I decided to leave in this clearing. Their meat had slid off the bone easily enough from where I had cut into it. They had no possessions other than their scalps to take with me, and Angus's had been beyond saving from its place in the fire.

I'd had to settle for his teeth.

But it was the wolf that had fascinated me, whimpering in the snare, unable to walk, eyeing me with the same fear that it had the men. I made a quick trip to my stage to deposit my trophies and retrieve the things that I would need.

The wolf was still there when I returned and a simple satisfaction came through me. I had expected him to chew through his own leg to escape the snare, to die on his own terms. Instead, the fates had entrusted that to me.

The stew boiled over Angus's blackened and charred corpse while I took the bowl that Bennie had been preparing to eat with and ladled out the contents.

The root I'd brought with me crushed easily along with the other herbs. I whispered old words that would not hold meaning to anyone who might overhear me and inhaled the aroma, feeling the tip of my nose go numb.

Satisfied, I took Frankie's pulped tongue from where it lay on the ground and added it to the mixture. I dug into Bennie's heart with my fingernails and added the warm red chunks. My knife cut a bit of cooked meat from Angus's rear to complete the meal before I stood and walked slowly toward the wolf.

It whimpered, baring its teeth at me, screaming as I got within inches of it. I placed the bowl down, just out of reach, before I dug into the folds of my coat and brought out a blank piece of paper. "You'll need a name if this is to work."

The red wolf's orange eyes stared deep, and I stared back, thinking about the bayou and the people that had lived here.

"Roux," I said finally. "That's your name."

He only responded by baring his teeth and growling.

I reached forward whispering, "Seal it."

The wolf obliged, biting down hard between my thumb and index finger, blood running between his teeth before he retreated, moving away as far as the snare would allow him to go.

I traced his name three times onto the paper in my left hand with my blood:

Roux

Roux

Roux

The match came next, dancing flame reflecting Roux's eyes, and I burned the bloody paper, letting the ashes fall into the cooling stew. Then I slid it towards him and stepped back to wrap my wound.

Cautiously, the wolf stepped forward, sniffing at the concoction. Greedily, he began to eat.

CHAPTER TWO

ROUX SLEPT SOUNDLY next to me on the stage bench, the roots and workings I'd put on him keeping him under. He had eaten his fill of the men who had hurt him.

I'd turn him loose when he was whole again, but for now, he would sleep and dream of moonlight and the wild.

There were more than a few looks as I passed; well-to-do couples taking a walk under the overcast sky in all their finery, coppers in their bright blues standing on street corners and staring at the strange stagecoach rattling down the cobblestone road. I could only hope that they wouldn't recognize the description of my coach, or the man who drove it, because if they did . . . well, it would certainly be interesting.

The Gun whispered to me. I hadn't been expecting it as the recent deaths should have sated it, but it spoke more and more these days, hungry for blood.

There were shops with glass windows displaying such things as DYERS & SONS, HOBS AND BREWERS, and CITADEL HOTEL AND SALOON.

I ignored all these things and made my way to the outskirts of the city where the homes were. It seemed like the smoke from the metalworks thickened in the sky the closer I came to my destination. This whole city smelled of soot.

The trees had been cut down in the city center, replaced by the veneer of civilization, but here the grass was cut between the stone paths next to the road, and the trees twisted, shining with light.

There was a somber tone. People out on their lawns glanced at me as I approached the house that remained solitary like the rest of the Quarter had built up their dwellings at a distance out of respect.

Candles burned on the porch awnings, more were held in the hands of the people standing on the street outside the home. It cast an eerie light over their dark features.

Drums beat, slow and deep bass notes ringing and echoing across the block. A fire crackled from beneath the tree next to the wooden house, I counted a score or more of people, all of them come to pay their respects, and none of them given entry.

I slowed the stage to a stop. People made room for the horses, and more than a few whispered to each other about this strange white man that had come to visit the great Voodoo Queen.

I stepped down, leaving Roux on the seat. A young boy stood with his candle, his mother next to him with one hand on his shoulder.

"What's your name?" I asked him.

He looked with wide eyes at the Gun in my holster, his mother stepping between the two of us. "His name is—" she started.

"I didn't ask you," I replied, the grit in my voice a warning.

The boy found his voice. "Micah, sir."

"Micah." I chewed the name over in my mind. "What's your last name?"

"Clement, sir," the boy replied.

"Well Mr. Clement, you look about thirteen, am I right?" My hand drifted to the inside of my coat and Micah Clement's mother began begging, looking around desperately for help.

The boy nodded his head, his eyes wide. "I'll be fourteen next March."

I pulled two silver dollars from my pocket and held them before him. "Watch my coach for me? Let no one touch it, can you do that?"

The gleam in Micah's eyes matched the two coins. "Yes, sir. I'll watch it for you."

He held out his hand and I pressed the two coins into his palm, grabbing his wrist as I did. "Don't let them touch anything. I'll know if they do."

Micah nodded his head furiously. I felt the chill bumps break over his skin.

I released him and turned, opening the door to my stage and retrieving a small basket, making sure that the contents were covered. Then I approached the house.

The crowd parted before me, but the half dozen or so men who guarded the house closed ranks as I approached. They were all black men, just like the crowd; the only difference was that these carried repeaters, Winchesters by the look of them. I didn't bother going for my Gun. Fire as they might, they couldn't kill me. And I'd be damned if I was going to cause trouble while my teacher lay dying. Unless they tried to kill me with something other than a bullet, then I'd have to apologize for the mess.

"Turn around, white man. She isn't seeing anyone, not at this time."

I stared at him straight but didn't bother saying anything. I wondered if he had children, what his home was like and where he had gotten his weapon.

"Did you hear me?" he asked. His voice reminded me of a bellowing bison.

"I heard you. I've come to pay my respects and if you don't move from my path, I won't hesitate to end you." I spoke calmly, letting my hand gently tap on my pistol grip, then I waited for him to make his choice in favor of living or dying.

He raised his rifle and aimed it at my face. "Big talk for a no-account son of—"

"JAMES!" A man rushed from the house, his white

beard reflecting the candlelight. He stepped between the two of us. "Mr. Covington, don't kill him, he's young and hot-blooded." He held out his hand, close enough that I could have broken his fingers.

I smiled and I saw the tension ease out of the older man's form as I held out my hand in return, shaking his, "I've dropped men for less than that, Scipio."

Scipio nodded his head. "All the same, you and I both know she wouldn't want you killing folks on her lawn."

I laughed mirthlessly. "That's the only reason he's still breathing."

James made a noise that sounded halfway between a growl and a sob, and he aimed the repeater directly at my head. "Scipio, why are you listening to—"

Scipio glared at the younger man. "James, look at him, look at his face real hard and tell me what you see."

"Reckon I can help him with that, Scipio," I said, flicking a match and illuminating my face. I didn't focus on James but instead found myself fascinated by the warm light as it slowly ate the pale matchwood.

The match flicked out at the same time I heard James come to the realization. "Sweet Christ . . . "

This time, he stepped back when I stepped forward, Scipio nodding as he looked at the door. "She's been waiting for you, only you."

My heart beat faster; I had never really lost my apprehension for my teachers. Or their approval even if it was long lost.

I looked back at James before I went inside. He seemed to have shrunk a size or two, but it wasn't enough for me. I wanted him to remember and I wanted to remember him.

"When I come out, I want his finger. One he can live without."

James paled and Scipio nodded, gesturing for two of the men who came forward and grabbed the young man, who began to babble and beg.

I nodded at Scipio then turned and walked onto the

porch, slowly opening the door and entering into the gloom of the house.

A few women stood in the parlor, all of them holding candles and whispering incantations and workings to help ease their mistress into the next world. A few stood as I walked past them to the bedroom.

I paused, then knocked twice.

"Come in." It was her voice, one that I hadn't heard since my last visit, right after the war.

I opened the door and looked inside, pale moonlight drifting through a slatted window. There was a dresser on the wall to my left and a vanity decorated with multicolored candles, all of them flickering.

A large snake slithered across the floor, but the woman who sat on a stool next to the single bed ignored it. A bucket of cool water sat next to her.

The old woman opened her eyes when I entered, and a smile etched its way across her face. "My, my. The Black Magpie come at last."

I nodded to her and took her servant's place on the stool. "Hello, Marie Laveau."

CHAPTER THREE

"**C**OME CLOSER, SALEM. Let me get a good look at you." Her voice was weak, barely above a whisper, like the hiss of the snake that was still creeping around the room.

I leaned forward. "Trail's been hard, Marie. Might have a few more lines than when last you saw me."

She reached out and tapped the skin below my left eye. "Still see you're wearing that petro mark. Wondered if you'd gone and seen the light yet, but word reached me before you even came." She winked at me. "Whispers in the reeds speaking of three dead men laying at a campsite. That mark ain't ever gonna go away 'less you stop the killing."

My warm smile disappeared, and I sighed, taking off my hat and running my gloved hand through my hair. I couldn't rightly say why her words filled me with regret and the Gun whispered to me that nothing good would come from what she said, that we still had plenty more souls to send off to the fire.

"Hush now," Marie said, staring at the Gun. "Ain't for you to chime in on with your poison, just me and my bokor student."

The Gun bristled.

Marie chuckled, a rasping sound that flaked spittle across her face. The smile didn't leave as I dabbed the rag across her skin.

"Glad to see that you're still strong enough to keep it leashed. Most men would be nothing but violence and rage now."

"Don't think so lightly of me, Marie. Plenty of violence and rage in me and I'm happy to apply it when the mood strikes," I replied, replacing the rag in the damp water next to the bed. "Think it's long past time that I changed my course. You know that same as I."

Marie shook her head, her bones creaking. "What I know is I still see that boy before me, that pale boy and his brother wearing murder like it was a Sunday shawl. Knew much, too much already, but wanted to know about the Ghede, the spirits, and every bit of magic that I knew. Oh, I taught you much, as did others . . . and fate is paying us back for that."

She coughed again and waved me off as I went for the rag, hazel eyes boring into me deeper than any knife blade or surgeon's needle ever could.

"But that's why I called you here; you've stayed on your path, you've spoken true, but fate is lining up to walk that path to its end."

She had my attention, and even the Gun was silent, whispers dying into a cold quiet as I whispered, "What have you seen, teacher?"

Her pupils dilated, unfocusing from me and looking around at the unseen world that I had stepped into a time or two, but to her, teetering on the edge . . . It was always easier to cross over when you were close to death.

"I've seen the cloak of murder you wear tied around your neck like a noose, thousands of souls pulling to string you up, the thing you love most dead at your feet. The Black Magpie joins those below ground." Her eyes focused on me again, and I wondered if she could feel the cold chill that ran down my neck or the sudden burst of fear that I tamped down.

She patted my cheek. "No man nor woman knows the day and hour, but I can tell you that there is no running from this. Fate has vouchsafed it, and it gathers for you like thunder clouds."

For a moment it was like time had rolled back and the

strength that I remembered from long ago had come on her again, but when I blinked, she lay against her pillows sweating and frail.

Her eyes fluttered, and her hand fell away from my cheek. "Dying ain't easy, Salem. Hurts too damn much, but at least when I meet Papa at the crossroads, I'm going to the place where all good mojo flows. What I've worshiped my entire life."

I squeezed her hand. "You deserve it too, Marie. Isn't a place I'm likely to see, even if my soul does get free of the fire."

I reached down and picked up the small pouch that I had been tasked to deliver. "Louisianne sent this with me. She prays for your health, and barring that, a peaceful transition."

Marie chuckled. "That old mambo was always soft. Hate we never had more time. Nature of things, really. Not enough time."

We sat in silence for a long time. I chewed the roots Louisianne Robichaude had sent with me into a fine paste that I spit back into a bowl I found on Marie's vanity. I combined it with ingredients from a small altar in the corner of the room.

"She . . . she done taught you . . . well," Marie whispered as I sat back down, dabbing my fingers into the mixture and rubbing it across her eyebrows and under her nose.

"Rest, teacher, just rest," I whispered, adorning her with the working, drawing designs with my fingers that would protect her from evil.

When it was finished, the paste twirled around the wrinkles of age and adorned her with a mask to ward off bad spirits.

And then I whispered the prayer.

"Papa Legba, who opens the way, accept your servant who comes to you, open the way before her and accept her offerings of goodwill. These things I beseech you."

There were more words, but Marie Laveau did not stay in the world to hear them.

I took time to compose myself, taking time to make sure the snake was fed before leaving.

The women's low conversation ceased as I entered the drawing room. Their eyes stared at me, hopeful that I would provide some comfort.

They had forgotten who I was.

I looked at the servant girl. "She's gone."

The cries of grief were immediate. I didn't bother pausing to tip my hat for politeness's sake. I felt the grief tugging at the pit of my own soul.

Scipio waited for me, holding the severed finger I had requested. James sobbed in a heap close to the porch steps, holding his ruined hand. I stepped over him with barely a glance.

"Best start planning a funeral." I said.

Scipio sucked in a breath, tears beading at the corner of his eyes. "Suppose I should start the arrangements. A woman like her shouldn't spend much more time above ground."

He handed me the severed finger and I shook his hand. "Take care, Scipio. Don't think I'll be coming back this way much."

The boy, Micah, stood watching with wide eyes as I inspected my traveling home. Not a hair or item was out of place.

"Well done, Mr. Clement; best you and your mother be about your grief."

He nodded, those full-moon eyes never leaving me as he and his mother scurried away. The drums were beating louder now, the silent spell of the death vigil broken by the celebration of transition into the next world.

My grief would be found at the bottom of a bottle.

I urged my horses on and I left Scipio and the body of my teacher behind, watching as the living danced for the dead.

CHAPTER FOUR

I COULD HAVE lost myself in any watering hole. There were plenty of saloons in this city offering cards, whores, and whiskey. But my teacher's words haunted my ears even now, and every stranger that watched as I passed stoked the coals in my mind. If fate came now I was ready to meet it with bullet and blood. No one on this street would be spared, no one in this city if that was what came to it.

Wanted to lose myself and reminisce about my brother and my learning with Marie, didn't want to dull my senses. A bullet could not kill me but a dumb man with enough drink to mimic real courage could do the job with a knife.

So it was I found myself easing towards the riverfront, the muddy water calling to me. I secured my stage, making sure that Roux would stay asleep and comfortable. Then I picked up a particular timepiece among my collection.

My teacher's words had wormed their way under my skin like wooden splinters, and I would not walk here and there without assurance that fate wasn't stalking me.

The pocket watch had a sigil carved into it, similar to the brand under my eye but with a flowing more beautiful script. A timepiece of fine craft, and supposedly would countdown to your death when it came calling. It hadn't always done such, but it had been a witness to death: including that of its previous owner back in Silver River. Witness often enough that it had picked up its own peculiarity.

I pressed the release and the watch swung open, hour and minute hand still pointed firmly at twelve. Some of the tension eased out of me, and I put the timepiece in my pocket

I strode among the docks, eyeing the fishermen as they cut at their catch. The dirty water under the pier ran with blood and lapped at the shore where a thousand rotting fish heads lay in final rest.

The riverboats were in full swing, but one could not enter their dens of vice without invitation.

The news would be spreading now, that the Voodoo Queen was dead and that the Black Magpie had visited her.

I had left quite a mess behind me in my travels, and even if my face didn't grace many posters, my likeness was well enough known that every two-bit bounty hunter or lawman could try to make a name for themselves. I'd almost welcome it if they tried. I wasn't averse to killing a man in my grief. It was a salve for the soul as the good book said.

Plenty of my old haunts in this city and not one that I had fond recollections of. Virgil and I had spent much of our teaching in the deep bayou, and Marie hadn't been one for allowing drink when learning her art.

I found myself drifting to one that was a few streets away from the riverboats. CARMINE GRIFFIN SALOON was plastered on a fine mahogany sign hanging over the entrance, clean glass windows revealing the lively clientele.

Habit had me take a measure of folks. There were maybe a half-dozen tables, each full up with the city's well-to-do, fine greens for the women, rich whites for the men. It had been a rugged trail, and the dirt clung to me, more than a few heads turned my way. Most turned back with a sneer, whispering to their ladyfolk, while others never looked away.

Didn't care if they recognized me or not. I wasn't here to jaw, just drink.

I went like a shadow under too much light, quick and

fleeting, barely pausing before I reached the bar. Two oil lamps burned at either end and there was a menu with their list of fixings. The shelf behind was filled with the finest things a man could imbibe, and there was a nervous man tending them.

The barkeep was average as far as things went. His dark skin complemented his black bowtie, his apron and clothing fine thread, reflecting the quality of the establishment. I'd stepped into many drinking holes in my life, fine ones in boomtowns, and bare husks on the edge of civilization. Never a difference if they were willing to give you firewater and peace.

Money went towards a fine bottle and an offer followed for a woman, one I refused. Dried blood from my earlier kills still clung to me and the wide-eyed barkeep's eyes never left. I offered another coin for a bath. I could soak myself and reflect on where the trail was leading.

"Indulge in your drink while I have the girls warm a bath for you, sir. Perhaps a hand of—"

I turned away before he could finish, didn't have an interest in money or the opportunity to take it from those willing to part with it. I could feel more eyes on me as I moved towards the stairs.

A man in a light-colored Parisian vest was busy speaking to a saloon dove who feigned interest. Her hand rose to her mouth as I approached, and the man turned, ready to come to scratch, only to meekly step back and let me pass. My spurs echoed off the steps as I made my way to the second floor.

The conversations that had stopped resumed once I was out of sight, excited whispering pecking at the tips of my hearing, like woodpeckers come morning time. A smooth pop echoed off the walls as I uncorked the whiskey, taking a long drink.

Let them have a look, a sight at the untamed wilderness they had forgotten. Where a man's life hung on his ability to deal death. They'd go to bed that night, frightened of what they had seen, wondering how a man could live this way. And when I left, they would avert their eyes and say I was a night terror and nothing more.

Paintings hung on the walls, like most saloons they were just bland expressions of some form of landscape.

One painting caught my eye, a landscape of sparse saguaro and dust, a lone coyote etched into the canvas, fur as dark as chimney soot, and two dots of yellow seeming to stare straight into me. I recognized the brush strokes, the artist was dead near ten years now. Her paintings sold, stolen, or burned. I poured a small bit of whiskey before the painting, tipping my hat and whispering, "Keep sleeping, Mary Jo."

A girl appeared after my dues, keeping her distance at the far wall where the grand staircase descended back down to the patrons. "Sir? Your bath is ready."

I followed her across the landing to the other side of the floor, a long hallway stretched after with maybe half a dozen doors, and the bath lay in the very last one. The girl held the door open politely and I took a moment to look her over. Her mousey hair done up to look attractive, her lips painted a deep shade of crimson. She didn't meet my gaze and closed the door as soon as I entered, but I made sure to listen to her footsteps until they were long gone.

The room was small, vanity in the corner, and a grand fireplace as swell as any I had seen crackling as the flames consumed the logs inside. In the center of the room was the copper tub, water still steaming inside.

I removed my clothing. The Gun whispered as I made a move towards my holster offering enough temptation that my hand wavered over it. Had to remind myself who was the master, and who was the weapon. It was harder to holster it, harder to quit the killing. Not that I was in the business of trading my swords for plowshares, but I couldn't slaughter the entire world.

But that was exactly what it murmured to me in my dreams.

WILE E. YOUNG

I kept my weapon close as I eased into the water, whiskey in hand as I let myself soak and lose myself in recollection. Thought about Virgil, usually did when I gave myself time. Hard to believe I'd planted my brother near seventeen years ago. Few folks in this world knew the measure of our grit, how far off trail we'd gone to acquire our guns.

Marie Laveau had been one of those, and even then, she'd only seen the results. When Virgil and I had come calling after we'd pulled up stakes, she'd near refused to see us.

Sold my soul and hadn't looked back.

Virgil had. He'd spent his power looking back and regretting what we'd done to avenge ourselves on those that'd wronged us.

We'd had ears, but I hadn't heard. Two Guns for two brothers . . . one death by fate shaped.

Wouldn't have been surprised if the entire war hadn't been concocted by fate for us to kill each other. Plenty of souls we still owed at that point, plenty of blood that called, and the devil knew I'd reveled in the killing.

But Virgil, he'd had a different notion thought that we'd gotten the wrong hog by the tail. Said that we should throw both our Guns in the darkest hole we could find, and rid ourselves of sin and strife. We'd done killed those who needed killing.

Coming to blows, and then coming to bullets, I'd planted him in battle at Marmiton River. I'd never gone looking for his body. Plenty of things I could have done to find it, but I hadn't thought to look. Hadn't wanted to look.

His Gun was all that had mattered.

The only thing that could put me under, the only thing that could shuffle me off to the fire as easy as any other weapon. I'd dug through the muck at the bottom of the river until my hands bled.

Never saw my brother after that day, in this world or the next, but his Gun . . . that I had seen.

FOR A FEW SOULS MORE

My thoughts about Jake Howe usually followed. A soldier from out in the territory, he'd gone through the mill with me killing some men. Got ahold of my brother's Gun by the time it was all said and done.

Fate has a way of laughing at you when you think your reckoning has made its jack, when you think that you'll go the whole way towards getting your wants. It laughs and reminds that you're just a man.

A man who couldn't pull the trigger and murder a friend.

I'd wanted to kill Jake. Had felt my Gun's loving caress stroke over that dark place that rejoiced in murder, but I'd let him go with a bag of gold and a pretty woman.

No doubt he'd done some killing since then, taking up a Gun meant taking up its debt. Virgil and I owed ten thousand souls, and it was a long trail to kill so many.

But that was a path that was coming to an end. I had it in sight, an end to the butchery. At least the butchery that I owed.

Wasn't the first time that I wondered what it would be like when I was out from under that yoke. Had always seemed like a distant thing, always just over the horizon and never getting closer.

But now I was close, and that tattered and ragged thing I called a soul would be owed to no one.

The old coffin-maker might've been filled with the devil's own cunning, but he hadn't seen that I didn't give a damn about my soul or my brother's. Only thing I cared about was killing. And so, I'd killed.

I opened my eyes and stared at the water, the steam still drifting and the bubbles floating on top of the grime like my very self was the opposite of something clean.

Money didn't interest me any, I had plenty of it, the payroll of a hundred different bank coaches waylaid in the west. I even had a home out there, filled with all manner of things.

But that wasn't my path. I walked the killing fields to

bring ruin, and until I shuffled off to the bone orchard, I was going to keep walking it.

Still, I could dream about another life, one with young 'uns and a homestead, and clean of a state's worth of blood.

My thoughts were interrupted by a knock at the door. My hand jumped, nearly before I'd even had the thought, the Gun was aimed and ready to end whoever had nerve enough to confront me.

"Mr. Covington?" The voice was soft, a woman.

"I don't want company. I'm not going to ask again." I said it calmly, keeping the Gun aimed at the door.

She knew my name. If she was just some good time girl looking for a poke with a genuine outlaw, she'd move along with my warning. If she was here looking to make good on a reward . . .

I felt a grim satisfaction come over me. Easy enough to wipe off blood in a bath.

There was a pause on the other side like the girl was trying to decide just what her next move was before she quietly spoke again. "I need to speak with you, it's urgent."

Not many would keep at it after I'd told them to leave, and I wasn't burdened by an overabundance of patience. But the girl at the door intrigued me. She had a need, I could practically smell it, and my curiosity always weighed heavy over my temper. I'd listen to her story and decide whether she could go on breathing afterward.

The bathwater ran off me as I stood, keeping the Gun aimed at the door. Too many now-dead folk thought that the bath was the opportune place to draw iron and there were plenty of men that had met their end that way. I wasn't going to be one of them.

I retrieved my threads, pants, and shirt still bearing the dust and blood from the trail. Didn't bother with my knife, shouldn't need it if I kept my distance.

"Enter," I said gruffly sitting easy on the resting chair facing the doorway.

The door creaked open, and a woman walked in. She

came slow, both of her black-gloved hands raised and kept purposefully away from the two pistols at her hip.

She had a rugged beauty, raven black hair falling in curls below a wide-brimmed bolero. A knife scar ran over her right eye, marring her tan skin and speaking to her time in the wilds.

I knew a genuine article, could smell the death on her. Those guns had killed more than their fair share.

Her eyes tracked the Gun in my hand like it was a coiled snake. I gestured with the barrel towards the only other seat.

"Divest yourself of your irons. It's been a long road to get here, and I'd rather not see a few new holes in the wall."

The girl nodded her head. "You can ease yourself, mister. I know better than to try drawing on you."

I didn't lower my Gun. "All the same lay them down."

She unhooked her belt, holding up both her weapons and laying them on the floor, then sat in the chair facing me.

I laid my Gun across my lap. "I'm going to let you talk, seeing as how you went to all the trouble."

She nodded her head, "Trust me, I wouldn't be here if I didn't have any other paths to turn to. Mother always told me to steer clear of you."

It wasn't an odd thing to say, I'm sure plenty of mothers had warned their daughters away from outlaws and desperadoes. But the way she spoke had a familiarity I wasn't used to.

"What's your name, miss?" I asked.

"Amaya, Amaya Shrike, though that isn't the name I was given when I was born." She said it quick, eyes tracking the Gun, a learned skill in her trade of bank robbing.

I'd heard tell of Amaya Shrike, the young outlaw who'd been striking every bank stage that passed close to the Rio Grande and scurrying back over to Mexico before any posse could be put together.

The only detail of this same story that intrigued me was

her apparent savagery. Amaya Shrike supposedly liked to leave mutilated corpses in her wake, impaled on the cholla strewn across the southwest, limbs twisted all to hell like a bastardized crucifixion.

She watched my eyes, glancing at the brand there. Seeing if I had an inkling of who she was. I regarded her in turn, wondering if she knew that her courting of death was nothing next to the long-term engagement I'd had.

I knew her type and had met and killed a good dozen. She'd felt the unwanted touch of a man, probably a two-nickel cantina rat who'd seen her busy about town one night. Had marked her face when she'd fought, and when she'd gone home had probably seen her padre cast her out . . .

Only two options for a woman then: take up whoring or killing. Obvious to see which one she'd chosen.

I smiled. There was no joy in it, just anticipation. "Tell me your story, Miss Shrike."

She didn't hesitate. "I've robbed plenty, held up rich gringos making their way out to California, skinned banditos and slavers selling their women in my country, cut their pelotas off, and fed them to the coyotes." All of this was said with a coldness to it, a nerve that doesn't come to someone too deep in their drink. She'd done the things she claimed.

I briefly wondered if any of that had driven away the pain. The gnawing worm in her belly that whispered weakness to her and had pushed her to live by bullet and gun smoke.

"Stolen lives and their riches, but the money goes back to feed my village, El Jardin. Have you heard of it?" Amaya spoke earnestly, genuinely curious, but she couldn't disguise the glint in her eyes, the hunger for my answer. She knew that I was more than familiar with El Jardin.

After all, it was there Virgil and I had gone seeking our Guns.

My weapon had heard its tale in my mind. It whispered to me, urging me to put a bullet into the scorpion that had wandered into the room.

I forced the feeling away, my eyes glancing from the Gun back to the young woman in front of me. "I know El Jardin, but I would like to hear why you knew I'd be familiar with it."

Amaya Shrike seemed to breathe deep, deciding to herself how much she had to tell. Whether she wanted to go above board and show her whole hand early. I saw her fingers grip the edge of the chair, chipped nails digging into the upholstery before she spoke. "My mother is Olivia Verganza."

The name gave me pause, staring hard into Amaya's eyes for any sense of a lie and coming up short. My smile had disappeared coiling back into a passive frown. I saw the corners of Amaya's lips quiver from across the room.

"I spent many a night with your mother."

Olivia Verganza had been much more than just another poke, but I wasn't inclined to tell this girl things about fiery nights in the saguaro that ended with a mutilated gospel-slinger.

"I know. I came along after you left."

My heart didn't beat any faster, trigger finger didn't dance to end her life. I'd had plenty of startlements in my lifetime and this was just one more. Curiosity seized me as I watched Amaya and she watched me, her dark eyes fixed on my finger. Always supposed the possibility had been there, plenty of ladies of the line over the years.

"Are you claiming what I think?" I asked quietly.

She adjusted her raven hair away from her face, finally glancing away from the Gun to look me in the eye. "Yeah, I reckon I am."

The Gun awoke in my hand. It had been a long time since I'd killed kin. I had the impression that this would go a long way towards squaring things, a mighty temptation, just pull the trigger one more time.

Instead, I rose and laid the Gun down. Amaya seemed to sigh until she saw me retrieve my knife. Her hand jumped to her boot, a hidden blade flicking into her hand fast, and thrown at me even faster. A slower man would have been dead from such a blow, but as it stood, just a graze of skin brought fresh blood spilling down my arm.

Amaya was quick; like a darting bird seeing a squirming worm; her fist found its mark, sending me stumbling. Her hand found the Gun, and as my vision cleared, I saw she was aiming it true. Her eyes were cold, like twin chunks of black ice. She wasn't afraid to cut me down if it came to it.

"I'm not letting you kill me, gringo. My mother, and everyone else, speak of you like you're the devil. It's the devil I need." She whispered it, her voice the warning of a rattler's tail.

I didn't drop the knife, just took a step closer. I felt a grin stretch across my face.

She pulled the trigger and the hammer fell in a resounding click. Her eyes widened, just a bit. She tried to fire again and found that no matter her nerve, it wasn't worth spit when it came to me.

My Gun wouldn't kill me, and I could almost imagine a mocking laugh from it as I slammed her hand against the table. She let out a pained grunt and dropped my weapon. My knife was at her throat just as fast.

She glared at me with naked hate, couldn't disguise that kind of loathing, and whispered, "Go on, kill me."

I shook my head, smiling. I could imagine the sight; she'd given me a good knock to my nose, drawing blood. Probably looked like a wolf after chewing on a carcass.

"If I meant to kill you, Miss Shrike, I would have done it as soon as you claimed to be my kin. I just mean to see if you're speaking truth."

She didn't have time to contemplate my meaning before I nicked her, just barely enough to draw blood. I dipped my finger, coating it in her blood, and stepped away taking the knife with me.

Amaya pressed her hand to her neck as I focused on the drops of blood running down my finger.

FOR A FEW SOULS MORE

Most civilized folk had forgotten the old ways, the secret rites done in the dark of night when not even the owl called. They turned to the answers that these so-called men of science and rationality gave, the ones that traded away terror for reason. But those men didn't reign where I walked, and I sought my answers from things unseen.

I found a bowl set on the vanity should I want to shave, scooped it up, and dabbed at the bottom of the bowl, smearing Amaya's blood across the base.

My blood followed, a quick swish of thumb drawing across the bloody line running from my nose. I smeared it across the opposite side. I felt Amaya over my shoulder as I began to draw the rite in the center of the bowl.

"What is this?" she asked quietly.

"Blood seeks blood, Miss Shrike, going all the way back to the beginning. We're all just the total of what came before, for better or worse."

She didn't speak as I muttered the secret words to an old hoodoo rite to find a child's true parentage. It began to take form immediately, my blood moving on its own accord to the center of the bowl, covering one-half of the symbol I'd drawn. Amaya Shrike's blood did the same, running across the smooth surface and finding mine, covering the other half of the symbol.

Can't say it surprised me, but it was different seeing the truth before your eyes. I set the bowl down and gestured for Amaya to sit, taking my place across from her again. "Well, Miss Shrike. What is it you want from me?"

CHAPTER FIVE

THE NIGHT HAD begun to rage, wind whipping through the wet streets, spreading the ash from distant smokestacks along the brick streets. I could hear the gale like a howl, as if a giant wolf was hunting lost sheep through the back alleys. But to hear Amaya tell it, much worse things were out stalking the world tonight.

"I thought we'd robbed some cabron's slave train. My men thought we'd get a decent payout. These traders get good coin for the women they sell."

Common thing, ragtag bands escaping a reservation; Comancheros, Mexican banditos, outlaws trying to trade in flesh . . . plenty of girls had been traded away across the border into lawless lands.

The wind howled again and Amaya's head whipped around to look out the window, her whole body coiled tight like Roux's had been when I'd rescued him so many hours earlier.

"What are you scared of, girl?" I asked quietly.

Amaya looked back at me warily. "Them who burned El Jardin to the ground. The same ones I escaped to come looking for you, Los Demonios."

I leaned forward, trying to get the full measure of her eyes. The scent of her story wafting off her like the musk of a deer that sensed its end was near.

"There was no money, Mr. Covington, just women. Two dozen or so, whores and girls, all of them swollen with their babes."

Amaya's fear evaporated her smile widening, a coy grin that spoke to the suffering she'd inflicted. "We set them free, killed every last hijo de perra that had laid a finger on them. Threw a few that turned yellow belly down a dark hole for the snakes and brought all the women back to El Jardin. Mama was happy to welcome all those that wanted to work and promised the rest safety. Brother Rodrigo even laid out a celebratory feast at the mission."

I could see it in my mind: overjoyed women, thinking themselves safe, joyous banditos and peasants who looked up to Amaya like she was a savior. El Jardin, the garden of empty promises that I had once wiped clean of the false prophets. But killing lying serpents didn't prevent more deadly things from finding their way to paradise.

Amaya continued her tale. "They came when the night was on us. There were five, they killed any man they saw . . ."

There were no tears from her. This was a woman who had moved beyond such things. Death came for us all and by her own words she'd dealt more than her fair share.

But it was the fear that intrigued me. I was of the notion that she didn't fear much, so to see the dread so naked on her face, these riders that had destroyed El Jardin would have been terrifying indeed.

I leaned forward. "Describe these devils to me."

Amaya glanced at the half-empty bottle of whiskey, rubbing the knuckles of one of her hands. "I could use a drink; the trail has been long."

I gestured for her to help herself. She walked to the small vanity and took a long swig, a small weary breath escaping her as she stared at a corner of the room.

"The first rode before the rest, a Chinaman by the look of him. His attire was strange, like caballeros from a storybook, si?"

I nodded, trying not to let her know that I already had an inkling to the man's name.

"They came firing into the mission, and this man, he

threw himself off his horse, no fear of death. He carried a strange blade, long and thin. He carved like a butcher. He smeared himself in my men's blood."

She took another drink and held up three fingers. "I put this many bullets in him, but he did not stop. I saw the blood, but he did not die." She paused and looked into the whiskey. "I have done bad things to men. But this man was like the devil had entered him."

I gestured for the drink and she passed it back to me. I wet my lips as I gave her the rider's story. "His name is Sagara Katsutomo. Reckon he could be called a caballero if one looked at it a certain way, but he was called samurai in his homeland. A vicious killer I was told, though from what I heard he went soft in the head as the years wore on him."

Amaya leaned forward. "How do you mean?"

I pointed to the brand under my eye. "They say he began to see this on everyone, went mad, butchered whole families." The wind seemed to cry out for the poor tortured souls as I spoke. "Skewered babes in their sleep, all for bearing my mark."

Amaya didn't shudder, not quite.

"His masters declared him dishonorable, took his lands, would have taken his head too. But he fled here, where fate delivered him to me. If there was a devil in him, it reached above its bend."

I offered the drink back to her. This was one of the finer stories I'd collected in my travels. Amaya took the bottle, finishing it off to nearly empty, and glowering at me. "You should have killed him."

That would have been the simple thing to do, and that was how most tales regarding folks I'd run against ended. But there were a select few, left alive to their shame. Shame led to hate, and hate led to thoughts of revenge, and when they came calling on me a second time, their soul was ripe for my Gun and me.

Monstrous men broken on the wheel of the world. Made for a much more interesting story.

But I didn't tell Amaya this, I just finished my account. "No use killing a madman. I took his armor, took his sword, and last my eyes laid on him, he was chained to another man putting iron down for the railroad. I rode away with what coin they gave me. I remembered the feel of his strange armor, the heft of his cunning blade, fine additions to the trophies I'd taken."

There was a ghost of a memory across my chest, right where his sword had tasted my blood. One of the better licks given to me. To know he was out in the world again . . . my trigger finger tapped against the Gun, anticipating when he would come.

Amaya watched me, the drink heavy on her, eyes blinking rapidly. "You are a cruel man, Mister Covington."

I didn't deny it, didn't bother defending myself. There wasn't use in such things. Sometimes it was out of cruelty, sometimes I just wanted to sate my thirst.

"Tell me about the others, Miss Shrike."

A large burst of laughter echoed from downstairs, loud enough that Amaya flinched, eyes flicking to the door like the law or something worse would come bursting through.

I realized that the wool had been pulled over me, not by intent or purpose, but by my own curiosity, so hungry for stories from this long-lost daughter.

"Pick up your guns, Miss Shrike. They're coming. Sagara and the rest, these people who killed your mother."

Amaya immediately reached for her twin pistols, fastening the belt around her waist. "Not killed, taken. They made sure that every woman was taken."

There was a cruel shimmer to her eyes, and I didn't need to ask why she had been spared despite her reputation and no doubt impressive efforts at putting El Jardin's attackers underground.

I knew what had happened to her, and I felt rage begin to simmer like coals deep in my belly. It had been years since I'd felt the sweet ire, and I already began to think of the violent delights I could visit on such men.

The Gun purred in my lap.

She was my daughter and that made her mine, woe be to the poor soul from now 'til trumpets sound who forgot that.

Amaya's eyes became hollow. "They chained us in a wagon after. I picked the lock easy enough and waited for my time. The caballero and the other four riders, they were not with them. This is the only reason I escaped."

Her eyes danced. "The bastard, the one who forced himself on Mama? I ripped his throat out the first night and stole his horse."

I nodded slowly. "Your ma told you to come find me., is that it? Can't say that I see you seeking me out otherwise."

Amaya pursed her lips, a decision not to give me an answer. "Mama told me stories of you, tales of my father when I was just a little girl."

I was curious why she would tell me this. "And what did you hear?"

"Nightmares," she replied.

There was more I wanted to ask her, wanted to learn. I could have spent a whole evening listening to her tale, but what little time she had garnered in her escape had been bought on luck.

The laughter downstairs died, the held breath of those who had not processed what had come. Then the screams began.

CHAPTER SIX

AMAYA WATCHED THE door as I put on my coat and hat, keeping both of her guns aimed and ready. The chorus line of pain downstairs had been silenced. I picked up my Gun and checked for bullets.

Amaya glanced at me, and I looked back as I strapped my knife to my belt. "Law will be here soon. I don't aim to find myself strung up on the leafless tree tonight."

She nodded, putting her back against the wall next to the door, guns clasped tight. "Where do we head, once we've killed them?"

I adjusted my hat, clasping the brim tight. "My stage is not far. We go there and then we head west. To find these men who took your mother."

A vengeance trail, a familiar path for me, but rarely did I go about the business of rescuing folks. I pulled the silver timepiece out as I approached the door, looking at the hands still rooted firmly in place. If death was gathering for me, it wasn't coming tonight. Though, the same could not be said for those in the saloon below.

I kicked the door open and stepped into the hall. Three men stood at the head of the stairs, all three with peacemakers in hand. They wore red hoods, and beneath them, their eyes widened. Their trigger fingers pulled, and wood splintered around me, an unlit gaslight shattering. No bullet could find me.

My first shot took the lead man in the gut, a stain spreading under his shirt and dripping to the floor. I heard his grunts of pain as he dropped, more tears leaking out the eyes of his mask.

The other two retreated, still firing, as they took cover at the end of the hall. I reached the man I'd shot and put a bullet between his eyes.

Amaya emerged behind me, twin revolvers firing. Both men ducked as she hurled curses in her own tongue. I walked calmly, mentally counting my tally; these men's lives would put me ever closer to being square with the house.

Two quick shots ended their lives, red masks stained with new streams as their blood ran from cavernous and tattered wounds. I didn't pause to take trophies from them: such things would come later if time and fate permitted.

The top of the landing had already been painted with the macabre visitation; two women were sprawled on the top steps, one face down, a bloody hole in her back marring the white lace of her corset.

The other stared at the ceiling with sightless eyes, mousey hair splayed behind her like a dead angel's halo. The young girl who had led me to her room. Her crimson lips were smeared, and her mouth yawned wide in silent pain. Someone had knocked her teeth out, blood from the pit where her nose and cheek had been drained into her empty mouth.

I heard Amaya swear when she saw the two.

I reloaded my Gun as I looked over the landing and into the saloon below. More than enough bodies to keep the local coffin maker busy. Some had tried to run, but none had tried to fight. They had gone to their death screaming like lambs in sacrifice.

A half dozen or more men in their red masks stood around the saloon, a few nudged their worn and mud-caked boots on corpses that looked like they might still catch breath. The rest aimed their irons at me.

The sound of pouring liquid caught my attention and I turned to see a man behind the bar. He was young, just saddled into manhood. A glass was held firmly in his left hand, missing the trigger and middle finger, and with his other he poured a drink.

"Should have killed that little viper as soon as we saw her. Damn bad luck, we come chasing her and run into you. The boss didn't want us to tip our hands but fuck it, I've been looking forward to this," the man said, just loud enough that I could hear him. Even with the bygone years, it was a voice I recognized.

Never could forget the victims left behind me.

"Hello, Thomas. Been a while," I said.

Thomas didn't raise his glass, tip his hat, nothing else in greeting. He stared hard razors at his glass. "Mama caught the wet lung the winter after you killed my Pa. Couldn't afford a doctor. No one pays a thirteen-year-old who don't even know how to shoot."

I didn't interrupt him while he spoke, least I could do. His Pa hadn't been someone who'd deserved to die, just a man in the way of my vengeance. And when Thomas had tried his own hand at playing killer I'd removed a few of his fingers.

With his styled facial hair, bright white vest, and pants, he looked like a dandy that pretended to draw iron but whose grit wasn't worth spit. But his eyes spoke a different story. Half a decade could change a boy just as well as it could change a nation. Thomas wouldn't hold back on doing the devil's work.

"You don't even remember him, do you? My Pa." He laughed bitterly and waved his glass through the air. "The Black Magpie! Taker of souls, stories, and lives! Except for the innocent, the folk just trying to live an honest life." Thomas took an angry swig, downing the entire thing and throwing the glass to the floor. It shattered and his feet crunched across the shards as he walked around the bar. "Isn't that right, Covington?"

Amaya came from behind me, her revolvers clutched tight. I heard her spit when she saw Thomas. She whispered to me, "That is one of them, the horsemen."

When he saw Amaya, Thomas smiled like he'd just seen his dead father come stomping from the pearly gates, his unmaimed hand drifting to his holster.

"That canister won't help you, Thomas. Thought you'd know that" I said, letting the Gun trail over to him, barrel pointed at his heart. My iron hummed, having long looked forward to the boy come calling. Seeing him here, now, stoked the killing urge something fierce. He would die braver than most.

Thomas grinned, like a coyote seeing a desert carcass. "That devil piece might keep you breathing, but it ain't got any claim on that girl behind you."

He drew iron and I put a bullet in his head. Thomas blinked, opening his mouth only for a gurgling stream of blood to splash out of his mouth, staining his white vest.

I'd killed three more men before he'd hit the floor.

Amaya tipped a wooden table at the top of the landing, decorated with lilac to give the Carmine Griffin a veneer of civility. The wood splintered as the three remaining men did their damndest to lay her in the ground.

I descended the stairs and let my Gun sing. The first shot took the leading man through his arm. Tendons ripped and bone shattered as he dropped his piece and cradled his ruined appendage, yowling like a tomcat.

The other two men realized the danger. They both began to hastily find their ammunition belts, their guns empty. I could hear the panting, the desperation. Their hands trembled.

I didn't end their lives, but my new companion decided to play her own hand. Twin shots and two bodies fell. Handfuls of bullets spilled from their hands out across the stained floor, rattling across the wood until they rested against departed flesh.

Her guns smoked and I tipped my hat to her. She returned the gesture and immediately went to reload her weapons. I mirrored her motions with my own.

Much more wicked things than simple death were on

my mind. Stepping through the carnage, I approached the last man, spurs slapping through the rivers of blood seeping through the floor.

The man I'd shot crawled backward, holding the remains of his right arm like a mongrel that had stepped on a thorn. He'd dropped his gun when I'd wounded him, and now he was just a fat worm trying to squirm its way back into the night.

My boot found his arm, spur pressing down into the bone. I watched as the man howled and thrashed like a babe left abandoned in the crib. Squatting down, I removed the hood and found a tear-stained face beneath the cloth, stubble caked with wet trail dust, eyes as wide stage wheels.

Recognized him as Isaac Blankenship, an ex-Pinkerton who'd once attempted to send me down to Yuma Prison. I'd put a bullet in his side and left him for the vultures under the hot sun.

I reached out and grasped his head, pulling it close as I whispered to him, "Need answers from you and when I'm finished, I'll kill you. A quick bullet or slow pain, your choice." I pressed my boot down and heard something pop as Isaac wailed, nodding fiercely as his feet danced on the floor.

"Where are you taking the women and what do you want with this one?" I asked plainly.

"P-paid us to ki-kidnap every woman who wouldn't be missed. T-taking them to someplace called Trail's End," he gasped.

I felt the blood run cold in my veins and even the Gun stopped its song. Couldn't say that it was impossible but hadn't ever thought anyone would go there.

The wounded man took my silence for tacit understanding, and he continued. "We-we didn't care about her. The boss, he- he didn't want you to know yet. He needs the women, needs them for something."

I heard Amaya's footsteps as she joined me. Keeping her pistols trained on the man, she spoke low. "What does this Bastardo need them for?"

The ex-Pinkerton shook his head, whining that he did not know. I let his head fall from my grip as I reached for the ruin of his arm. "Wrong call." My gloves dug through the flesh, making sure I had a good grip on the bits of bone my bullet had left intact. Then I began to twist.

Behind me, Amaya's breath quickened like a roadrunner's swift feet. I felt the bones splinter in my grip. Felt tendon and muscle ripping as I twisted the arm full round. Those who had never inflicted real pain didn't know how a man could howl like a mourner seeing her dead children. It was the sound of folk who couldn't rightfully endure anything more and had to regardless.

When I'd bent it true, I dug my boot into the man's head, spur cutting across his eyeball as I braced myself. Then I tugged hard and listened to the wet drip as his arm came clean off, and the blood ran fresh. I breathed deep, holding the limb, feeling the warmth drain as the ten-cent man beneath me shuffled off to hell. Didn't need his name, or his story. Had enough of both, just wanted the look of fear in his eyes. I always looked for some inkling if they saw their eternity there.

The foxes were in the henhouse, my years of collecting possessions and lives had yielded all manner of things like my own city of gold. All of them left in Trail's End, my home, and these men were heading there.

I retrieved my Gun from its holster, dropping the dead man's arm. Wondered how I looked to Amaya, staring at my weapon. My weapon and I spoke, unheard by anyone except the dead. It growled in my head to kill her, abandon my notions of rescue. Always had been said that all lives came to Trail's End.

"What is Trail's End?" I heard Amaya ask the question and I half-turned to regard her, wondering if she could see my finger snaking around the trigger. Couldn't say if I would've killed her, though the thought certainly was there.

It was Thomas' pained laughing that brought me back.

Both Amaya and I looked, her eyes wide, nose flaring like she'd just caught a whiff of something rotten.

Thomas rolled over, glass crunching as it tore into his vest. I met his gaze, ignoring the hole in his forehead. His grin was a rictus, a dead man's joy. "You're not the only one who a gun can't kill. Not anymore, Salem. The senorita put one in my heart not three days past, but now, I can't die . . . none of us can die."

Thomas howled like a traveling show performer, and when he had finished, he held my gaze, thinking he had me quivering. Thinking that I hadn't walked with dead men.

I put two bullets in him the second time.

"God in heaven," Amaya whispered.

I barely heard her. Time had gone out to pasture as I realized just what my teacher had been trying to tell me. Death came for us all and she was out stalking these streets. I'd kept her waiting for a time.

I began to walk towards the door, glancing at the timepiece I carried, the hands as still as the grave. Amaya came after. I could hear her boots falling in close behind me. She was smart, and didn't stand directly in front of the swinging doors so the light would illuminate her. Couldn't say the same for me.

The night wept. Rain that had been kept in its airy safe by the storm came down, lighting flashed and showed me the waiting men. And throughout this city, around massive bonfires that not even the deluge could quench, men and women mourned for a voodoo queen.

"Aim true and kill every last one," I said.

Amaya nodded, and together we left The Carmine Griffin behind.

CHAPTER SEVEN

SAGARA KATSUTOMO WAS waiting when we stepped out of the saloon.

He roared like an angry boar, and I saw the blade glint against the gas lantern hanging from the awning. I turned, quicker than most men, but still felt the slicing pain.

He'd cut through my coat, drawing a long line of red up my arm.

I pulled the trigger as he brought his blade around to take my head. His armor splintered, the shot sending him stumbling back. A killing wound, even if I knew that whatever power rode with these men wouldn't let them rest. Not while I was still drawing breath.

More of the red-hooded men were mounted up, trying to keep their horses steady as the thunder rolled around us. Amaya spat a curse and began firing. A few horses panicked, her bullets lodging in their thick flesh, tossing their riders who tumbled into the mud.

Amaya didn't show mercy, chewing through the men and sending their guts into the mud when they tried to stand. There had been eight that I could see, and she killed five before needing to reload.

The remaining three spread out, one held a scatter gun clutched tight, Amaya had gone into the storm, laying near on her back in the muck behind a trough, digging in her belt for her ammunition.

The thunder masked my shot and half of the man's face went splattering down into the muck. He blinked with his remaining eye, trying to comprehend his situation before he toppled into the mud.

Amaya rose and the nearest man's throat and jaw disappeared; he made a choking sound, his tongue flapping against the ragged tendons, his eyes rolled up as he died.

The last man attempted to run but found himself staring down the city's law. Two dozen or more figures in blue illuminated by the lightning flashes, whistles blowing like prairie winds. He put his hands up, sinking to his knees.

Horses milled about, Amaya and I didn't speak as we mounted up, urging the animals forward. I spared a glance back at The Carmine Griffin just as Katsutomo was pulling himself to his feet.

And Thomas emerged through the swinging doors.

Plenty of nights I'd spent hunkered inside my stage listening to the rainfall while I worked the art. My teachers, they'd all labored that this was the true way one should work, while creation screamed and threw its fury.

I knew of many magics that could throw these men off our trail, but they were not the men that plagued my thoughts. If I thought the two deathless men we'd left at The Carmine Griffin weren't coming for us both, I'd be a fool.

We rode down the Quarter, hooves clattering on the cobblestone streets, the mud left behind as we rode through the crowds. The whistles sounded again like the pleas of sinners as four men came on horses. A wagon had pulled ahead, blocking the streets, a garden's worth of deputies leveling rifles.

A long wall ran to our right, grotesques perched every few feet, rictus grins mocking. An iron gate was ajar, and tombs and mausoleums framed like dark mountains against the furious sky.

I heard a shot and felt the horse shudder under me, the two of us tumbling across the stones. Both horses fell with pained whinnies while I staggered to my feet, stumbling over to Amaya. Her horse breathed painfully, each exhale heaving fresh blood into the street.

"Covington! You and the woman lay down your weapons!"

Couldn't be sure which lawman had opened his mouth, but I didn't rightly care. I fired, taking one of them through his head. The rest didn't hesitate, their shots ricocheting around me.

Never had to worry much for anyone else when the shooting started. But while a gun couldn't kill me, the same couldn't be said for those standing close. Over the rain I heard the soft splattering of flesh and Amaya's cry of agony.

The lawmen who'd been pursuing us dismounted, each one heeled and firing. Mists of blood puffed out of each horse's corpse as I reloaded and Amaya crawled behind them. She held her guns close, staring up at me with hard eyes. The meaning there was as clean as a freshly scrubbed boot.

The Gun laughed, and we killed.

I wasn't sure if they'd added something to my broadsheet or they just believed the stories, but a few were running down the street, knives held out, but all fired for my hide like stampeding cattle.

It was the smart choice if a man wanted to kill me proper. As it stood, their meat decorated the cobblestone streets. I didn't stop when their blood ran through the cracks between the stones, I didn't stop when they pleaded to God, I didn't stop when I perforated their backs with as many shots as it took to make sure they'd never walk again.

I didn't stop.

The Gun purred in my hand as I returned to Amaya.

I eased Amaya onto my shoulder, hearing her suffering as she tried to move her ruined leg. She looked up and down the street at the dead as I helped her toward the graveyard.

"These aren't getting back up, why did the others?"

Didn't bother responding as I wrenched the gate open, hearing the squall of the hinges as the thunder boomed overhead. Amaya dug in with her one working foot when I made to enter.

"My leg's gone. I'll just slow you down if you keep dragging me, no better than a hay—"

I didn't let her finish. "Got workings enough to fix flesh, soon as we make it to my stage."

She panted hard; her face already pale. "Don't think I'm going to make it that far."

I ignored her words, pulling her forward. She stumbled with me, hair dripping like dark moss over her honeyed skin. The sight brought me back to Marmiton. There had been plenty of boys pulled from the river looking just like this, ragged death wounds crawling with beetles and the fish who swam in their hollow bodies.

My brother had died there, amidst the water and screams, the cannons sounding like thunder. But at the time, and every year since, I remembered the stillness that had settled over us when we'd drawn on each other like death had laid a blanket over the whole damn world.

The cemetery carried that same quiet, the sky ceasing its weeping when our feet found their way onto the stone path between the tombs. I could see the trees waving in the distance, far over the tops of the stone mausoleums.

This wasn't some two-bit boot hill in a nowhere desert town; this was decadent death. Worshipers who'd thought to flannel mouth the end and the devil when they came calling.

Didn't suit me and I spat as we came to a crossing. Each direction was lit by small flickering candles, the names of their occupants under the dirt catching the shadows as the flame threw them. The air was heavy and humid, deep enough that I could smell the working in the air. I learned everything from the greatest shamans and magic workers across the length and breadth of the land, so I knew the scent of it, creeping through the stone and Spanish moss that draped over the tombs like a widow's shroud. It maintained the quiet, kept the shouts of distant lawmen like echoes off a canyon wall, and made the sky hold its fury.

I heard her humming before I saw her.

A light melody, but one that carried with it the wailing of a thousand mothers crying for their dead children. A shadow came from a path further down, and when she stepped into the dim flicker of the candle's glow, I felt the chill race through my heart.

She was clothed in a fine dress that seemed to be cut from the black sky overhead, a corset of dark leather wrapped around her waist. She was heeled, a pallid white peacemaker jutting from the holster like a dead man's finger. A wide-brimmed hat supported a mourner's veil, obscuring her face, and what little flesh showed between her dark gloves and silk sleeves was paler than the unseen moon.

My heart raced, the brand under my eye burning like the iron had just pressed into my flesh and I gripped the Gun tight while a creeping fear came over me. I was afraid of nothing that walked this world or the next except her, and I watched her like a man watched a coiled snake.

Amaya wheezed in my grip, sagging a little bit more. The blood dripped out of her leg in a staccato beat but even so, she aimed a gun at the woman. "Out of the way, senora."

The woman laughed, a dry sound, and spoke. "You're close, Amaya, I can smell it on you. Tell me, can you smell the sweet earth yet?"

"The girl is with me. Plenty of souls here for you, Lorelei," I said, keeping the Gun pointed straight at stone. I was more than sure I'd best her drawing iron, just like I had when I was barely a man.

FOR A FEW SOULS MORE

I couldn't see her face beneath the veil, that pleasure belonged only to the dead and dying, but I sensed she was smiling. "No wealth or ruin sways me, Salem. It is a sweet drink before you, I've waited for so long." Her hand drifted to her holstered weapon, the fabric of her glove rubbing across the handle. "I've walked amongst your prizes, so many tormented in restless death. You, my love, I've come to reap."

I felt the weight of my Gun. "I can't be killed by a gun, Lorelei, not even yours."

Silence filled the space between us before she spoke, her voice as soft as a billowing shroud. "I know, that's why I brought help."

The gate behind us squealed; Thomas and Sagara Katsutomo had caught up. Thomas waved his hand I'd maimed so long ago. Katsutomo's eyes burned like prairie coals, his blade scratched against the stone as he trailed it across the graves.

I leaned Amaya against the nearest tomb, the occupant's name long since faded from the white alabaster stone. Her eyes fluttered, struggling. Then I aimed at the two men who'd come seeking their satisfaction.

"How many times do the two of you want this? If you have the stone and nerve, come and kill me, but I swear this to the both of you: the bullets I put in you this time will be the last."

I didn't make idle threats. I'd tear them to pieces this time, see if they could get back up with their innards spread all over the damned city.

Thomas' mouth split in a wide smile, the gaps between his teeth stained with his own blood. "Keep talking guff, Salem. We ain't scared no more. Too many souls crying for your blood, for justice." He leaned against a tomb, staining the wet stone with his own blood. "And Miss Lorelei has a hold on more than just us."

I heard the rustling. A corpse stepped from behind a towering crypt along the left-hand path, clambering like an animal onto a headstone. It was Gwendoline Bell, her face mottled and near formless from the past flame that had consumed it, strands of hair clinging to her head, black as the mud her bare feet stepped in. Her clothing was handmade, sewn from the pelts of animals that she had no doubt killed with her hands, but it was the string of skinned faces hanging from a bandolier that caught my attention. They were always mentioned in the stories men told in the saloons when the night was darkest, and their liquid courage was strongest.

She'd been a beautiful woman once, before her time with the Comanche, before a shaman named Dead Bear had worked on her. Before I had ritually ruined everything soft and lovely about her with fire. I could still see her flesh peeling back from the flame like a peeled apple, left to wander the world ugly after.

Brown eyes gleamed from beneath her tattered locks. No barber or cutting man laid a hand on her, not with her coat of many faces so close at hand. Word was that she added to it whenever she ran across a new friend.

And her friends were usually children.

"Magpie . . . Black Magpie!" Her voice was chipper, higher pitched than it should have been.

Didn't have time to answer her before the figure that had been trailing behind her stepped out. His shaggy black hair rolling into large mutton chops, a weary smile splitting his face; all snake oil and lies.

"Hello, Salem. Been a while," Charles Marland said.

"Since I killed you, I reckon," I replied.

He adjusted his charcoal tie, mist grey frock coat pulled tight against the chill. He tipped the brim of his cap. "Guess it didn't take."

"Play with him again?" Gwendoline asked, looking down at the man from her perch on the grave. Marland closed his eyes and from beneath his hair came the whispering.

Amaya whined at the sound, gritting her teeth. I tried

to make out the words of hell that crawled from underneath those long and dirty locks, but they were as gibberish to me as they were to my daughter.

They called it an affliction, Marland's mumbling. Word was the devil himself had come to dwell on the back of him, telling him all the secret paths and trails that hadn't been carved in tomorrow yet. Met a sawbones once who'd said it was all ignorance and fear, product of your birth and nothing more. Either way, Charles Marland had been born with a face jutting from the back of his head.

He'd once been an act in a traveling show. I could still see the posters they'd passed out in every town: DR. ODDICO'S CARNIVAL OF ODDITIES AND MUSEUM OF MARVELS.

Marland had worked telling fortunes, and in the night when the tents grew dark and the entertained townspeople slept, he'd crept through the night and visited his pleasures on the girls.

I was present when he'd been found out. Practically the whole town turned out to lynch all the performers before I'd convinced them that if they meant for real play, it was me they'd be drawing against. Persuaded both townies and oddities to give the two-faced oracle to me.

He'd sobbed and begged, said it wasn't him, it was his other self, the one that whispered, but I didn't pay much heed to his claims. Truth be told, I'd come looking to kill him. There were plenty of folk looking for my brother's Gun and I couldn't have some double-faced soothsayer whispering the wrong thing in the wrong man's ear. So, I'd dragged him out of the show and put a bullet in him.

The performers looked to their own when it came to burial and knowing they hadn't buried him deep enough curled my hair like a dog smelling blood, especially after they'd stopped me from cutting the deformity from the back of his skull.

Gwendoline Bell seemed to have cottoned to Marland's mumbling. She smiled and nodded, crouching to whisper into the man's hair, right where his double was said to grow.

"Thought you were rid of all of us, Salem. But Miss Lorelei has reach below the ground, and in hell," Marland said, his voice like a man trying to comfort a lover. "And that's where we are going to send you. Straight as the rails, I've seen you die."

I bared my teeth in a devil's grin. "Hell? Where is it you think I came from?"

The smug smile disappeared from Marland's face as I fired, the shot catching him in his belly. There was a small mist of blood and he fell backward into the mud, hands cupping the wound.

I stepped forward, clearing the way for Amaya who didn't hesitate; three shots found Thomas' innards and he slumped against the stone tomb.

But Katsutomo didn't stop, never saw him coming, focused as I was on the charred woman leaping at me. I felt the pain, hot and searing, saw the trickle of my blood flowing down his blade, saw his bloody smile.

He collapsed to his knees at the same time that Gwendoline's kick sent me sprawling across the stone.

I hit the tomb hard and felt my ribs break as blood flowed out of me.

Lorelei was there, her veiled face looming over mine, the barest hints of pale skin visible beneath the cloth. She moved like a whisper or an early morning mist.

Every breath was pure agony. The blade in my side felt like a bayonet wound I'd taken a long time ago, but this time, there wasn't any strength or grit left in me.

Still, I tried to raise my Gun.

Lorelei traced a hand of velvet across the brand under my eye, her finger following the scars. "You've kept me waiting. Through all your killing and bullets, I've waited. Now you've come in pain, so close you can feel the flames at your boot heels."

I wanted to raise my weapon, tell her that she could

come see those flames with me, but only managed to cough up something warm and wet in reply. I felt it dribble down my chin as I struggled to breathe.

Gwendoline appeared, dragging Amaya behind her, the girl's guns left behind in the mud. The burned woman's face leered as she reached toward me. "Let me play with him before he can't move."

Lorelei turned, her peacemaker in her hand, bone white barrel pressed to her lips. "Shhhhhhh." Her whisper drifted out into the night and Gwendoline's eyes rolled back into her head. The bruise from the rope that had killed her bubbled up from beneath her skin and she toppled backward, an alabaster stone tomb cracking under her weight.

The Lady of Mourning lowered herself to look me in the eye. "I was called, Salem. Called to kill the Black Magpie, the one thing you couldn't kill in return. But if you die now, you suffer the punishment of the grave and the torment of fire . . . " Her hand clasped around my wrist, felt like the bite of winter had reached down and settled underneath my skin. Her other hand found Amaya's, and she began to drag the both of us across the wet paths of the dead.

My Gun whispered to me, urging me to find my nerve, to take it up and put Lorelei into her beloved grave. But I could barely move my arms, could barely draw breath. Each bump in the path felt like the wound in my side had opened just a little wider. Didn't know how much longer I had. I felt hot, each headstone we passed shining like the damn sun had come down to earth. Felt angry, I'd come so close, ignored every shot and cannonade that'd come my way, only to be felled in a dark boneyard by a foreign blade, my killer a man with his feet halfway into the next world.

Lorelei looked down at me, the dark veil parting just right, enough to see lips as red as a fresh battlefield. The fabric obscured her again. A chill numbness set about my lungs and penetrated my guts.

"Can't have you slipping away yet. The fires of the pit can burn until all of creation weeps, but I won't let any take you from me, oh killer mine," Lorelei murmured to me, though I heard her words like they were pressed against my ears.

Distantly, I heard the whistles, the shouts of men who had come to see justice done for all those going to the boot hill come morning sun. Thunder rolled in from the storm, like it had taken a nap in the long night and just woken to resume its fury.

We passed through another gate, and beyond my stage sat waiting, old horses straining at their bits, a mist from the passed gully washer floating across the deserted quarter.

Lorelei dropped Amaya's hand, hoisting me until my boots touched stone. "Your nest of workings, Salem. Had Thomas Grail bring it here. Your beast is safe inside. Now, you ride, you rest, and you come home to release me before I come for you on the day I have anointed your death."

I shouldn't have been standing, but the woman's touch had chased away the agony. Death no longer sat on my chest like a fat vulture ready to gnaw at my innards. Now it circled close, but far enough that I could drive it off.

Lorelei bent down and placed her hand on Amaya's leg. Color flooded into her cheeks again.

Leaning against the black wood of my stage, I watched her. "Been a while since Dust. I called you there, who called you now? Who's holding your reins?"

Got the sense that she smiled under her veil, that she reveled in the knowledge, but when she uttered the name, it was with all the hate of a curse. "Granger Hyde."

I felt a savage satisfaction wash over me, the Gun in my hand stirring. Another man I'd left living, though I thought I'd killed him at our first meeting way back in Lawrence.

"Too much to reckon that he brought together your riders? Or sent you looking?" I coughed, feeling the cold she'd pressed into me beginning to melt. She didn't have to nod; her silence was all the answer I needed.

She picked Amaya up from the ground and leaned her against the stage. My daughter's eyes never left her; all it took was a touch to know the deadliness that came with Lorelei's attention. But she did find her voice, asking, "This man took my mother?"

"And so many others," Lorelei said, her hand drawing close to her holster. "Now, I must raise the four you killed. When I'm finished, your bullet will only find a specter of me. I rest in the dark of Trail's End waiting for you."

She pulled her peacemaker and whispered to it. "Come from the four winds, breathe on these slain that they may yet live."

We were too far away to hear their gasps, to see life enter their bones again.

I felt the Gun in my hand, hadn't been aware I drew it. I guided it until it aimed straight through the mourning woman's veil. "What does old Granger want with these women, Lorelei?" I had a feeling I knew the answer to the question but didn't want to believe that it was possible.

Lorelei traced her gloved hand along my Gun's barrel, and I felt the shadow of death pass through it to me. "He wants what you have Salem, to transform from what you made him." I could almost hear the laugh in her voice. "Plucked chicken to Black Magpie."

I pulled the trigger, felt the kick of the Gun, and watched the woman sink in on herself, until the black silk lay flat against the stone, any trace that it had once held anything blown away by a west wind.

CHAPTER EIGHT

I **DIDN'T HAVE** time to look for Lorelei's piece in the folds of her empty dress. Whatever working she'd put on me was wearing off quick. My blood began to pool around my wounds, my guts beginning to remember that they couldn't function cut open by a blade.

I tore open the door of my stage, the light flickering like ghosts behind a row of glass mason jars full of ingredients for things good and bad. Both of us would need to sleep under the ground tonight, let the soil keep us close, but for now, I needed something that would keep us breathing.

Found the worms easy enough, rummaging past the still-sleeping Roux, and grabbing the mason jar. Thick nightcrawlers each one, squirming through dirt from a dead man's pine box, gnawing their way through whatever scraps of soul still lingered.

I fished through the jar, feeling the oily black dirt beneath my fingertips, the slimy muscle of the worm contracting when I pinched my fingers around it. Kept going until I had six wriggling in my hand.

I had a small trunk that I'd filled with salt for curing and preserving innards, both man and animal. I drew the dried heart from it, the former wet redness replaced by a long-dead brown, cured for a time such as this. It was a pig's heart; this working would have been permanent if I had to use the heart of man, but needs must for the desperate, and this would work for my purposes.

I slipped the worms down the heart's opening, three of

them, letting them nestle and squirm deep. I whispered the words to myself, holding the dry and round organ high. "Devourers of flesh long dead, eaters of life broken and ended, nestle and writhe in that which lays still. Give me your struggles so the grave flees from me."

I bit down hard, feeling the gristle sink beneath my teeth. I gnawed until I felt the wriggling of the heart's new occupants, slimy earth joining the toughened meat as it slid down my throat. I ate until there was nothing left, and when it was done, I felt the strength entering me again, my ribs wriggling back into place, my side stitching whole.

Three hours they'd given me. More than enough time.

I repeated the process on a second heart I'd stowed, then stepped back out into the night. Amaya breathed soft, her dark eyes looking up in confusion as I crouched over her, heart in hand.

Shots rang out from the graveyard. The law on our trail meeting those whose souls were as black as all hell's fire.

Amaya watched, confused, as I offered her the heart like it was straight from the tree of life.

"Take and eat, every scrap and morsel, or die. Doesn't matter to me."

Amaya glared at my offered hand. But in the end, she accepted it. They always did.

I hoisted her into the seat, taking my place at the reins and urging my two old horses. The wheels turned on the wet stone.

A brown worm writhed from the center of her hands, jutting out of the meat like a newborn struggling for life. She didn't pause as she plucked it up with her teeth and swallowed it whole.

And I didn't pause as we left New Orleans behind us.

The trails and paths of the bayou are treacherous to those who don't know the way and I was counting on that to keep us safe for the night, letting the Spanish moss and cypress bring us into their embrace.

Lorelei walked the next world, but she'd whispered life back into her riders' bones and they wouldn't stop until I was dead. I knew that sure as a bullet.

We made camp in a hollow between three trees, kudzu vines drowning us in green as the Spanish moss blew in the light breeze. There was a fog on the ground tonight, mist rising as the heat crept back in. The moon shone through the tree limbs, white light creating a haze.

Amaya shivered, staring at her injured leg. Still had an hour or so before the magic wore thin, but already the marks of the wound were beginning to manifest. Wouldn't be long before the two of us were laid up dying slow.

When we'd finally stopped, I'd immediately handed her a shovel and told her she'd better dig two, just shallow enough for the two of us to lie in. She looked like she wanted to protest but I simply stared until she started digging a good few yards away, sheltered underneath the cypress limbs.

As she dug our shallow graves, I dug through my stage until I'd found what I'd come for: a few mirrors, broken glass, and jars filled with clear mountain water, all of them tied to thin strings. I hung two each from every tree that circled our camp, listening to the clinking as they swayed in the breeze.

"There was an old man who used to do that when I was young. Said it warded away bad spirits," Amaya said, panting as she rested on the shovel.

The last two went above the graves she was digging. Workings to turn away prying eyes.

When I finished, I looked down at her. "Deeper, Miss Shrike. Unless you'd prefer to listen to the buzzards pick at you."

A scowl darkened her face, the scar chasing her lips as she frowned, but she kept digging as I made a fire and tended to the horses. I kept an eye on the woman as she worked.

FOR A FEW SOULS MORE

Hard to believe this was my whelp, taken to violence and killing like coyotes took to new death. I was sure she told herself late at night that it was to help her village, help her people; justice served to the gringos who'd come down marauding and raping.

But she wasn't a juniper anymore. She had iron tempered down to the soul. She dealt pain raw, the pit of hurt that gnawed at her growing deeper with each kill. She could ride hard, but each new act of agony would dig her a bottomless grave.

I had half a mind to teach her, show her all manner of ways there were to kill a man, sit her on the other side of the elder fire, and whisper the secrets of power. She'd take to it; she was blood of my blood.

Amaya finished her task, embedding the shovel in the ground as she climbed out of the hole and panting hard as she limped towards where I sat at the fire. She collapsed opposite of me, pulling off her boots with a pained wince.

We didn't speak. I had gathered my mortar and pestle, and the few herbs that I needed, crushing them into a fine pulp. I had retrieved a pair of tongs and clutching the mortar tight I held it over the fire.

She watched me, shrugging out of her jacket, the white cloth of her shirt underneath stained with sweat and dirt, "What is that?"

I didn't meet her gaze, instead watching the dancing flames. "Medicine for our wounds. It's going to burn but can't have us dying before we rescue your mother."

I brought the mortar close, careful to avoid touching the heated and bubbling broth inside. I spit in it once and stirred it with the pestle, glancing at Amaya who watched the dark around our hollow.

"No use looking for trouble. We will sleep sound beneath the ground." I stood and dabbed my fingers into the mush. "And we will kill those death has fled from." She watched me close, tense, staring at the vaguely green pulp dabbed on my fingers. "Your wound . . . "

Slowly, she began to roll up her pant leg, and when she reached her injury, the flesh was already beginning to peel back. She saw the shot beginning to reopen, the stolen scraps of life that had sustained her unbinding like frayed rope.

I watched it too and I knew the medicine wouldn't take until one more thing was seen to. I grasped my knife and brought it close, watching her instincts tell her to kill me.

I wiped the blade down with the green paste. "The bullet's still in your leg. If you want to live, it'll have to be retrieved." I squatted in the dirt, reaching out and holding her leg still. "Won't lie to you, this is going to hurt. I don't have any whiskey to take the edge off."

She nodded and I listened as a distant owl hooted, breathed in the deep humidity, heard the hordes of insects and frogs from the creeks and streams close by. Then I dug the blade into her leg.

I watched her as she gripped the dirt, a strangled cry escaping from her lips. She kicked her leg as I peeled back the muscle, cutting hard as I searched. "Still yourself, tell me about your mother."

Her eyes rolled about her head, reflecting the firelight, dancing marbles trying to find an escape from the agony, but they snapped into focus again when she heard my question.

"She lived good; the gold you gave her stretched long."

I felt her warm blood gush, the tip of my blade tasting her muscle, gnawing on bone. Amaya paused, stifling a scream. She'd bleed out soon, would have already if it wasn't for the stolen life the worms gave her. But I'd found the bullet.

I reached down and plucked the deformed lead from her wound. Paleness seeping back in as death crept into our camp, unwilling to wait any longer for the two of us.

Her voice was faint, each word coming slow but determined. "She tried to make me proper, I looked like a right princess every opportunity she could grab."

I dabbed my hand into the mortar, taking more than a thick glob of the green paste and spreading it onto her wound. She hissed as the medicine did its work. I nodded. "Going to burn, like a fire that'll eat the hurt right out of you and leave you whole."

Amaya nodded, gritting her teeth, "I have felt worse pain."

Her past hurts called to me, stoking my curiosity like I stoked a log on dying coals. I rose and picked her up in my arms. I felt her tense up, trying to fight only to find the medicine sapping her strength like a creek drying.

I carried her to the hole that she had dug and laid her into it, her half-lidded eyes snapping open, looking around the hollow earth in fear. "I . . . This . . . I've seen many things. B-butchery like you cannot imagine . . . "

I chuckled lightly as I began to cover her with the dirt, her wound disappearing beneath the cool soil. "I can imagine a lot."

A small smile made its way across her face. Her eyes closed, fighting with all of her might to cling to the waking world. "I do not . . . doubt that . . . Mr. Covington. I just have . . . never seen . . . real magic."

More earth buried her, and she took a deep breath as I covered her neck, leaving only her face above ground. Her breathing softened and unconsciousness took her. I watched her for a moment, tracing the familiar curve of her chin in my mind, her mother's features. I couldn't see much of myself there, except for those eyes; Virgil's eyes, her grandfather's eyes . . . The eyes of bad men, killers all, given over to the devil and every sin that a man could ever commit. Every evil. And all of it was like the finest swill a saloon could give, and no matter how much of it you drank, or how much you wanted to put it down, in the end you weren't nothing but a drunk. And there was no putting down the Gun.

I felt the pain in my side, reminding me that if I didn't tend to myself my daughter would have to claw her own way out of the earth. Covering Amaya until only her nose jutted from the dirt, I used the last bit of the green paste on my wound. Pulled my own flaps of skin apart, unable to reach my ribs but trusting the medicine to do its work. I was used to the pain; in the end, it would just be another scar. Pain usually made a good tale, and it was always interesting hearing the stories of wounds.

I doused the fire with water from the nearby bog. The warm glow vanished leaving only the pale light of the moon through the mist, the smoke billowing up into the dark.

Something rustled out in the night. Could have been a pole cat or fox, owl or crow, or the swish of a dress as black as the sky. A cold washed over me that had nothing to do with the wind and I reached for my Gun, letting it whisper its iron comfort.

I reluctantly turned my back on the night and limped to the hole dug for me. I remembered Lorelei's words a few hours past and wondered just how alone I'd be beneath the ground.

I laid down, feeling my strength going. My ribs were cracking as my previous working wore away giving room to the new medicine and magic. I pulled the earth over myself, slowly, until everything was covered but my nose. I let the quiet of the grave have me.

Dreams never seemed to come for me. In the dark of unconscious infinity, I floated like a castaway. But tonight, the dreams came vivid. It was home, Trail's End, where those who'd sought to hide their sins went to air their iniquities.

I walked down main street, cutting through past the saloon, café, and general store. Virgil came with me, both of us slinking like coyotes, pups who hadn't even seen ten years yet. Both of us had already killed in those days.

And now we had come to watch a friend die.

Trail's End called to the hollow hole at the bottom of a man, the place where the devil lived and whispered. Our father had founded the town, and within its streets, everything was permitted.

I remembered the fear of having to run faster than the men who looked at you with hungry eyes from the shadows between buildings. How you only took little bites of Herr Adler's sweets for fear of poison. The screams of animals being sacrificed up at the church as you tried to close your eyes and beg sleep to take you, especially on the nights that the screams weren't animal. Especially on the nights they were familiar.

That was why we'd snuck out that night, to try to play hero. Our Pa's guns divided between us.

Father had been up there that night, indulging in the preacher's words, same as the rest of the men. They'd caught a girl coming home. Her name was Mary-Ann; she'd just celebrated her sixteenth year, and every boy and man worth his pecker lusted after her.

That's why they'd come for her, and that's why Virgil and I had made plans to save her. We walked sure and true, thinking we were the heroes in the books our mother snuck to us when Pa was out doing the devil's work. He'd put out her eyes years ago so she couldn't see him going to seed.

In my dream, we ran the streets of Trail's End with a purpose, Mary-Ann's screams nipping at our heels like spurs urging an old nag, guns nearly too big for our hands.

The church in my dream was just as I remembered it, an inverted cross displaying the corpse of a naked woman, snatched from towns far distant and crucified.

Old Dusty Tillman was there like he always was, naked as a jaybird, pecker in hand as he stared up at the fly-ridden corpse draped from the steeple, grasping at himself until he'd spilled his seed. Blackened teeth smiling up at the dead woman's hollow gaze. There'd come a time Virgil and I would kill him, but it wasn't this night.

Tonight, we'd come trying to be heroes and had been

found wanting. My fingers broken, memories of the punishment Pa had inflicted on us for our real play, Mary-Ann naked and dead on the altar, surrounded by equally naked men.

The men circled Virgil and I. Our clothes were torn from us, hot breath creeping at the nape of my neck. I hadn't screamed then, just cried silent tears as I stared at the girl's dead face, eyes of pain and shame, devoid of light.

But it wasn't Mary-Ann's face there anymore. The dream twisted. Amaya's face stared. Her dark hair laid over her like a veil, her brown skin bearing the burns and bruises from torment and lust.

My rage charged forward like a herd in a storm, and I was no longer a child playing gunslinger. The decadent men of Trail's End fell away, frightened whimpers escaping them as Virgil, and I rose.

The people of Trail's End had worked a mighty debt, and the time had come that their darkest sons came to collect. As each bullet found its place in the bastards' flesh, I screamed my rage until all of them were dead, reduced to nothing but empty flesh.

I left Virgil behind, walking forward and calling Amaya's name. My voice echoed like it was halfway across some distant field. The altar never seemed to draw closer, time stretching out like a wrong note.

Time didn't have any meaning in the dream. I could have continued my pursuit for an eternity, but the hand on my shoulder ceased my steps. I saw the black velvet glove and I turned to see Lorelei, her veils falling around me, drawing me in like a curtain of rain ushering livestock home.

She whispered her black deeds, and I whispered mine in return, and as my dream fell back into that grave where all dreams go, Lorelei worked her way with my soul. When she was finished, I was no longer man or magpie, just something that mewled for succor, squirming and screaming.

CHAPTER NINE

I CAME BACK to the waking world in the early morning. My eyes snapped open beneath the dirt and I rose from the hole like a drowning man clawing for air. Roux jumped back from where he had been pawing, large orange eyes fixing me in place as the Gun woke in my hand.

The clearing was still empty, a light smoke drifting up from the extinguished campfire, the dirt next to me undisturbed. Soil fell from me in large clumps, and I shook my head, clearing out the prairie coal that felt like it was clogging my thoughts. The red wolf watched me as I stood and walked slowly to the blackened logs and brush of my fire.

A few embers still glowed under the grey ash, and I blew softly, coaxing them back to life. There was a crack of flame on dead wood, eating its way back to life. Roux came and sat on the other side of the fire, far enough away that if I made a move towards him, he'd vanish into the trees. But he stayed, fur rippling as the flames grew higher. It looked like his whole body was shaking, the pain of the previous day still fresh. Couldn't say why he didn't make out for the bayou, what kept him rooted here with me.

Marie Laveau had once told me that I was a brother of wolves, companion to crows; collecting stories and lives like a man hoarded gold, never to submit to the yoke of another man for deed or dollar.

I retrieved a few strips of dried jerky from my stage, gnawing on the meat like a savage. Roux's eyes watched hungrily on the other side of the fire. A toss of jerky and the red wolf joined me in communion, tearing into the meat with greed. I threw him another scrap and retreated to my stage, retrieving the ingredients for what came next.

The tins were bubbling over the fire when Amaya came gasping up out of the ground. Didn't even glance her way as I cooked, watching the strips sizzle on the skillet I'd retrieved.

She immediately looked at the wound on her leg, standing up like a newborn deer afraid it was going to fall. She stared at the new scar marring her leg. Her hands grasped at her hips, looking for her guns left behind in the New Orleans cemetery.

I picked at the bacon, listening to the grease run and pop and watching Roux happily devour his portions. He growled when Amaya walked over, trailing dirt like a veil. She ignored the wolf as she claimed her place.

"Drink this," I said, passing her the tin cup by the tips of my fingers.

She gingerly took it, blew away the steam, and set it down on the dirt. I noticed the bags beneath her eyes as she stared at the liquid, trying to make heads or tails of what I'd given her.

"What hoodoo is this?" She asked.

"It's coffee," I replied, picking up my own tin cup and taking a sip of the bitter brew, feeling the burn as it passed my tongue. Amaya drank slowly and I handed her a few strips of bacon.

Neither of us spoke, ruminating over the previous evening. My thoughts turned to Lorelei and her riders. I knew each of their stories by heart, and each one was written in a book of blood.

"Who was she, the woman?" Amaya asked, her voice small and quiet.

Thought about spinning some yarn to satisfy her curiosity and keep her from feeling the fear that came from knowing the truth. But that was the thing about knowing;

there was no turning back the way you came if you didn't like what you found. There was just the time before and the time after.

Answers were out there if she chose to go looking. Turning over those dark stones could take years. She had ironed the whole way through, but a killer from this world was worth less than spit against a woman from the next. Taken or dead, either fate awaited Amaya without me. And I owed it to her not to sell her swill or the chance to fold her cards and quit our journey before it started.

"How many dead, Miss Shrike? How many have you laid in the ground?"

Amaya glowered, her eyes flaring like dry lightning on a prairie night. "That ain't an answer."

I stared back, letting her glower roll off like oil. "It is an answer, you just haven't learned how to discern it. Every shot, every grave, every time you wore black up to the cemetery, she was there watching you. She waits for anyone that picks up a gun and makes their mark killing."

Amaya stared right back. "You ain't going to see me going yellow just because some devil bitches keep herself from the same."

I laughed. It wasn't her fault that she didn't understand the full extent of it or the fact that Lorelei would come for us again soon enough. "She isn't dead. Can't kill what was never alive to begin with. Right now, she's just making the journey back, waiting for us to come calling."

Amaya finished her drink and set the cup back down. "Who is pulling her strings? Heard her name him."

Finishing my own drink, I stood, rounding up the camp's accoutrements as I put out the fire. "Old victim, killed his son in Missouri more than a few years back. Cut off his hand, took his leg, and melted a bullet straight into his eye."

The memory came to me like it was yesterday. I could still remember the smell, the acrid smoke wafting everywhere as the boys torched the buildings, the women screaming as we dragged their boys out into the street to send them off to meet the Good Lord.

And there was Granger Hyde, roaring with all the thunder of an old bear as I scraped the knife across his son's skull, tearing away his hair and skin to decorate my horse. I recalled it well and had occasionally wondered what the elder Hyde had become in the long years since the war. Now I reckoned we'd find out.

Amaya retrieved her belt, cinching it tight. "Why does he need the women? How are they meant to kill you?"

Pouring the grease into the fire, I watched the flames bounce and lap up the fuel like a horse gone weeks without feed, and in those flames, I asked those same questions. Couldn't have been more than twenty women in El Jardin capable of birthing, if Amaya's recounting of their previous raids was true, could have been sixty or more women taken from all across the border.

Looking into the flames one bit of knowledge nagged at me, magic I knew all too well, one that called for plenty of women's bellies swollen with babes.

The ritual that had given me the Gun in my hand.

The pieces were out there if one had a mind to pledge themselves to murder. But getting a full reckoning of the rite . . . folk could go a whole lifetime and still come up short. It didn't seem possible, but maybe I just didn't want to think there could be others carrying around the same hand as me.

To steal the Gun and its oath from me, it'd take a soul near as black as my own, but any who called Lorelei had the nerve.

I felt the eagerness in my bones, ready to collect Granger Hyde's tale for my own. "Don't think that those women are meant to kill me, just like I'm sure Granger's men didn't know your kinship with me. Fate has a way of driving things; betting Marland's heart stopped beating when his second face told him where you were heading when you escaped."

FOR A FEW SOULS MORE

It was Amaya's turn for her own grin, reminding me of a hawk perching high in the desert, "You will take me to them, Mr. Covington. I will kill them for what they have done, and I will make them hurt if they have harmed my mother."

I kicked dirt into the fire, holstering my weapon. "I reckon you will."

CHAPTER TEN

WE HEADED NORTH following the flows of the Mississippi, intent on making Patois Landing and its port. The plan was to catch a steamer and head upriver, keep off the trails. Didn't want to be fighting for my companion's life in every one-horse town between here and my home.

I recalled the men, not the ones Lorelei had brought back, but the others who'd worn those crimson hoods. They must've been Granger's men, gun hands, a few ex-army, whatever cowpunchers that he could scrounge up. Nothing but gravy on the biscuits; the main meat came from Lorelei and her four riders.

I hadn't had much schooling on the good book. The gospel-slinger in Trail's End hadn't been one for teaching the holy words, but doing his damndest to live in opposition, same as the rest. But I read the whole thing years later, even sat in the back of a gospel mill, and listened to a preacher's words. To hear it, we were all fearfully and wonderfully made in the image of the Lord above. I could see that; after all, he wasn't the only one who'd killed a passel of firstborns.

Now I was brought back to those words, thinking of my pursuers. Not one rode a colored horse, but they were bearing down on me and Amaya like my own personal apocalypse. Always thought that death would flee from me, but now it seemed like it was steaming ahead like a train on the railroad.

FOR A FEW SOULS MORE

I expected Granger's men to be waiting along the trail. There was also the law to worry about. Our escape from the Carmine Griffin probably had every juniper lawman from here to Ogallala looking for us, and it was a long way to Trail's End.

The journey to Patois Landing took us most of the day. The cypress trees closed in thick, most of it covered by the green kudzu that was slowly but surely strangling everything. The occasional sight of muddy brown water through the trees gave a measure of our trail, and from all around us came the croaking of frogs and bird calls.

Roux trotted beside us, the red wolf keeping an easy pace, occasionally darting off into the green and returning with blood-stained teeth and fur, rabbit or rat carcass clutched between his teeth.

"Never seen a wolf take a shine to people like this," Amaya said, her hand drifting to her pistols, replacements for the ones lost. She watched Roux vanish between two trees in search of more food and turned back to look at me, the accusation clear. "Doesn't seem natural."

I whispered comfort to the two horses to keep them calm and on the road. "Reckon he sees what I really look like past my skin."

Neither of us spoke much after that, couldn't say whether she cottoned to my thoughts or kept to her own. Didn't much matter either way, as I was dwelling on one thing: how to kill something that couldn't be killed by a gun.

The sun was setting low when I spotted Patois Landing's tallest building through the trees. The steeple was silhouetted against the dying sun, drowning the three or so other buildings in shadow. The town was just a muddy street separating the saloon and general store on the left from the ramshackle church and warehouse leading to the steamboat dock on the right. The river stretched out, brown and curling like a serpent squirming its way through the swamp.

WILE E. YOUNG

A few men stood on the saloon steps, dots of orange fire lighting their cigarettes as they watched us pull equal to them. I tied off the reins and listened to their slurred words, all of them heavily in their cups.

As I climbed down from the stage, I heard the faint whisper of a shooting iron pulled from its holster. I spun Gun in hand and aimed it directly at a man who looked like he could put away an entire fried hog. His jowls bounced like a working whore; eyes wide as he raised his empty hand. "Easy, mister. You've got a wolf trailing you."

The man pointed down the street where Roux was waiting near where the town limits met the trees. I didn't lower the Gun. "He's mine. I'm giving you one chance, put it away."

Another man stepped forward, face red as mulberry. "Listen you cock-sucking son of a bitch. Wolf's gonna eat—"

The third man cold-cocked the mouthing man across the back of his head, sending him sprawling across the saloon porch. The fat man looked at his friend, who was young and blonde, reminding me of a sheriff's deputy I'd sent off to hell years back, and he stared pointedly at the brand under my eye with knowing.

Big difference between hearing and knowing. You could hear all manner of things, sit around the drink house after a day of sweat and toil and tell yourselves all the stories you'd heard. But a story was safe, a story wasn't supposed to step to life in the twilight of the sun. Now here I was, and I brooked no insult.

"Look at him, Willis, look at him real hard," the younger man said.

The fat man stared, inhaled sharply, and then I smelled the bitter scent of fresh piss. The fat man stepped back out of his puddle, muttering, "Oh Christ."

He holstered his gun quick, holding both hands up. His younger friend stepped up; hands held far from his piece. "Willis didn't mean nothing by it, Mr. Covington."

I nodded holstering my own Gun, but I noticed that Amaya kept her aim, both pistols marking the men.

FOR A FEW SOULS MORE

"He didn't shoot, no harm there. But your other friend—" I gestured down to the red-cheeked fool holding his head against the bloody knock that the young man had given him. "Let his flannel mouth get the best of him. The lady and I are going in to have a drink. When I come out, I want his tongue. Expect it in my hand when I return."

I let them chew on that as I motioned for Amaya to follow, ruddy cheeks looking up with mule eyes at his two friends, both orbs jumping like toads between each other.

Amaya holstered her pistols as we pressed through the doors and into the saloon proper. A few candles kept the place dimly lit, and there were a half dozen or so mud-caked drivers enjoying what they could afford.

A few heads turned our way as we walked in, but most went back to nursing their drinks and engaging in half-whispered conversations. The barkeep was a matchstick of a woman who looked like she'd spent too many years on the wrong side of the saddle.

"Girls are worn pretty thin, but I can send for one," she said as we took our places at the end of the bar.

I shook my head and laid the coins flush against the hardwood, "Just whiskey and glasses to drink it."

The woman eagerly scooped up the payment and scampered back down the way to fulfill her obligation. When she returned, I poured Amaya's drink then my own, watching as my she lifted her glass. "Gracias."

Nodded my head and both of us drank, letting the comforting burn wash through me.

"Why the tongue?" Amaya murmured; her eyes turned back out to the sunlit street. If you looked right, you could see three dark figures arguing amongst themselves on the saloon porch.

"Lot of things you can do with a man's tongue," I said, tipping my drink back. "A tongue can bind your speech, take the truth from those unwilling to give it . . . "

Amaya tried not to look eager, but I could see it

crouching ugly behind her eyes, the yearning to know things done in secret places.

"Can even tell you a man's own secrets if you rip it out of them," I finished, listening to the pained scream outside that set every head but mine turning.

The cowpunchers cleared out, some running on steady legs, and some stumbling with vacant looks of concentration. Either way, they'd do what I want.

Amaya watched them go. "They'll bring the sheriff."

I poured another drink and set the Gun on the bar next to it. "That's the other use of a taken tongue. Folks either gather up their sand, or they find someone who will."

I could hear the commotion outside; a few lost their drink, vomiting it up, and the rest went shouting down the street, calling for the sheriff at the top of their lungs. Amaya watched everything, keeping her gaze on a few of the men brave enough to keep a watch through the windows.

"These are like buzzards; they wait for their pound of flesh." She spat on the bar's floorboards as she spoke.

"Your boots more like," I replied nursing my drink and listening to the clamor. I finished my second glass and heard the rattling as the saloon doors opened. It was the young cowpuncher and his fat friend, Willis. Willis' hands were dripping, thick blood running from the fat hunting knife he clutched vise-like in a trembling grip. The younger one stood with steady hands and a fresh tongue in his palm.

Watched both. Amaya looked at me, no doubt wondering what I wanted from these two. My daughter spoke. "Leave it on the bar."

The younger man stepped to my right, pressing the dismembered organ firmly onto the paneling. My finger paused its tapping and the man flinched. I kept my gaze fixed on Amaya. I didn't usually brook others to make my decisions with useless lives. Instead, I indulged my curiosity. "What's your name, kid?"

Heard him swallow. "Norm, sir."

"Norm . . . " I chewed the name like day-old grits. "Sit and tell us your story."

He didn't fidget, but he didn't look thrilled by the prospect. Willis shook his head just slightly, trying to hide the fact he'd even done it when he caught me looking. Wasn't sure if they were Patois Landing's river hands or if they were with the cowboys crowding the windows. Both groups had heard stories of me, they knew that there were only two ways this was going to end.

He leaned opposite of me, his left side facing the windows. The barkeep reappeared, trembling hands presenting a new glass for Norm. The glass rattled against the bar as I reached over and filled it, small drops splashing as Norm's trembling hands took it.

"Your story, Norm," I said taking back the bottle. Amaya retrieved it to fill her own empty glass.

So, he told me his story. His father had died of consumption when he was just old enough to start learning about the world. His mother had been killed but he couldn't say by who. He'd been taken in by a traveling steamer captain, taught the river man's trade, and had been jumping from boat to boat ever since. He, Willis, and their third friend, Morris, were working the one docked here. One that was taking on passengers.

I listened to everything he had to say and when it was finished, I flipped over my drinking glass and stood. Amaya watched me close, but Norm watched me closer, eyes wide, unsure of what I meant to do.

Bennie the pig farmer's wedding ring still danced in my pocket; the band stained with his dry blood. Had his story and no need for gold.

"Your hand, Norm." I said.

I let the ring drop into his trembling hand. "For the story. Now find your way home. Might want to take your friend with you."

Norm's head bobbed like a half-killed chicken, walking smart to Willis who stood, mouth gaping like one of the fish he took from the river. Norm pawed at his friend, ushering him out of the saloon.

Called after him. "Norm, your mute friend . . . leave him on the porch."

Didn't have to keep watching to know he'd do what I asked. Bravery and wisdom walked as brothers and Norm wasn't afraid to save his friend, just smart enough to think better of it.

Both men vanished and I looked over at the barkeep. She was keeping as much distance between us as she could, her hands shaking like a rail with a train coming. The sweat pooling on her brow could have been from the humidity or her fear.

"C-can I get you something else, Mister Covington?"

Fiddled with my drinking glass. I pondered on the fact that I wasn't the only bad man walking the trail who couldn't be killed. Only difference was that my four old enemies had made tracks into the next world. Could come at us time and again as long as Lorelei bothered to bring them back.

My hand fidgeted, glancing at the silver pocket watch, hand still firmly rooted at the midnight mark. Still, I felt like a man facing down the rope, gallows waiting. I'd been told once that my path wouldn't end in anything but rope, something I agreed with, and I briefly wondered if Lorelei thought the same.

"Mister?" the barkeep asked again, interrupting my musings and realizing that there was only one choice.

I held up two fingers. "Your name, ma'am. And if this town's got a telegraph."

The barkeep hesitated, then her eyes flicked down to the tongue laying like a dried worm next to my hand and I saw her swallow the lump in her throat. "It's Mary, sir. I come down from Shreveport after the war. Sheriff has a telegraph, right at the jail."

I nodded to her and offered another coin. "For your name, and for fetching the sheriff."

Mary pocketed the money in the folds of her dress, her ear cocked and listening to the faint shouts coming from outside as the sun finally crept beneath the shadows of the cypress trees. "No offense, mister. But I expect the sheriff to be coming through those doors before you pour another drink."

I filled up my glass and watched the whiskey run dry. "All the same, go fetch him for me." It wasn't a request and Mary walked swiftly out from behind the bar,

Amaya and I were alone, and I immediately picked up the tongue and held it bloody in my hand. The severed organ felt like a tough sponge, old nerves twitching with every new incision. This was old magic, designed to loosen the lips of those keeping secrets, and I had just the person in mind.

Amaya watched my handiwork. "That's not the name of any from this town."

"Isn't meant for any of them," I replied, drawing a fresh cut across the increasingly pale appendage.

"Then why bother learning their names? Why're you sending for the sheriff instead of just waiting?"

It was a wagon's worth of questions, and as I cut, I thought of how close to the vest I wanted to keep things, what I wanted from Amaya Shrike, this daughter of mine. In the end, I decided that she'd killed enough to warrant some truth. "To know a name and a story gives it meaning makes it yours once they die. I've heard tales from doctors cutting through soldier's legs as they begged for a bullet, promised those same soldiers I'd end it if they told me the same. Then I'd kill them. That's the power of it, Miss Shrike. By and by it's yours once the worms come squirming to eat them down to their bones."

I stared deep into my daughter's eyes, wondering if she felt the gnawing hunger of the Gun, how if I let it indulge its want, we'd be sifting through the bodies of every man, woman, and child in this town. Wonder if she knew that the closer I got to squaring my debt, the stronger that need to kill was.

"I see the question in your eyes. How many I've killed just for their names and stories? You've heard me as a killer of men? It's true, but I've also killed women pawing at their men to save them, killed children clinging behind their mother's skirts, and I've even torn a babe from the teat and fed it to the fire."

I couldn't tell if she believed me or not; she didn't speak, and in the end, it didn't matter. She spoke as if I was the devil. But I wasn't the devil, I just kept him fed.

Anything else was left unsaid as the doors behind us swung open and I heard muttered curses, and one deep voice breathe out, "Ah hell."

I smiled at the bottom of my glass. I recognized the voice, just like I'd known I would.

"Evening, Luther," I said.

CHAPTER ELEVEN

SHERIFF LUTHER MOON had two deputies with him, one more than I expected Patois Landing to have. The two men were jumpy, I could hear their breathing coming out short and quick.

Amaya had spun, her hands lurking close to her guns. Wasn't sure if she was quicker on the draw than the two men with rifles already aimed. I could see their reflections in the glass, deputy stars pinned to their dark vests.

"Put them away, boys. Wouldn't do you know good no how," Luther said. His voice was just like I remembered it, charred like meat on a spit. He'd survived a fire and it had mutilated his throat.

His two deputies looked at him like he'd just told them to feed their dog to a bear. "You saw what he did to Morris? His fucking tongue is right there!"

Turned around and saw their cheeks go red, anger turning to rage, and the one on Luther's right took up his rifle butt. "You sick son of a—"

Saw Luther's hand dart out quick, faster than a breeze, grabbing at the man with wide eyes. "Morris done brought it on himself. He's being generous with you already, Harris."

Luther looked to me, trying to warn his deputy. "You take one more step, son. and he'll kill you."

I slowly stood, picking my Gun and the tongue up from the bar. "Too right, been a long time, Luther."

Luther Moon had once been a wiry man, but it looked

like his time here had put him to seed. He had a bit of paunch that showed beneath a vest green enough that it reminded me of faraway Kansas fields.

His breath came out in wheezes, throat rattling thick and wet like he had consumption. But his eyes still watched me like he had back then. Like I was a bear come down from the mountain. He leaned hard on his deputy's shoulder. "Not long enough; my leg still hurts something awful."

A brown brace wrapped around his right leg, a testament to the man's skill more than a hindrance. He'd killed plenty of men in his time. Before I'd put a bullet in his leg.

He spit. "Didn't expect to see you fighting with the Cheyenne back then. They weren't your people."

I regarded him, looking up at his hat pulled tight over his skull, knowing what he'd lost. "I go where death is coming, thought Virgil had told you plain."

Luther licked his lips, nodding, one hand rubbing the crook of his leg where the bullet still rested. "Yeah, told me to not come looking if you killed him, said to let him lie and let some other unfortunate take up what he owed. If I'd known you were anywhere near Fort Phil Kearney, I would have deserted first chance. Gone on down to Mexico."

The two deputies who had accompanied the sheriff looked at the man like they were just seeing him clear for the first time. I could understand it; the wind getting knocked out of you when you realized that the man you thought invincible was just a man.

Every so often I'd look to Amaya. She watched all three men warily; thought she might pull iron just to get the two deputies to quit their aim. I felt the tension crackling in her like fire.

I tapped the brim of my hat, right where he had his own. "Would have been smarter had you quit when you saw me coming, could've walked away whole."

Luther stared for a moment before he removed his hat,

revealing the mangled and scarred baldness around trains of still dark locks that fell to the side and rear of his head. The scars from the suture lines followed the grooves where I'd cut into him, taking his scalp.

He finally broke his gaze to look at Amaya. "You take a good look, Miss. The man you travel with don't play games, them pretty pistols ain't going to save you when he gets what he wants from you."

Amaya looked back unwavering. "It isn't what he wants from me. It's what I can get from him."

Luther seemed taken aback, I nodded when he looked my way, tipping my hat to Amaya. "Bad folk about need killing, sheriff. That's why we're here. If you haven't been told to be on the watch for us, I expect that to change before too long."

The old Indian fighter sighed and made to rub a hand through his hair before he remembered that I had taken it from him. Instead, he replaced his hat and looked at the two of us with defeated eyes. "Expect you'll be wanting me to turn a blind eye?"

Nodded, pocketing the tongue. "And I need you to send a message."

Luther hobbled out of the saloon, his deputies scurrying past him, arms held out and admonishing the small crowd gathered to go home. There wasn't going to be any lynching tonight.

I heard the anger, the accusations that he'd turned yellow, but when the sheriff pointed inside the saloon and urged them to try their hand if they felt they had the sand, they looked down and drifted away like wood in a slow current.

I gestured for Amaya to stand clear just in case some juniper trying to prove himself decided to take a shot.

Mulberry cheeks, or as I now knew him, Morris, still

writhed on the porch. He was curled up tight like a calf laid down to sleep. Blood had pooled on the boards, flowing around my boot when I stepped out into the humid twilight. The man mewled like a babe, trying to form words as he looked up with wide and helpless eyes at the congregation of men standing over him.

Saw the hurt when Luther glanced down at him and looked away, the pain when the two deputies wouldn't meet his gaze and the fear when he saw me step over him. Morris opened his mouth, and a bubbling whimper came croaking out of his throat as he tried to keep from choking on his own blood. I could see the severed stump at the back of his throat waving around like stones before a stampede.

I felt Amaya step behind me as I crouched over the man, taking his chin in my fingers. "Going to bleed out soon if you don't get that looked at."

The man muttered something unintelligible through the gore and I took my hand away. "If you ever pick yourself up from this porch, you come find me." I left him there as I followed Luther who had already hobbled halfway back to his jail, motioning for his deputies to bring my stage. Amaya stared at the man still pitiful on the porch before she followed.

I stared at the distant street and the bridge stretching over from Patois Landing to the trails that would take travelers north to Shreveport, watching the shadows. I could feel it deep down, smell it like I could a rolling thunderhead. They'd be coming soon.

Luther lit a few lanterns hanging around the interior of the jail, casting the four cells in a half-light. There was a small cast iron stove in one corner with a chimney stretching up and out of the stone. On the opposite wall were the wanted posters, some fresh and others like ancient scrolls. My own hung behind a few of the newer ones; doubt that the old sheriff drew much attention to it.

I watched the man sit down behind his brown desk, positioned so that he could have an equal view of the cells and street through the glass window. He groaned when he collapsed into his chair, rubbing at his leg, keeping his hat firmly placed on his head. "Hasn't been the same since them years. Every time a storm comes, I feel it ache."

I nodded with him. "Not many people walking with a bullet I put in them."

Luther didn't deny or ask further, just looked towards the flame of one of the lanterns, the small cinder of fire dancing like a woman. "I have nightmares about you and Virgil sometimes, see things that I tell my missus are just old war wrongs come calling, a bad dream. I've seen you kill that sheriff up in Colorado . . . the one that had your brother's Gun."

She tried to hide it, but I saw Amaya look at my Gun holstered and hungry, the greed and possibility seeping into her soul, the thought that she could be like me.

I leaned forward. "Best go back to dreaming, Luther. Don't want to have to finish the work I started with you all those years ago."

If he wondered about my sincerity, he didn't ask it, didn't doubt it. Luther Moon had spent enough time around my brother and me to know that we didn't give a threat we weren't afraid to play to the bone.

As it stood, he wrested his eyes from the flame, breathing hard, memories and visions running rampant behind his dark eyes even now. "Reckon you're right on that. So, who're these fellas after you?"

I told him, watching his face go from curiosity to fear fast as a train passed over the plain. When I was finished, I saw Luther rubbing his leg something fierce, mumbling to himself. "Fucking peace is all I've wanted. Not this damned horseshit . . . " He sighed heavily, face going red, but his hand finally left his leg.

He asked, "When are they coming?"

Night had fallen outside, the lightning bugs coming to life out in the honeysuckled woods. Looked like the stars had jumped down out of the firmament and were burning around the Landing. That feeling of fate or Lorelei coming.

"Couldn't say, could be they come after the boat leaves. Could be they'll ride over that bridge before the end of the hour. Your two deputies, can you ride the river with them?"

The old Indian fighter shook his head.

I decided to inquire about my other purpose. "Got any writing tools?"

The sheriff produced a pencil and paper, and I began writing down my message. "Luther, when I leave here, you're going to send this message to every telegraph station between here and California."

I slid the completed message across his desk, followed by a small pouch that I fished from my pockets; the coins inside rattled as I dropped them next to it.

Luther tucked the pouch into the folds of his desk. "I'll make sure the word gets out."

I made to stand and had turned my back on the sheriff when I heard him continue. "Course after what you did in New Orleans, I'm sure every bounty hunter between here and California is going to be coming for you. Don't see why you're making claims of outlaws heading to Fort Smith."

Wondered if I should tell him the truth, that this was just the play of a man placing chips on a desperate bet. Decided it wasn't worth the words. "Address it from yourself, Luther. Keep my name off it."

The sheriff nodded, looking at his cigarettes. "Should say it's you riding the trail, the bounty is high enough to tempt most."

I'd killed plenty of bounty hunters. Didn't matter to me what the price on my head was anymore, but it was Amaya who asked the question. "Had a price on my head since I was fourteen years old. Why should they come looking now?"

Luther chuckled. "Senorita, after you killed all them folks in the saloon, the bounty has shot up to $30,000."

CHAPTER TWELVE

I **LEFT LUTHER** behind in his little town. Wouldn't grace it again in my life or Luther's, but I imagined that sat well with him. I'd become a bad dream, a brief nightmare that had nested with them for the evening.

I drove my stage across the boarding ramp of the steamer, the name Dixie Queen on its bronze plate reflected by lantern light. I paid my fare to the boatmen who waited to accept my coin with trembling hands. I noticed Norm and Willis working to haul in the lines as I settled both my horses below the deck.

Deep inside, bellows began to work, the great boiler burning as the gargantuan paddle wheel on the back began to churn. Black pillars poured from the smokestacks and the ship belched out a droning horn that echoed across the bayou. I patted both of my loyal beasts, whispering comfort. "Enjoy the ride. Reckon this is the first time the two of you have enjoyed much rest."

Maestro snorted, shaking his head back and forth. I smiled at the beast and patted them both one more time, leaving them to their rest and returning to the humid air of the deck.

Amaya stood at the stern. I'd seen the great merchant ships in Charleston Harbor once, and she reminded me of the figureheads on them, carved to appease the powers that ruled the sea. Beautiful and terrible.

I joined her there and together we watched the lights of Patois Landing disappear, listening to the distant cicadas and the lapping of muddy waves against the hull.

"The sheriff, why is he bothering to help you?" Amaya asked.

I pondered on how to answer her, what answer would satisfy the hunger in her. Trying to make sense of the stories she'd heard, the crumbs of my past fallen like scraps.

"He has an understanding of me. Spent years with my brother, and watched him die. Fate brought him to me, and by its hand, he lived."

She picked through my words, trying to separate any lie resting there. There was none. Luther was just one of the few alive who understood me.

Thoughts of Virgil crept in. I stared off into the black night; there wasn't any moon to grace the sky, and I whispered to the wind and let it carry my words to the other side as I spoke to my brother, letting him hear my confessions on the far shore.

The deckhands present kept their distance, no doubt wondering what I was doing, whispering to the air and the dead. But like most times, no answer came drifting back to me.

"Best be getting inside, get settled," I told my daughter and I walked toward the center of the ship and the ballroom that made up the interior. A door opened as we approached and a man stumbled out in the arms of a woman, slurring his words and pawing at the woman's breasts as she giggled and tried to lead him past me.

I made to move past him as the well-dressed man whistled. "Wowee. Lookie here, Madeline. Got ourselves a reeeallll pair of desperados." He laughed at his jab before whipping swift out of his woman's arms and airing his paunch over the side.

The woman, Madeline, looked disgusted as she turned to me. "He went hard with the good stuff. Rich little whoremonger gets handsy after a few drinks."

I looked from the man who was emptying his innards into the river to the woman, thinking about what I wanted to do next. No choice at all really, I'd killed plenty for less.

FOR A FEW SOULS MORE

"What is your last name, Miss?" I asked politely.

The woman smiled sweetly, her green eyes shining, deep black hair matching the ebony of her gloves. "Don't have one, mister. Was raised by the other girls of Madame Giry's."

I inclined my head to the man who had slumped down to the deck, his joy having transformed into a dumpish melancholy as he rubbed his belly. "Do you have any desire to follow through on what you promised him?"

Madeline stepped towards me, running her hand down my vest, tracing her hand down my coat and towards my belt. "You willing to pay twenty greenbacks? Whoremonger there likes to spend on a classy lady such as—"

I had slipped my hand into my pocket and brought out a gold piece, the unasked answer to her pondering passing between us as she reached for it.

I moved my hand just out of reach. "Before you take it, there are things I require."

Madeline's eyes gleamed, the greed plain as day as that coin shimmered in front of her. I could feel her other hand tighten around my belt. "What manner of things are you wanting? For a piece like that, I'll put some effort in."

"I expect you would, but that isn't what I had in mind."

There was only a bit of fear, the kind folks who've seen more than their fair share of trail hid, trusting on their sand to get them through the danger. Course, I wasn't like most danger and my words were like a rattlesnake's tail, warning of the venom that coursed through me.

"Imagine you've been working this boat since you boarded, and I imagine that was back in the Quarter. You place yourself on my arm all night, tell me every tale you've picked up on your journey, and afterward, you tell me your own. Do these things, I promise a matching coin."

I searched her eyes, diving deep into her soul and trying to find her roots, and whether she was apt to blow away when danger came or stand firm. She worked for money, and if those looking for us came calling and paid her more, I expected her to sell herself for it. That was the way of things, but giving her the chance to help me, to live with an interesting tale. Well, I couldn't resist offering.

Madeline took the coin at the same moment that the man on the deck dragged himself to his feet. "You can't take my-"

He threw a punch, slow, and I caught it easily. The man struggled in my grip as I looked at the woman. "What's his name?" I asked.

Madeline held the gold piece like it was manna from heaven, quickly stashing it between her breasts as she answered, "Alfred Bullock, why?"

I angled him just right. "So I can remember."

He was easy enough to tip over the side; only screamed for a second before he hit the water. I heard him sputtering and gasping before the paddlewheel's never-ending cycle covered the sound.

Amaya stared over the side, her eyes searching for Alfred, to save him or witness his likely death, I couldn't say. Madeline stared with wide eyes at the edge as I turned and offered her my arm. "Shall we?"

The inside of the Dixie Queen was a maze of blue hallways that eventually made their way into the grand ballroom. Stained mahogany floors ran the length of the room, leading up to the ornate bar that had engraved figures of gold holding up the overladen shelves of drink.

Chandeliers and lamps hung down from the ceiling, illuminating the tables where rich johns played with their livelihoods, wandering off in loss or victory to the shadowed tables where cigars and opium were consumed.

The three of us made our way through towards the bar, where there was room between a fat man and a woman laughing at the jokes of two men in cheap threads. The bartender motioned he'd join us shortly.

Madeline's arm was rigid against me. She hadn't said a word since I'd killed Alfred. I leaned in, feeling her hair brush past my face as I whispered, "Don't hold your tongue, miss. I don't aim to harm you tonight, so long as you follow my direction."

She swallowed, taking a deep breath. "What do you need from me?"

I inclined my head towards the group surrounding a table at the far end of the room. "What do you know about them?"

Madeline's green eyes followed mine and she saw the four clustered around their cards; three men and a woman.

My companion shook her head. "They're wanted men. That's the Crogan brothers, oldest is that one sitting next to the lady."

I'd seen men like the Crogan brothers often, caked in dust, what little coin they had paying their way onto the ship, looking for diversions from trail life.

But the woman, she intrigued me. Her black coat and pants complemented her near-white hair. She didn't carry any shooting irons but I saw the blue-uniformed staff glancing at her like she was a coiled rattler. Her left cheek bore a mean scar, weaving its way up to her brow, meeting an eyepatch.

The Crogan brothers were laughing at her, drowned in their tongue oil, cheeks rosy red like the setting sun, and words slurring out like horse droppings.

I leaned in close to Madeline. "Who's the woman?"

Madeline grinned. "You have an eye for danger, mister. That's Sadie Faro. Half the cells in the Quarter are full thanks to her. It's said she's the best bounty hunter this side of the Mississippi . . . "

"What'll it be?" the bartender asked gruffly, interrupting us.

I raised three fingers and inclined my head at the top shelf and the whiskey sitting there. He poured three glasses, leaving the bottle, and I handed over the coins. I saw Madeline savor it, drank it down like a damn trail head six months dry, and she kept talking of the woman with the silver hair.

"Alfred was going on and on about her; killed Jose Flores and his rustlers two years back and saved that paper man, Cornelius Wells, after he'd been lost in the wilderness for a whole week. Alfred said she had the grit to take on the Black Magpie if he ever showed his face here."

Amaya stiffened. She'd only been sipping at her whiskey, ready to let fly if any of these here recognized us.

But Madeline giggled, her eyes unfocused, pouring her fourth drink from the bottle. "You heard of him? Hardly seems real. One of my regulars read me a dime he'd written about how the Black Magpie slaughtered a whole congregation on the devil's word. Took the preacher and nailed him to the front door."

The idea that some wordsmith was telling tales stoked my curiosity. "This writer, did he say whether he'd ever met the Black Magpie?"

Madeline took another drink, nodding her head. "Said that he'd traveled with him for a spell. Been party to some of his worst things, stories all, or so he said."

There were very few who had ever traveled with me for a time, and most of them were dead. Those that were left I was certain weren't the type to go spilling my deeds or their own. So I asked for his name.

"His name is Tatum Beasley, and from what he speaks it's a wonder he survived the man." She looked me up and down. "You could be a spitting image I suppose, even that marking under your eye could be mistaken, but it's not like what Mr. Tatum describes."

I could hear the whispers in my head and I tapped a finger against the hilt of my Gun. "And just how does Mr. Tatum describe him?"

Madeline giggled behind her drink. "A monster right out of even your nightmares, mister. Wearing human skin, with the devil's mark carved across his whole face like a mask, filed teeth to rip out the throats of God-fearing folk, the devil's own gun telling him to kill a thousand children so his spot in Hell will be assured."

I watched as Madeline shook her head, laughing a little. "Utter nonsense, but good reading for a working girl." She dismissed the bad thoughts and stories as easily as a child waking up from a bad dream. This wasn't Graverange, Furnace, Silver River, or Dust, we weren't more than spitting distance from New Orleans, and the savage and bloody had been driven out from here.

There were no monsters anymore, only men.

I took a drink, feeling the fire as it washed down, and wondered where it was that I could find Tatum Beasley and educate him on what things I really had done.

"Of course, he is making good money off the whole thing. Folks back in the Quarter can't seem to get enough of it. You don't see things like that around here, not with the city police."

Madeline finished the last of her drink and watched me. "Suppose the bounty woman could mistake you, mister, if you're worried about her. But she seemed keen on those savages. You just tell her your name and I bet you won't be sent swinging."

I chuckled darkly, finishing the last of my drink. "I doubt that. More than a few would be mighty pleased to see me swing."

Madeline trailed her finger around the edge of the glass, looking shyly at my reflection in the glass. "I gathered that after what you did to Alfred. Didn't think he was your first as you seem to be a man accustomed to killing." Her hand wandered across the bar, soft velvet glove drifting onto my hand. I looked at her and those deep green eyes promised wicked things.

"A madame named Helga runs a place at the next stop. She keeps a safe practically bursting with half of what the girls make. A violent man like you might be persuaded to relieve her of it, and her life if she makes trouble?"

Madeline spun pretty words, a fine plan for any man wanting to turn thief. I'd known a woman like her.

I produced another coin, the gold held in Madeline's gaze. "Let me tell you a story about a woman named Ruby Holloway. Working girl like you, she killed plenty of men in her parlor. Then she entered my service, struck a bargain, same as you."

My hand grabbed hers, lightning quick, like I was drawing to kill instead of give warning. And I made sure that an understanding passed between us. "She decided to sell what she knew and now her head sits in my stage. Remember that when you work from now on. Tell your story truly and you won't suffer the same."

Madeline made a small whimper, fear creeping in as she realized that the money I'd given her hadn't provided safety. I leaned close and whispered. "I don't wear human skin, and if the devil calls, I don't pay heed. What I did for this—" I pulled the Gun from its holster, and I could feel its touch on my mind, a soothing lullaby that urged me to deal out her last hand. "What I did would send you screaming. And all that's keeping you breathing right now is the word I've given you."

I released her wrist, watching the tears in her eyes, the realization creeping in, and I asked her. "Do you know who I am?"

Madeline nodded, her breath catching quick, looking around the room, eyes imploring. But I released her wrist and whispered again. "Then you know more than Mr. Tatum Beasley. Remember that."

I slid the coin across to her. "This is where we part ways, think I've gathered enough of your story to satisfy me."

She practically scrambled to grab the glimmering gold and move away from me. Then a thought struck me; she needed more than a sense of who I was, she needed to send a message. "Miss Madeline?"

The woman stopped like a whip's lash had torn straight

through her. I raised my glass to her. "If you see Mr. Beasley, tell him I intend to call on him. I'd like to hear his stories firsthand."

A shiver passed over her and she hurried away, leaving Amaya and me at the bar, aware of the Crogan brothers eyeing me.

"I think this writer is going to head for the hills knowing Salem Covington is coming for him," Amaya whispered beside me.

I tapped the bar and poured another shot, one I gratefully downed.

"They are still staring, those men at the table."

I slid the bottle to her. "Enjoy the rest. Reckon I'd like to learn more about them that have taken such an interest in us."

I strode over to the table, watching as the younger brothers averted their eyes the closer I came but the oldest glared like I'd spit in his grits. The open seat next to the bounty hunter called to me. I didn't speak to any of them as I took my place in the chair, pulling out a roll of greenbacks and placing them in the middle of the table. "Deal me in."

The Gun whispered as the oldest brother began to cackle, unpleasant like a black lung just come to coughing up his guts. "Risky play, stranger, sitting next to the bitch. And across from a couple of gunhands ready to air her innards."

The other two brothers licked their lips, staring at the woman. Her gloved hand trembled as she looked at the cards clutched tightly in her fingers. Any card sharp worth his sand would clean her out.

I wondered how much of her had been built up; the shivering thing next to me didn't seem to be the famed killer Madeline had told me. But I'd seen plenty of dangerous things wrapped in the guise of weakness. A catamount hidden amongst the trees.

I ignored the older Crogan brother's guff, picking up

the cards dealt to me. I barely glanced at what I'd been given, keeping my eyes on Sadie Faro. Realized that I had mistaken her demeanor for fear. It was tension. The poise of something seasoning its kill. While the Crogan boys were busy slipping their sand away into their drink, she was preparing a new cup for them to drink.

"Know who I am, Miss Faro?" I asked.

She nodded her head. "I didn't expect the Black Magpie."

A stillness came over the table. The younger brothers looked between themselves, uneasy, but the oldest brother spat onto the wood. "Bullshit. He ain't real, just trail talk."

I smirked and threw my cards to the table, letting the middle brother bask in his momentary joy of money. "That so? Then tell me, Miss Faro, are you worried about killing the wrong man?"

Heard the telltale sounds of springs popping, each brother lusting over their winnings not paying attention, I saw a block of wood rise up out of the green felt of the table.

Sadie Faro shook her head. "Not at all, sir. Just never thought you'd ever come sit at my table."

I watched the dumbfounded looks of the three brothers, each one staring blankly, trying to realize the truth of me despite their oldest brother's previous claims. "I've heard the stories of you, Miss Faro, even watched you from the dark where your fire couldn't stretch, that rifle of yours draped across your chest . . . "

I glanced at her right wrist, the hand holding her cards. "That hidden blade cutting out the hearts of them that think you sweet."

The words gnawed their way under her skin like maggots trying to get to the bone. It wasn't a lie; I reckoned she was one for picking up the truth in a spoken falsehood.

The Crogan brothers looked between themselves, and I saw Sadie Faro's left arm tense, pushing levers unseen under the table, four slots lowered from the wooden block that had risen out of the green felt.

Saw the barrels inside the wood, short little pistols that wouldn't have killed any man standing further away. But unfortunately for these men, they were sitting, and their drunk heads were grateful targets.

There were three shots, then the screams as three small holes appeared in the foreheads of the Crogan brothers. The youngest slumped across the table, a small river of red soaking into the green felt and his good hand of cards. The oldest one had tried to go for his pistol when he'd seen what was coming and now he decorated the floor. The middle brother was last, he made to stand, blood dripping from the tiny hole in his forehead like a dribble of piss from the end of his pecker. He stumbled backward. I was impressed he managed to cling to his life this long. Wasn't but a temporary strength, tricks played on the mind like he could go on living, and in time he finally toppled just like the rest.

Sadie Faro was quick to her feet. I saw the glint of the blade underneath her glove as she lunged forward, but she stopped when she found herself staring down the barrel of the Gun.

"Misfire, Miss Faro?" I asked quietly.

She glared at me for a moment, fear and anger cooling; most folk erred towards keeping their breath in their lungs when staring down a bullet. She stepped back, raising her hands as a half dozen or so men came pouring in, each one raising a rifle like it would help them.

Sadie glanced at me, reaching to close the blade at the same time she raised her hands. I lowered the Gun, hearing its disappointed murmurings. I didn't mind these rifles staring down my back, I was just fascinated by Sadie Faro's killing table.

I heard her explaining the state of the departed Crogan brothers to the boat security, who she was, and how no one had been in danger. She was accurate in her assessment. I had seen many things in my travels, but this was something extraordinary.

I could rustle up many a working. Call things from the dark, but I never had been one for engineering. There was a small button used to raise the hidden pistols and four strings running to the dealer's chair where they had been curled around the bounty hunter's fingers. One pull and four men could be reciting their wrongs to the devil. Except no bullet could kill me, and only the Crogan brothers were experiencing the never-ending fire.

Amaya had drifted over to me, her hands resting on both shooting irons as the men dragged the dead Crogans away. There were still a few whispers from the booths around us, these swells who had paid well for a trip upriver interrupted by the bloodshed. I looked up at my daughter, pointing to the strings and pistol contraption. "Never seen such a thing."

Sadie Faro had returned, standing over her chair and looking ready to throw it should the cards fall towards shooting. "Fine compliment, coming from you. Took some years to craft, and half a year's wage to get it put on this boat."

I examined the small gun pointed at me. "A compliment to your grit as well. Aren't many with the nerve." I tapped the Gun laying on the bloodstained felt. I saw her eye the weapon like a trail hand eyed a rattlesnake.

"I heard the stories, even believed them, but to have you sit down right in front of me . . . I couldn't resist."

"I would have killed you for it." Amaya said.

Sadie looked at her hands, a small smile playing over her lips. "I promise you, little senorita, you don't have the same sand in you. Seen your broadsheet and all you're known for."

She reached up slowly, her gloved hand snaking its way under the eyepatch covering her eye.

My daughter's hand twitched when she saw the lidless orb staring out at us. I heard the Gun whisper for the bounty hunter to receive its gift, and for that eye to join the tongue still resting in my pocket.

"But when you come from the place where this was given to me," Sadie started. "You wouldn't be anything more than a chirping bird."

I lashed my hand toward Amaya to keep her from killing the bounty hunter. Time would come for that. She had tried to kill me, but that scale could be balanced yet. And her story fascinated me.

"I'll make a deal with you, Miss Faro. It'll keep you breathing, keep you sane, and I won't have to kill any of these on this boat."

Sadie tapped her fingers,, and I saw her unmarred eye blink, pondering her odds at killing the both of us before a bullet could find her. She swallowed once, calm. "I'm listening."

I didn't hesitate in making my offer. "When we make port, you'll leave with your bounty; neither she nor I will follow you on the trail. You'll go your way and I'll go mine. It'll be another night when the dark crawls in around you, your fire clinging to the logs, that's when you'll see me sitting on the other side of it."

I picked up the Gun, and for a moment I thought I saw the bounty hunter's lidless and useless eye focus on it as if in its infinite blindness the weapon was the only thing to be seen.

I made to finish my offer. I could almost feel the working in the air, the vow I was making. "You'll owe me your entire story then. In exchange, the bullet I have for you won't ever come to rest in your flesh."

Saw the gooseflesh run across her skin like a herd of bison on the plains. She reached up for the eyepatch, drawing it down until it covered her mutilation, and nodded.

I nodded in return and stood, gesturing for Amaya to join me as we left the boat's gambling hall. I tipped my hat to Sadie as we went. "Until then."

Silence had come over the Dixie Queen. The cabin I'd paid for the two of us wasn't much, just a bed and a chair. I let my daughter take the bed as rest eluded me.

I sat facing the door, the Gun cradled in my hands, thinking of Sadie Faro and her attempt to kill me. Wasn't sure how much money I had taken from the dead. More than enough that I could have lived like a rich man back East. $30,000 weighed heavy, money like that could bring a heap of trouble calling.

I hadn't given promises to Amaya. If she died, I would go on. A likely outcome with the amount of money being offered for us. So, in the humid darkness of a paid room, I sat with my Gun and let it whisper. Hours passed while I considered how many more I owed, and I stared up at the ceiling, listening to Amaya breathe lightly. Her guns were in easy reach.

She was trail weary and sleep had come quick. I felt the same tug pull at me, the urge to let go and lapse into the rest, but I kept my vigil.

Couldn't account for the time when I saw the flickers of light pass through the window and play out their dance on the wall. Knew the light of torches, but didn't know the number of men carrying them. Didn't matter either; they'd come up like waves on the shore and be found wanting.

A floorboard creaked out in the hall. Amaya's soft breathing ceased, and I saw her hands reach for her pistols. I rose from the chair, silently making my way to the window looking out onto the deck and the blackness of the bayou.

I heard a whisper beyond the door, whoever was there trying to work up their nerve.

They never got the chance; as soon as I heard the first scream, I put a bullet through the door. Heard a grunt and a body topple to the floor, and someone mutter something before they began firing in return.

FOR A FEW SOULS MORE

Amaya ducked behind the chair as I waded into the hall. It was Norm, his hands held out like he was praying for forgiveness at Sunday service, his shirt was a curtain of red, bubbles of blood popping on his chest as he sobbed.

His partner, Willis, was close at hand, his hands held out, revolver already clattering to the floor as he squealed unheard pleas for mercy. He jerked as the bullet blew his head apart, a solid spray staining the wall behind him. He slid down and fell into his dying friend's lap, a wanted poster with my name on it clutched tight in his hand.

I saw my name at the top of it.

Greed could drive a man to stupidity, greed had betrayed kings, greed had killed the people who had once roamed to and fro over the earth, and gospel-slingers told that greed had sold God for just thirty silver pieces.

Bullets chewed through the wood around me. Four men had toppled tables and positioned chairs, cowering behind them as if it would save them. Each of them wore a crimson mask.

I fired twice and the first man slumped against the banister rails overlooking the card tables, laying against them like a drunk full as a tick. Both shots took him through the eyes and blood poured from both sockets like he was weeping when he'd gone to death.

Another bullet turned the jaw of the next into unusable meat, teeth rattling out amongst the acrid smell of smoke and gun powder. He made a sound, a choked gargle before he too joined the dead.

The last two had emptied their guns, pistols running dry. One tried to raise his hands, give out pleas that he hadn't believed the stories of me. The final thing he heard in life was the shot that ended his life. He stumbled backward, toppling over the wooden banister and falling out of sight. The bottles of whiskey decorating the bar underneath shattered.

I reloaded as his partner made for the stairs, my bullet catching him in the leg. He jerked, a short splattering of blood spraying against the wood before he screamed, falling end-over-end like a tumbleweed.

I heard spurs and turned to see Amaya emerging from the room behind me, her revolvers clutched tight. I put a finger to my lips and gestured for her to remain there. I had a feeling that there would be more waiting below.

Amaya didn't press the issue, especially when another shriek pierced the air, sobs following like a sinner come to die. Doled out plenty of pain to recognize its work on someone else; a woman below us was suffering.

I followed the scent of agony, smelling the blood, the salty tang of sweat and tears, and when I reached the bottom of the stairs, I saw Gwendoline Bell rip the skin from Madeline's finger.

The woman's stolen face was wrapped tight, the decaying flesh gone brown, flies buzzing in and out of the folds that separated her mutilated features from the putrid skin. A half-dozen more crimson-masked men stood around the gambling tables, all of them heeled.

I saw that each one of them was handling a woman, ropes binding arms. They were the wives of the swells who had watched Sadie and I end the Crogan brothers and lying dead all around us were their menfolk, their money still clutched in hand. I imagined they had offered it to them that had come calling and learned what little power it had on those who wanted nothing but killing.

Gwendoline had already taken eight of Madeline's fingers, the red stumps curling and uncurling like scorpion tails as she sobbed incoherently.

The grotesque woman looked over at me, lidless eyes hollow beneath the mask of flesh. "A handsome woman, this. Not like some bonny straight out of girlhood, but she'll do."

I traced with my gaze the mottled and distorted flesh on Gwendoline's bare shoulders, the ragged dress she wore occasionally showing hints of the grotesqueries within. "More woman than you, Miss Bell. Playing like you're still alive."

FOR A FEW SOULS MORE

A rasping laugh came from her throat, the damage that long ago ritual fire had done still holding strong. "I am still alive, the beauty that couldn't hang. Except I did hang, didn't I? Ordinary folk killed me, I went under, and I thought I would be beautiful again."

Her hand quivered around the butcher's knife held tight in her grip. My own hand tightened around the Gun, whispered warnings floating through my mind. The vacant lips of her flesh mask trembled and I knew that Gwendoline wanted to shed tears. But she couldn't, her slow turn around the fire all those years ago had stolen anything that could offer her succor for her agony. After all, I had cut off her eyelids and then I'd carved out her soul.

Gwendoline brought the knife close to the sobbing woman's face, scraping the blade across her skin just enough to prickle but leave the flesh unblemished. "But that wasn't to be. I drank the punishment of the grave, but when the veiled woman called me here, I wasn't beautiful again. And you were still living."

I heard the pleas and the impact of hands from the fine women who had been removed from the room. Thought of the two boat workers lying dead above me and wondered if Sadie Faro had sold us upriver.

I heard the creaking on the floor behind me; Amaya moving to get a good view. Gwendoline's eyes rotated like billiard balls, looking up, the slackened mouth of her mask curling upward as her lipless teeth bared themselves into a wolf's grin.

"Is that the pretty bird? I so wish to fly like her, soar away with a stranger, beauty that never ends. A final perfect face."

Her fingers danced across Madeline's dress. She bucked at Gwendoline's touch, reminding me of a fish trying to dance off a hook.

"What do you say, Black Magpie? You give me the girl and I give you back this innocent? You like those deals, don't you?" Gwendoline's stolen face twisted into a sneer. "So you can feed on their sweet pure souls?"

Madeline turned towards me, and I studied her face, age lines just beginning to show, her maidenhood long since gone transforming into mature beauty. There was just the barest streak of grey amongst the blonde tresses, testimony to a life lived, but with more than enough vigor still in her bones. She was pleading for me to help her, could hear it like a fly's buzz against my thoughts, persistent and useless.

I looked into her eyes and measured her fear. Had the means to save her, a quick bullet would send Gwendoline back off to Lorelei's arms. But that was the thing with fate; when it came time to call your chits and play what hand you'd been dealt, there would be no rescue if your cards came up short. I'd known that from the moment I'd first picked up the Gun. When the time came, there wasn't going to be any help coming to me.

I ignored Madeline's eyes as I kept my gaze on Gwendoline. "Wouldn't deny a killer their due. I won't stop you, but when you're finished, step outside and we can settle this."

Gwendoline didn't hesitate; her hands slithered to the folds of dead skin around her neck, pulling it up and away, rotten flesh separating in her hands, dead blonde hair falling off in clumps as the flies decided to find better prospects at her feet.

I heard Amaya stifle a gasp, but the same couldn't be said for Madeline whose scream pierced the night like a soldier's whistle. It was a natural reaction to seeing the monstrosity my teacher and I had created.

Her flesh beneath was completely devoid of hair, but not smooth. It was mottled and splotched, wrinkled like old leaves come winter. Her eyes stared without pause, unblinking marbles empty of color. I'd cut her ears from both sides of her head and now all that were left were dark holes. Her lipless mouth revealed teeth angled and broken like headstones in some old boot hill. There was other damage, things unseen that had been done before the ritual. Virgil had cut through her cunny, and I'd cut off both breasts.

And now she stood in her terrible glory above Madeline.

I gestured for Amaya to come down, heard the footfalls on the stairs at the same time Madeline began screaming. Gwendoline pulled hard, yanking the woman's head up, knife sliding underneath the nape of her neck. She began cutting, the flesh slicing away and spilling blood over the already ruined table. The blade carved the whore's skin and Madeline never stopped her wailing and I never blinked.

Gwendoline had finished with Madeline's scalp, the bloody bone of her spine showing. The woman's arms fell like limp stalks and her eyes rolled up. Her head twitched and shook with every new cut.

"Shoot her," Amaya whispered.

She stood close, both her guns trained on Gwendoline who ignored us both, busy pulling at her victim's scalp. I heard the wet tearing as she pulled at the sinew of the woman's skull.

"She'll be finished soon enough," I replied, leaving Gwendoline to complete her work.

Amaya trailed behind, close enough that I could feel her hot breath on my ear. "You let that woman die for what? She hasn't done—"

I turned and stared hard into my daughter's eyes. Anyone else I wouldn't have thought twice about giving the local gravedigger some new business, but this girl was blood, and I thought to give her a true measure of who she was to me.

In that time that passed faster than the beat of a wing on the air, I wondered if Amaya knew that I would kill her if times came calling for it. Her life was different only in that she was my child, kin to me and the Gun I held, born from a night inked in killing. But family only stretched so far . . .

Needs must, even if it was her death.

But Amaya didn't give into fear. Her hand snapped up, I saw the flash of the bullet, and Gwendoline fell, her bald head opened up like a canyon, blood running out a small flow.

Amaya looked back at me, hands trembling, staring down the barrel of my Gun. It whispered and jumped, I felt it stroke my mind like a woman's touch, grabbing hold of my fingers and urging me to end her there.

She'd cheated what was due and I aimed for Amaya to learn that there was no reprieve for those fated to feel the soft dark of the earth come sunrise. I lowered the Gun, slowly, feeling the rage in me course its way like a flooding bank and I whispered, "You haven't saved her."

Whatever venom she might have flung, it was kept to herself as Madeline coughed on the table, her whole body quivering, her dripping blood keeping time. Her moans reminded me of a cow led to a butcher, lowing cries for life that would go unheard.

She wasn't going to live. Gwendoline was an artist with a knife and before Amaya had shot her, she'd made it down to Madeline's nose. The whore's skin held to nothing, bloody bits of skull and muscle visible in dark pools of blood.

When Madeline turned her head at the sound of Amaya's footsteps, her face sagged like an empty flour sack, skin folding in and blocking her eyes from seeing anything but the wet hollow of her own flesh. She muttered some words as Amaya placed the barrel against what used to be the woman's forehead and fired, replacing the spent bullet even as her head fell back against the table.

"Well done, Miss Shrike," I said as I walked past.

"Wasn't a test, cabron. This is not the first I've put out of their misery."

I looked down at Gwendoline's unblinking eyes,

mocking that it wouldn't be long before she was called back to work another woman with her blade. By hook or crook, I meant to make sure she stayed dead.

I looked out the window, hearing the screams from outside the bar, the smell of smoke and charred wood. The Dixie Queen was burning.

And I aimed to add more than just wood to the fire.

CHAPTER THIRTEEN

I TOSSED GWENDOLINE Bell's corpse onto the deck. It rolled until it landed face down, blood spreading across the planks. Plenty of her gun hands milled about, handing down the women they had taken to the boats below. More walked the breadth of the boat, setting fire to every room they came across. I counted thirty or so of these men, each one wearing a crimson mask and busy mutilating the women they'd come for.

I saw a woman dragged from the huddled mass of swells. The gun hands heated long blades of metal in the fires of the swiftly burning ship. A wooden block had been laid out on the prow, little more than a stump ripped from the ground. The woman babbled as they stretched out her hands, howling as they laid the edge of the white-hot blade against her wrists, flesh charring, peeling back like it could escape the heat. His mark made, the man slashed the blade down and the woman shrieked as both her hands fell twitching to the deck, rolling with the listing deck until they disappeared over the side.

The masked man laid the blade back into the flame and the woman fell back, sobbing as she stared at the seared stumps. One of the gun hands shoved her over the side and into the waiting hands of the men below, then selected the next one.

They had the boat's men on their knees, about half the number of the gunhands that had come to take their lives from them. Those that had fought back had gotten a good crack over the head for their troubles and blood streamed down from their scalps in dark rivulets. They looked to me, their eyes like gateways to nothing, the death of having found purchase there.

Could only imagine what I looked like against the flickering light of the fires, like death's own shadow had come unstuck and had arrived to send all of them screaming down to hell.

I walked out of the ship's inside, planting my boot directly on Gwendoline Bell's back, feeling her spine break under me as I put my weight against her. A few of the gun hands paused, fingers twitching towards their irons as if it would save them.

But one waved them off, going to the nearest kneeling man. It was Luther Moon. I imagined he'd been taken when we'd left port, taken by Gwendoline along the river. He'd been stripped down to his union suit and taken a beating that left his right eye swollen. Blood dripped from his nose and a tooth protruded jagged over his lip.

One of the crimson masks stepped forward to meet me, a rifle held tight in his grip, Luther's sheriff star pinned like a prize on a sash displaying seven other law badges. "Not so fast there, Covington."

The man had a rippling voice, like a flapping mule skin. I didn't heed his request until he pointed the rifle at Luther. With his other he pulled off his mask, revealing a thick head of black hair, muttonchops running into a sparse beard.

"Reckon this is a familiar face?"

Truth be told, it wasn't, but I didn't care who he was. He began to speak again, but his words passed over me as I stared at Luther, letting him know what was to be done. To pray if he so chose it.

The gunhand spit, looking between the two of us. "So, here's how this is gonna go." He tapped his trigger finger against his rifle as he spoke, the air punctuated by a scream as another woman's hands were removed. "You throw that piece of yours over here, then you jump in the fucking river, we haul you back to your little nest of death, and we fucking end you. Do that and these fine folks plus the lawman will live."

He spoke with an easiness that came with a man who'd seen his fair share of blood. There was no bluffing his resolve; he wasn't afraid nor was he a juniper with his rifle. He'd shoot Luther as easy as a man could chew.

I gripped the Gun and felt its joy as it realized what was coming, eager to drink the blood of innocent and guilty alike. The sheriff locked eyes with me, and I asked him the only thing I cared to know. "My message, Luther?"

He nodded, and I tipped my hat. The gunhand shouted for me to look at him, to answer him. Luther closed his eyes.

The mutton-chopped man was telling me that he would kill them, he would kill this sheriff, the children, the women. "I will do it, I swear to God!"

I smiled and watched the man's blood run cold. "Let me make this simple for you." I fired. The bullet took Luther through the eye, the orb splattering and running clear fluid down his cheek as he fell, lifeless.

The gun hand's eyes widened, trying to turn his rifle to fire, but before he could, his kneecap exploded. A piercing shriek erupted from his throat amid the crackling flames of the burning ship. He fell to the deck, hands clasped around his ruined knee like he could pray healing into the bleeding appendage. By that time, I'd already killed two of his friends.

The ground ran red, blood from bodies tracing through cracks between the deck planks, forming small ponds of red in my boot prints as I fired. Some of the red-masked men attempted to fight, but they died. Some attempted to flee, but they died. To their credit, none pleaded for mercy, and I gave none.

I fired the Gun and it drank in the dead and damned, it guided my hand and I knew that some who fell under its sight did not wear crimson masks. Some were husbands pleading for their families; every woman who'd had her hands removed by these men found a bullet nestled inside them.

I paid my devil's due one life after another, my hands trained for killing, my fingers for murder. It had been a long time since I had given myself over to the slaughter, unconscious of my reloading, uncaring of stories or possessions, just lives, picked clean and left to burn on the shores of fire.

I remembered Lawrence, Centralia, Marmiton River . . . all the times that I had given into the power I'd bartered. All the times I'd left wounds on the world.

The world came back into focus. My breathing was heavy. I felt the warm sprinkles of fresh blood against my cheek as I looked at the work of my hands and my weapon. Bodies lay mutilated and empty of life, but a few walked around in a daze; three men, one woman, a girl, and two boys.

The gunhand trembled, still clutching his ruined knee, eyes shut, his breathing coming out in quick puffs. No doubt wondering whether the next shot was for him. I put the Gun against his head, breathing hard. The urge was still there, like a dog thrown a bone after eating supper scraps.

Tears stained his muttonchops, hands collapsing to his side when he heard me release the hammer. There were no parting words between us, just sobbing as the water began to lap over the edge of the sinking pyre. He'd never make it to shore.

Amaya stood behind me, she had Gwendoline Bell bound at her feet, rope digging hard into her wrists and ankles. I didn't know the burned woman had come back until I heard her laugh, her lidless eyes rolled up to look at Amaya. "You see now? Cuts a real swell, doesn't he? Look hard, pretty bird, he ain't nothing but the Devil's bast—"

Amaya kicked her. I heard the rib crack and the mocking cackle transform into a wet cough. My daughter looked out to the river, the burning ship highlighting the few living stumbling around the deck. All of them wondering what they would do now, where they would go, how they could go on . . .

Suppose one or two would come after me, unable to weather the nightmares and anger at being left alone in the world weighing them down until they came looking to die.

Amaya found the words stuck in her throat. "You killed the children."

"Yeah," I replied, hearing the edge in my voice as I shoved past her to stand over Gwendoline Bell, matching her glare with my own.

"COVINGTON!"

It was Sadie Faro. She fired at the last few of Gwendoline's men as they attempted to row away. I heard the splash of their bodies as they fell into the river.

She took a running leap and jumped into the water. She swam to the boat, pulling herself up, throwing a line up to the listing deck. "Get in!"

I turned to my daughter. "Don't wait for me. Take those that are left and get to shore."

I didn't wait for her to respond as I sprinted the length of the deck, remembering my other companions.

I waded through the lower decks, making my way down to the cargo hold. My horses thrashed in their reins, the water nearly up to their mouths.

I stared, feeling the flash of anger sear through my mind like the touch of a branding iron.

There were no tears from me as I swam close, whispering soothing words, feeling the pull of pain in the pit of my stomach. But it was quickly replaced with the fury that burned for those that pursued us. I pulled the Gun and fired quickly, whispering the death prayer for both.

I turned, pulling against the current of the rapidly

filling room. My stage was drowning, everything it carried doomed to the darkness of the riverbed.

I felt the water inside my coat. My ingredients and workings floating in the low light. I busied my hands with taking what little things I could; it was a long way down to the bottom of the river.

Soldier and Maestro had sunk in their stalls, but I could smell the copper tang of their blood, stronger than the scent of the wild water. I gritted my teeth, then left them behind. The wet darkness took me into its embrace, like the darkness of Hell swallowing me, the current sweeping me out of the depths.

I came to the surface like a guilty man coming up from baptism, seeing the lanterns burning on shore.

Gwendoline Bell cackled as I pulled myself from the river. "A serpent for the devil, here to spread his sin wherever he roams," she said from her place in the mud.

Amaya pulled the woman to her feet, tossing the rope binding her to me. I looked to Sadie who was tending to the business of making a fire. "Keep your watch, Miss Faro."

The bounty hunter nodded, reloading her rifle and staring at Gwendoline. "She cost me my money. Won't be no mercy from me."

I started pulling Gwendoline into the cypress, Amaya following me. I called to Sadie. "Might change your mind when you hear the sounds she'll make."

We walked into the dark, and I felt satisfaction when I heard Gwendoline stumble and fall, crying out and gasping for air as my pace made her chew the dirt.

I tied Gwendoline Bell to a tree some ways from the bank. These kinds of things could not be done amongst the survivors, in the places where folk thought they were safe. No, pain like this carried all the way to the tables of real power, fueled workings and magic. Agony deserved to be carried out in the pitiless dark of the wild.

I found a half-dead oak that would do.

The mutilated woman just stared, lidless eyes following me as I built the fire, Amaya standing close, holding what I had rescued from my stage. I wondered what my daughter thought of me now; there was a difference between hearing stories and seeing them performed. Her mind had seen me as just another outlaw like her, driven by the same wants and needs of greed and lust. Dangerous, but just a man.

I did not want comfort; it held no appeal to me. And the only thing I lusted after came with me after I'd put their former owners under. Their possessions lined my home, their blood fueled my craft, and their souls lived in my thoughts when I stared into my future of brimstone. Eternity was long, and I aimed to feast on their stories until the timepiece stopped ticking.

The sticks began to smoke as the tiny flame that I nurtured finally began to catch, a thin band of smoke drifting up to lose its form amongst the stars. I poked at the flame with a branch, watching the orange sparks dance, deliberately not looking at the woman before me. Gwendoline had been speaking the entire time; my mind had been too busy wandering in its own counsel to notice, but I noticed when she went silent, her gaze locked on the fire.

I reckoned it made sense; it may have been a rope that had sent Gwendoline off to hell, but it was the shaman fire that had made her worthy of it. Felt satisfaction seeing that she still feared it.

"Have some questions that need answering," I said, tending the flame.

"This where you offer me some painless death if I turn yellow? Have you forgotten so soon? The mourning season is over, the time of dying is done. Where is your sting now, Black Magpie?" I saw her fingers bloom in her bonds like a flower opening to the sun, eyes still fixed on the flame. Her charred skin stretched, lidless eyes crinkling at the edge, and I got the sense that she was grinning.

She was laughing when I produced Morris's tongue, but the rattle died away quickly when she saw the rotting organ in my hand. Her name was cut into the tissue.

"Don't need your sweet talk to come willing, Miss Bell."

I hit her, fist driving hard into her mouth. I hit her again. Then again.

Blood trickled from her gums, and my knuckles smarted. My skin had cut against her teeth. A belt's worth lay in the mud around my boots, reminding me of headstones at a boneyard.

With my knife, I cut the tongue into smaller pieces, thin slices between the bloody letters of my victim's name, easier to swallow that way.

Gwendoline mumbled, blood oozing from the new wounds, her mottled flesh swollen over one of her eyes.

I cupped her chin between my fingers, tilting her head back until her mouth lolled open, and with my other hand, I dropped pieces of the tongue down her throat.

"A taken tongue, for taken truth."

Wasn't sure if Gwendoline could hear the words, didn't know if she could feel the magic strangling her will, but it didn't matter either way. I would get my answers, then I would make sure that Lorelei heard Gwendoline's agony in the next world.

The last piece of the tongue was swallowed, and Gwendoline leaned forward, lidless eyes dilated, her breathing labored, coming out in long billowing wheezes. Like a mule that had taken an arrow to its neck.

"Who are your gun hands, Miss Bell? What's Granger Hyde paying them to die on his behalf?"

Silence. Gwendoline clamped her jaw, mewling at the pain as some of her teeth drove into her bloodied gums, throwing her head like a sinner come to the cleansing creek. Trying to resist the working as it hitched her mind.

"They're . . . they're yours. Your orphans, widows, and desperate men. You go around killing, stealing lives, butchering good people. Now those scraps you left, they've done turned over like bad apples, and all of them are eager to come for you." The rasping laugh returned, words tumbling out of her like a cracked gourd. She twisted in her bonds and howled at the dark sky.

"Nettie Hays, you killed her father after a hand of poker. Dallas Gray, his father was a sheriff who tried to run you to his calaboose. Frank Dickerson, you killed both of his boys when he was guiding settlers, young pups of fourteen both." She listed more names, more stories, men and women signed on with Granger Hyde's outfit, an army of sins come back to see me trussed up and ready to meet my maker.

I listened to every word, feeling the pit in my stomach growing. It wasn't a lie, my working made sure of it. It just meant that Granger had gone across the nation, following the dust of my trail. There were many united by their hatred of me, some with eyes that had seen the railroad march across the land, the natives turned back and confined to their barren reservations, others just barely old enough to ride or lift a gun. All of them swearing a blood oath they'd see me dead. Flattering, and foolish.

I've killed a passel of men, so many that their stories would feed my damned soul for eternity should I not escape the black circles waiting for me. These souls made sinners and their graves would square my debt. Granger had offered them all a chance to right their wrongs, and all he was really doing was offering up a feast for me.

Counting those back in New Orleans, I reckoned Amaya and I had already killed plenty of them. Despite their anger and bullets, at the end of the day, they were just men. And men couldn't run from what was coming for them, what was coming for me, what came for everyone at Trail's End.

"Granger found your nest. Wasn't deterred by all the graves, so neatly made, or those you left to rot under sun and sand. Got to roam your pretty house where your Ma brought you squealing into the world. Saw her too, and oh did the Mourning Lady tell us all about her . . . "

Gwendoline leaned forward, her eyes rooted on mine. "Hired hate is easy, Black Magpie, but to bring her up from deepest bone and darkest death, from the same womb you crawled from? She'll sing you a bullet lullaby and nestle in the cold of your corpse."

I gestured for Amaya and she came, sweat staining her face as she brought what I'd asked her: a hammer and a large railroad spike. I nodded to her as she laid the implements next to the fire, pausing to listen to Gwendoline's defiance.

"You think she can't see you, Magpie? Even now? Just because you sent her home to rest? You never paused to reason why I'm walking proud? Your precious Gun . . . " She tried to spit, thick drool running off her tongue and down her lipless chin. "Ain't worth nothing now. Kill me as much as you want, I'll be on your bootheels like a hound from hell. My soul is hers to keep."

I reached for the railroad spike. There were plenty laying around this country, remnants of a time before progress had passed this land by. I put it into the burning coals and let it heat.

Amaya looked like she'd had the piss kicked out of her, eyes dull, mouth open just wide enough that I could see the tips of her teeth. I could see her trying to shake the scent of blood.

She'd killed bad men, she'd raided towns, and she played with pain and cruelty like a babe just learning its first steps. Unused to the truth of the world, the only truth, one that I aimed to pay out unto Gwendoline Bell.

I watched her fingers fidget like worms. I doubted she even knew that she was doing it. "Thank you, Miss Shrike. Now, if you would be so kind, gather up every piece of dried brush you can find and bring it here." She nodded and disappeared back into the black.

Gwendoline watched her go. "Pretty bird. You won't save her, you know? Just like you couldn't save your sis-"

I wrapped my hand around the railroad spike and

drove it into the woman's gut, the white-hot metal peeling apart her flesh as the cloth of her dress began to singe, catching flame. Gwendoline's voice trailed off into a hollow gurgle, trying to scream, her agony arresting what little sanity she had left. I could feel the heat beneath my glove, and the flesh beneath my eye hurt, a reminder that nothing burned hotter than perdition's flame.

Gwendoline sobbed and stamped her feet, hands wriggling in their bonds like headless snakes, and I leaned in close, whispering my question. "What does Granger Hyde want with the women?"

I looked into her lidless eyes. Unable to meet my gaze, she answered through hoarse cries. "I'm not afraid, I'll kill the pretty bird and be beautiful when the Lady of Mourning comes for me."

The railroad spike began to cool in my hand, tempered in her blood. I pulled it and smiled as a charred and blackened loop of intestine came with it.

Crouching low, I held the intestine tighter than an owl gripped a mouse, Gwendoline groaned as I pulled inch by bloody inch. The dirt was hard here, far enough from the river's touch, and the blackened loop in my hand became caked with dust as I pressed it firmly into the ground. I stepped down on it hard with my boot, the gut felt like a giant worm underfoot and reached for the hammer. I angled the iron over the intestine and Gwendoline cursed, spewing every obscenity known to men, but she quit just as fast when I drove the still-hot metal through.

The railmen hummed tunes when they drove their hammers, whistled joy to their sweat. I timed my blows to her screams until the spike was entrenched fully into the ground.

Her head turned like an old windmill, making deep circles as her tongue brushed over dry lips, her breath coming like a dead man's sigh. Then I decided to share a truth with her, the truth of why she'd even gone on living all those years ago.

"Virgil let you live; he always did have a soft heart. My teacher had already decided on you and yours as a sacrifice. He was determined to get every drop of pain. Remember your little ones? Sounded like sows when Dead Bear hauled them high, your husband's innards decorating the stones around the fire . . . "

I heard Amaya coming, dragging thick brush and brambles. I barely paused as I pulled my knife and placed it on the edge of the flame.

"You roasted over your family's innards, I watched your skin crack and peel like skinning a sweet potato. And we wouldn't let you die. Comanche knew how to draw it out, keep someone living past all reason to die. If it wasn't for my brother going soft, you'd have joined your family feeding the dogs."

Gwendoline Bell screamed, hoarse like some bear or wolf, her reason fleeing in the face of her rage. She tried to bite me, tried to kick, only to scream as it tugged her loose intestine further from her gut.

I left her to her despair, turning to my companion. She'd done just as I'd asked, large dry pine branches and dead shrubs ripped straight from loose soil. She'd found good handfuls of Spanish moss, threading it amongst the dead pine.

I nodded to her as she set the last of it down. "Tend the fire, I'll get the rest."

It took the better part of the night to gather enough dead brush. Gwendoline was dying slow; she'd been dying slow ever since Lorelei had raised her up from whatever potter's grave that town tossed her in.

I aimed to keep her alive just a bit longer, if only to feed her the last truth she'd hear.

She'd stopped her screaming, her gnashing, and Amaya sat in front of her, legs crossed and listening to whatever Gwendoline had to say. I didn't stop my task, didn't waver; what was said between the two of them was their own business. No words would avert fate tonight, no promises that were worth less than spit. If Gwendoline expected Amaya to intercede for her, she was a damn fool.

Amaya wasn't a shavetail when it came to killing, her pistol handling was a testament to that. She didn't shy away from blood or the need to pull the triggers and end a man's life.

But whatever padre had a hand in raising her up with Olivia had schooled her to believe she wasn't just another killer. Given her false righteousness, imagined herself a hero like some dime novel character. I wondered if she knew that justice and mercy wouldn't follow her, that the good folk of the Dixie Queen would have seen her hang just as swiftly as they would have accepted her saving guns.

I could sense it sure as the wind blew; fate had a way of calling a man's cards when his hand was only barely known. Come sunrise, I imagined that Amaya would be thinking of pulling stakes, heading back for El Jardin. Be killed by some Pinkerton or rail man finally getting the drop on her someday. Or she'd find the killing urge running deeper, colder than a swift mountain stream.

I'd piled the scrub and limbs around Gwendoline, still hanging and barely clinging to life. If she'd found some way to unwind herself from her bonds, she'd still have to pull the spike from the ground and stuff her guts back in.

Amaya rose as I approached. I saw her questions there, but Gwendoline had my focus. She gasped, breaths coming slow, reminded me of an old mongrel still wheezing by in a twilight life.

"Told . . . her . . . what you did, Black Magpie. Who . . . you . . . killed. My children, my . . . husband . . . " She was breathing hard, every word slower than the last. I just pulled my hot knife from the fire where I'd left it.

"I'm not the only one to be killing young'uns, Miss Bell. You tell her about your own journey? About the girls rendered faceless for the buzzards?"

I didn't give her the chance to answer before I dug the blade under the skin of her wrists, watching the blood splash over my gloves and sizzle off the burning blade. I sawed through her tendons, making sure each hand would be useless.

She screamed and from somewhere off in the distance, a wolf's howl answered.

Gwendoline had hardened in her time; she didn't pass out, didn't let the pain undo her no matter how she must've wanted it to. I whispered to her as I cut the bonds of rope keeping her tethered to the tree. "Never learned the truth the Comanche were trying to teach you, Miss Bell. The only truth of the world. Suffering is all there is. We come into the world accompanied by it, and we all leave with it. Pain is an old friend. I aim to reacquaint you."

The singed rope snapped, and Gwendoline fell to the dirt, more of her guts pulling out of the open wound. She pulled herself to her knees, and I stood watching as she feebly threw her hands over her own innards, limp fingers unable to grasp the loops of bloody intestine.

I picked up a branch from the small fire, looking at the palisade of wood and Spanish moss I had created, making sure there was no opening she could go crawling from if by some miracle she pulled the spike from the ground.

Then I began to light each palisade of brush around her, the fire jumping greedily. Gwendoline, already touched by old flames, began to howl as the inferno surrounded her. She'd become an idiot, scrambling on all fours and screaming into the rising flames.

Amaya fled through the small corridor I'd left open, the flames already beginning to catch there. Soon it would engulf the dry moss I'd left strewn across the ground.

I followed her through the opening, standing clear of the flame and watching Gwendoline Bell scream as the flames began to lick the barest edges of her dress. I shouted into the din. "The fire remembers, Miss Bell. I reckon you remember what it feels like."

A person could last a long time with their guts nailed to the earth; my teacher had taught me that when my brother and I had lived among the Comanche. This had been a favorite death for white settlers caught on the wrong side of fate, warriors casting lots to see how some chose to die. It was beast instinct, the torment of fire euchring all senses, giving saddle to only one thought: escape.

Gwendoline Bell didn't disappoint. She came running, the heat peeling at her hide, and her bowels unlooping themselves out of her belly as she came. She reached the end of the trail I'd left her, bloody viscera hanging behind her like a butcher's rack, and I saw the relief in her eye when she cleared the fire.

I smiled when I heard the wet sound, the spray of blood from her belly as the last bit of her entrails came tearing out. Her carcass toppled into the mud, staring unseeing as her funeral pyre raged behind her.

I walked over to it, feeling the satisfaction come through me faster than saloon whiskey, squatting to whisper to the empty flesh. "Give Lorelei my regards. I'm eager to kill her again."

I gestured for Amaya to join me and together we threw what used to be Gwendoline Bell into the din, flesh and flame come together once again.

CHAPTER FOURTEEN

I **DIDN'T LEAVE** the pyre until every bit of flesh was nothing but ash in the breeze. I watched Amaya cringe as the scent of charred flesh drifted through the air, turning her brown skin a shade lighter.

Flesh smelled like pork when it cooked; known many a man that had turned in shame when the succulent smell caused their hunger to rear its head. Amaya's stomach gurgled, supper long since disappeared, and I smiled at her, watching the look of disgust flash across her face. I stayed with the fire, watching it try to chew through the dirt to continue its destruction.

It was the same with me, a fire destroying everything in its path until there was nothing left to destroy but my own self. Could see it on the horizon, but there was still plenty of blood to spill yet.

"A bullet would have been kinder," Amaya said.

"Bullet wouldn't have been permanent," I replied, eyes fixed on the body burning in front of me. I didn't think Lorelei's working could stand the fire, but I wasn't one to kill with a lick and a promise.

I took my place in the dirt, legs curled like this was just another solitary fire burning out in the endless plains. Amaya joined me and the two of us stared at the shadow that had once been living as it collapsed in on itself, sparks and ash carrying the dead woman's soul off to hell.

"She told me what you'd done, back when you were living with the Comanche."

I chuckled as I wiped a bead of sweat from my forehead, the heat from the flame creeping under the folds of my coat like a pig roast. "She didn't know everything, not even close. Miss Bell and I were acquainted for a short time. She spent four days on the sacrificial fire before she escaped."

"Before your brother let her go, more like."

I nodded, remembering my brother's guilt, the brutality he hadn't embraced. "Yeah, Virgil was tender that way. Course, he did his part when our teacher called for her young 'uns."

Roux emerged from the shadows, trotting to meet us, nudging up under my arm. I ran my hands through the blood-stained fur; the red wolf had eaten well tonight, same as me.

Amaya watched, and I could see the fascination and curiosity laid bare. "I'm a brother to wolves and those that choose to walk as them, same as you'll be."

She shook her head, feeding herself a lie as if it would save her in the end. "I won't. I'm not like you. I don't kill children."

The wolf lay down beside me, a yawn exposing his wide maw, bits of gristle from whatever he'd managed to kill still hanging between the teeth. I scratched behind his ears and whispered another truth I'd learned. "When the chips are called, Miss Shrike, you'll find there isn't anything you won't kill."

She shook her head, raven hair falling across her face, reminding me of Lorelei and her veil. "I heard my mother's stories, but I didn't believe her."

I kept my hand on Roux, feeling the rough fur pass between my fingers. "If you didn't believe, you wouldn't have come looking."

A log cracked, sending sparks swirling up to flare and vanish in the night. Amaya's eyes reflected the fire, like her rage had taken shelter there, as if the memory of the women floating dead not even a mile behind us would burn away.

FOR A FEW SOULS MORE

The longer the trail was, the less you tended to keep regret and guilt in your saddlebags. But looking into the fire, I saw the bodies clear, their death spasms as the Gun ate their souls down to the bone. And in the night's quiet silence, I found that things long discarded weren't as gone as I'd hoped. I couldn't change from my path now, not after so long given over to wickedness. Plenty of times long by still clung to me like sweet honey, but I couldn't see this one doing the same. I'd remember, that was my way, but this bloodshed would turn to bitterness in my mouth.

The Gun slept, sated. Better than a whore eager for the coin, it drove away the guilt and the scraps of remorse, giving me back over to my black curiosity. I gave into the feeling, indulged the interest that nagged like a buzzing horsefly. "Did Gwendoline tell you about her own deeds, Miss Shrike? About the women and girls she killed?"

Amaya looked up from her curled knees, her hair and the darkness keeping her face hidden. "No."

I nodded, leaning back to look up at the night. "It was quite the ride for her. She'd wait in the dark, find a woman alone, and lurk in her house while whatever menfolk drifted to rouse a game of cards. Then she'd creep slower than a serpent slithers, on her belly to the missus' sleeping in bed, taking her knife and butchering them. Then when the man would come home, senses more dulled than a man in the jakes, she'd greet them, all sweet, thinking he'd never be able to tell the difference."

I looked at my daughter, watching the firelight dance in her eyes. "She killed more than a few."

I watched her chew on the thought, the shadow of her face swallowing the scraps of truth I'd fed to her. And in that darkness, I could almost envision another life.

I saw a house, a ranch. I'd become a damn sodbuster. I toiled in bitter earth and labored through the sweat of my brow. And I was happy. A woman as pale as fallen snow brought me a jar full to the brim with tea to slake my thirst. I did not recognize her, though I got the sense that I knew

125

her. And beyond that I saw Amaya sitting on the porch, pregnant, her husband out in the pens breaking horses. Her holsters were empty, and as I sipped the drink this pale woman provided, I checked my own. I didn't hear the Gun's loving whisper; my debt was paid, and what was in my holster was nothing else but a weapon.

It was a fool's dream, a young man's dream, one who imagined that there was something like a good man's life at the end of the trail. Such a thing could have been true for Virgil, had he lived, had I not killed him the same as I had our father and our sister.

I felt the Gun whisper to me, curious at my longing for something that didn't involve it. And the juniper's dream was blown away same as the ash carried by the dying fire. It would not abide any future that didn't include bloodshed.

No more talk passed between Amaya and me, not until the witching hour was passed. I'd seen her head, slowly lowering until it was near cradled between her knees, sleep close to taking her. I pressed on her shoulder, and her head shot up, her hands immediately going for her guns.

"Best be getting back, see how Miss Faro is getting along and get you some shut-eye. I imagine we'll be continuing on come sunup."

I saw the fight behind her eyes, trying to decide whether it was best to keep her watch or follow my instructions, but it didn't take her long before she rose, looking back at the shore, the smoking remnants of the Dixie Queen still funneling up into the star-strewn sky.

She paused before leaving. "You might need to get some shut-eye too. No stage to catch some rest if you start dragging."

I matched her gaze and held out my hand. "I've ridden days on end without shut-eye, won't be dogging my boots."

She nodded to me and went on her way. I watched her recede until she faded into the dark, waited longer to make sure she wasn't doubling back, then I rose. Roux looked up at me, yellow eyes irritated at my movement.

Better that Amaya was gone. A working was a secret thing, a pact between you and the powers and principalities of the world. I had plans for Gwendoline Bell even in death, and it meant trading in the only scratch of her left in this world.

There wasn't much that I salvaged from my stage, but this one jar would suit my purposes.

I crouched down where Gwendoline had burned, a few charred bones jutting through the ash like fingers. Red embers glowed around the pile of corpse dust, and I began to take handfuls, pouring what had once been flesh into the jar. The bones joined the ash inside the glass. One more thing and all was done; a lump of burning coal still glowing red added on top of the rest, the warmth of the death fire keeping Gwendoline's soul quiet.

I stood, holding the jar carefully, and I left the burned ground and charred tree behind.

CHAPTER FIFTEEN

SADIE FARO HAD piled the bodies along the shore, four separate bonfires blazing in the dark. I saw Amaya leaning back against a log, hat drawn low to guard against the light, far enough away that the scent of cooked flesh wouldn't interrupt her dreaming.

The survivors huddled amongst themselves, dead eyes staring at the boat wreckage. The Dixie Queen sat like a squat beetle in the middle of the river, smokestacks still stretching tall above water while the wreck burned.

I saw a few eyes look up at me, quick looks of hate turning to fear when they realized I'd come to put my own boots at the fire. They moved, scurrying away into the dark like prairie dogs when the wolf came calling.

Sadie glanced over at me, white hair falling down the left side of her cheek like mountain ice, her eye reflecting that same bitter cold. I didn't doubt it had been the last thing many an outlaw had seen.

"I gather Gwendoline Bell ain't going to be fetching me any coin," she said.

I presented the jar, the hot coal only now beginning to lose its luster. "If you can prove those bones and corpse powder are hers, you've got yourself a bounty."

I watched the bounty hunter snort, her small smirk disappearing as she turned that icy gaze my way. "You and I have never crossed paths. I never took a job from any said they were gunning for you. I've been called a coward, yellow, more than a time or two, but I believed the stories . . . " Her hands drifted to the brace around her wrist, a little pull from the cords wrapped around her fingers and the knife would spring.

She lowered her hand. "You know what happened to all those men? Can't say I heard of one of them ever coming back. Imagine their endings were about as easy as Miss Bell's."

She'd hit the truth, could nearly lose track of the posses that I had sent off to an early death.

"Manner being, your past sins cost me my living on this trip. The Crogan brothers are feeding the damn gators now and I'm out the reward. Heard you were a man who kept his word and paid his debts, and the way I see it, you're in mine now."

I leaned forward, tasting the scent of the burning flesh as her bonfire crackled and I turned over her words My gaze shifted to meet hers. She was ready to meet bullet with blade should the need come.

"Speak plain, Ms. Faro. What is it that you want?"

"I want payment for my losses, Mr. Covington. Those boys were worth $8000, and a payout like that could've set me for years."

She gestured to Amaya, sleeping soundly. "The senorita there is worth more than that."

I didn't respond to the question, looking away from my sleeping daughter and back into the fire. The skin beneath my eye itched.

Sadie Faro narrowed her eyes, her fingers twitching. "More than $25,000 last time I saw a broadsheet. Heard tell that the Pinkertons were trying to enlist a cavalry regiment to hunt you down."

She reached for the Lancaster; a cloth full of gun oil wiping the mud from the metal.

I made my offer. "I will pay you three times the amount, gold or dollars, whichever one will suit your fancy. In return, you ride with me and kill the rest of the outfit you met tonight. I imagine they all have bounties, and you can claim as many as you can haul off."

The bounty hunter's hands stopped their work and she looked up at me. "I'd say you were spitting a pile of horse turds, but from all I've heard, you're not one to shoot your mouth off."

Kept my gaze rooted in the flame, seeing Amaya's sleeping figure through the dancing glow. "I'm not one for offering more than once, same as I'm not one for warning more than once."

The Gun woke at my side, the vibration passing through me. Sadie Faro might have decided to try for real play. Her contraption hadn't given me a measure of her speed, and while I was safe from that Lancaster, her knife was another matter.

There was a long silence, but then the bounty hunter leaned back. "We're going to need some help to kill that many, devil gun or not."

I leaned back from the fire, feeling the humid night and listening to the bullfrogs keeping watch. "That, Miss Faro, I've already taken the liberty of arranging."

Sunrise saw a whiskey boat trolling down the river, little more than two stagecoaches in length. A half dozen men stood on deck; coats caked with old mud. Saw two tarps pulled tight over their cargo.

The Dixie Queen rotted in the river's current, a plume of black smoke billowing into the sky. I reckoned it wouldn't be long before the scavengers came calling like flies on horseshit. This whiskey boat was only going to be the first.

I saw the deckhand on top of the cabin point, hollering his sighting to the rest of the crew. His long rowing pole embedded itself into the deep river silt, pushing the whiskey boat closer to shore, finally coming to a rest on the bank.

I had seen the back of my eyelids soon after the pact

with Sadie. Hearing her tales about folk coming after me just to die had put my mind at ease.

It was a dreamless sleep, but one I was happy to put behind me once the rays of the morning sun tickled my eyelids. It was Amaya who woke me up, and I'd noticed that those I'd let live had disappeared, saw their tracks vanishing into the trees, following the shore.

Those that were carrying guns had them drawn. A man I pegged as the captain stepped forward, spitting his quid into the river when he smelled the lingering stench from the bodies.

"Have a reason why I shouldn't have my boys here hang you three?" His voice was gruff, and worn, a reflection of the life that he lived. A few fishing hooks were embedded in his coat fabric, a long black tie hanging askew, and all of it was covered with tobacco stains.

"They weren't any innocents. Outlaws one and all," Sadie said easily, keeping her rifle aimed at the dirt.

The man rubbed a hand against his patchy facial hair, tanned skin showing through the black bristles. His upper lip peeled back, chewing juices rolling into his hair as pointed at the charred corpse of a child floating along the bank. "Suppose that one was a hardened killer too?"

Sadie glanced at it, hand grasping the Lancaster tighter. "Victim of them that attacked the boat you see sunk yonder, they weren't discriminating when it came to women and children getting in their way."

The man's leer changed, more of his chewing juices running as his eyes looked over Sadie. I decided that he reminded me of a fat nightcrawler, glistening with whatever moisture his putrid skin could produce, looked like he'd been chewing earth his whole life.

The rest of them were the same, and I noticed that their eyes weren't just settling on Sadie, but looking like hungry mutts at Amaya, tracing her curves beneath the black leather of her jacket, greedily probing at Sadie's sarape.

I knew then that a few more would be joining those

already burned. The captain removed his hat, revealing his balding head, and smiling with intent. "And you three were the only ones to live?"

It was Amaya who answered, pointing with one gloved hand down the shore. "They lit out; thought they could make it back to Patois Landing to get assistance."

The man spat into the water, glancing back at his men. "All high and pretty, boys. ASSISTANCE, ain't that something?"

There was a smattering of laughter amongst the river men. The captain sighed deeply before waving one finger. The other men drew their own six shooters, all of them aiming true.

"So then, I think it would be best if all of you started grabbing air. Nobody has to die today. You women folk might even be wishing to stay on by the time we're finished." He grinned again, his hand gripping his groin. "Been a long time since we had a poke from two ladies such as you."

Amaya raised her hands. Sadie hadn't dropped her rifle, but I saw her eyes moving, calculating how many she could kill before they did in kind.

I stepped forward, and most of the guns pointed my way. The captain sucked at his lower lip, holding up one hand, the other making for his shooting iron. "That's fucking close enough, 'less you want me to carve a head canoe between your eyes."

I held up my trigger finger. "One chance, that's all I'm giving you."

A smattering of laughter passed between the men, and I didn't hesitate, was barely aware of my hand moving. The Gun fired, a bullet chewing a path right through the captain's heart.

The other men shouted and then let fly. Amaya and Sadie both ran to the woods, ducking behind the trees, and I stood like a rock in a creek.

I could smell these men's deeds on them, the same as

a man could hear a lie if he knew how to listen. Evil beat like an open wound, like a key struck wrong on the piano. They'd murdered, they'd raped, but only on those that couldn't fight back, those that could be left for the gators. They thought themselves men, rather than rats scrabbling for their place in the dirt.

Their six shooters ran dry and I stepped onto their boat. Two men dropped their weapons, praying for grace, their hands clasped in supplication to the sky like there was salvation to be found there.

The closest man's hands were fumbling with his ammunition. He stared up at me like a dumb mule when I placed the Gun's barrel between his eyes. His face opened, flesh following the bullet as it journeyed through bone and brain. His eyes bulged, sockets loosening. I saw one fly and roll across the wooden planks. His brains wet the deck.

I'd killed another before Sadie and Amaya joined in the slaughter. The man wailed, dropping his gun to the deck as he clutched at the ruined leg, toppling backward and off the boat.

The gators waiting patient tore him limb from limb.

Amaya killed two quick, both revolvers running dry, and both corpses stained the wood red. She and Sadie both mounted the boat, following my tracks as I approached the last living crewman.

He was younger than the rest, sawdust colored hair and a soft face suggesting he hadn't seen a hard life yet. His face was turned away, eyes squeezed so tight that his sobbing couldn't even release his tears. Both his hands were held palm out like they were shields that would prevent death from finding him. He was whimpering, begging all the saints to not let him die like this.

I stared at him, weighing the cost of keeping him alive, and decided that for a few days more, his soul was his own. I tried to take my hand off the trigger, but I felt the Gun whisper, urging me to kill the kid. It wanted it, longed for this kid's death like a dry county yearned for just one drink of bathtub gin.

"Covington? Covington!" It was Sadie's voice, though it sounded like it was coming from the other side of some canyon, distant, but distracting enough for me to wrest the Gun's bloodlust. It howled across the prairies of my mind as I lowered my hand, looking down at the blubbering shell that made play at being a real man.

I reached out and grabbed a fistful of the boy's hair, slamming him down to the boards, soaking his cheek in the blood of his friends. I could smell his piss as he soiled himself, and I stood, pressing my spur down into his spine, just deep enough to draw a string of blood from his neck.

I turned to look at Amaya. "Miss Shrike, check their cabin. I'd rather not have some coward find his manhood and kill the both of you."

Amaya nodded, reloading both of her pistols as she walked to the cabin. It was a squat structure built into the boat, just barely large enough to stand, saved for the captain's use. She opened the door and entered the dark room, re-emerging and shaking her head.

I looked down at the squirming kid. "You got a name?"

The kid sputtered, swallowing a bit of thick blood as he answered. "Dewey, mister. Please don't—"

I pressed down with my spur, digging the sharp points into his skin, hearing him squall as his fingers dug new lines through the pool of blood.

"None of that. Have a family name?" I asked, keeping the pressure on until he managed to sputter out, "Powell."

"Well then, Mr. Powell. Answer me, and you'll live a short time more. Were you boys outlaws, or just idiots eager to wet your peckers?"

Dewey Powell nodded. "Idiots, sir. Nelson always charged women a poke for passage. Their men folk see a gun and they just roll over, let it happen." The eye that wasn't pressed to the deck rolled up to stare at me, his breathing coming fast like a fish held tight as the flaying knife came for it.

"The law drove out everyone, we didn't think there was

anyone with real game traveling these ways. Just heard rumor of strange folk . . . "

They hadn't the sand for killing. I wanted to sneer at the kid; I could deal with a man trying to kill me, but knowing that he and his compatriots had been scaring folk into submission . . .

Anger uncoiled in me like a snake bearing fangs, and I meant to make the little shit pay for every poke he'd taken part in. I took my boot away from his neck, but he knew better than to move. I reached down and pulled him up by his coat, shoving him over to the side where his row pole hung from its crook.

Dewey glanced over his shoulder, probably wondering whether he should take his chance with the gators or wait for the Gun to devour him. He sniffled, wiping his nose, and I holstered my weapon. He breathed easier.

I nodded at the row pole. "You're going to take us upriver until I decide we're done. And when we're there, I'll kill you. I'll make it quick, so long as you don't try to run. If you do . . . Well, the gators are going to be eating their dinner in courses."

Dewey's eyes were cast down, staring at the ragged eye sockets of his friend, the one Amaya had killed, placing her shots so his soul would wander blindly down to hell.

"Why don't you just kill me now, I . . . I don't know if I can do this . . . "

"Your decision, but I'm not in a hurry today."

The kid had paled, his hand reaching up to his eye and spreading the blood of his comrades across his cheek, like art on a cave wall. I shrugged my shoulders and smiled at him. "The last one screamed for hours. Maybe you're made of stronger stuff?"

Dewey Powell didn't speak another word, picking up his row pole and standing stock still. I saw fresh tears struggling down his silent face before I left him to his post and making peace with his life.

The sun was shining, the morning dew boiling away.

I'd spent plenty of time in these swamps, learning from Marie Laveau and Louisianne Robichaude. I'd floated on rafts made from whatever driftwood and vines I could scrounge, speaking to the gators and dragonflies, begging the elements and the beasts to bring two starving boys food.

Amaya helped me load what supplies we had left; ammunition, and the jars full of ashes. All the while, Sadie watched the kid, ordering him to dispose of his crewmates. The gators enjoyed the corpses tossed over the side like a stable hand baled hay.

Once he finished and stumbled back to his position at the row pole, he looked to me for approval before he pushed the boat back out into the river. We floated past the wreck of the Dixie Queen, water lapping through the broken windows. Smoke still stretched up into the sky from the blackened deck boards, still burning close to the water line.

It would probably become a haven for any bad men operating in these parts. If the teetotalers were making a stink, the wreck of an old steamboat would be good territory for a moonshiner. And if they dove down far enough, they'd find my stage, and the things claimed by the dark river mud.

I heard a yip and looked back to the shore. Roux was standing between the corpses we'd left behind, before turning and following from a distance.

CHAPTER SIXTEEN

WE SPENT THREE days heading north on the river. The goal was to make it to Fort Smith, rustle up a few horses, and head further up into Kansas. I stared into the muddy water, the murk only disturbed by the occasional splash of a fish.

Gwendoline Bell had a mind coming apart like a sod field, so I couldn't bet that Lorelei's other riders were going to make the same mistake of coming at me head on. Especially with "Mumbling" Charles Marland looking for us.

Katsutomo wasn't anything but savagery and Thomas Grail was wrapped up in his newfound font of life, eager to see vengeance done. But both were green when it came to matters of the spirit.

Marland's second face was a gift from hell, the power to see unstained truths and the ripples of terrible deeds past, present, and future. But that kind of sight could be obscured if a man knew the proper ways; water, mirrors, anything you could surround yourself with that cast a reflection. Marland could try, but as long as we floated here, he wouldn't see anything but his twice-damned faces.

A situation like this couldn't last forever. Like any good game, we were both building our hands and I meant to see mine played straight. Magic could see you through but kicking a man in his cherries when he wasn't looking worked just as well.

I stared at the stars reflected in the water's rippling

surface, knowing what I had to do but dreading the risks. Walking with your soul wasn't supposed to be done drifting like we were. The currents and streams ran strong in the next world and could sweep away a man's self.

I knew this moment had been coming, knew it since I'd gathered up Gwendoline Bell's ashes. I had an appointment I meant to avoid, and I aimed to see her who'd made it.

We made camp on the shore. Caught fish and cooked them in a small fire pit, and felt my belly rumble as the scent wafted over to me. Sadie boiled a pot full of crawfish she'd caught.

Sadie let her nearly white hair flow freely down her face, helping herself to a cup of whiskey from a cask she'd opened. She wasn't quite half seas over, didn't measure her a woman given over to getting herself soaked.

Amaya handed Dewey a plate, fish laying across it. She hadn't bothered to remove the head and he grimaced before picking at the steaming meat with his hands. I hadn't allowed him a knife.

It was a hard thing living knowing that time was short. I'd seen lungers, lepers, and other desperates head west, hoping the Good Lord had provided reprieve there. That there was a shaman or holy man waiting with the answers, the cure, the promise that there was still a little more time they could forestall the judgment. A few had even come to me, and I'd revealed that what little time they had been allotted could still be taken away, a truth they had taken to the grave.

I spit into the river, gritting my teeth as I pulled out the watch taken from Silver River, breathing a soft sigh when I saw both hands firmly fixed at twelve. There was still time for me yet. And there was a place close by where I could find answers. I could feel it.

I pulled off my coat, letting it drop to the deck behind me, rolling up my sleeve, and dipping my arm into the water. The coolness washed over me and my quarry latched on.

FOR A FEW SOULS MORE

Counted five leeches suckling at my skin. I retrieved Gwendoline Bell's ashes and a bottle of rum the dead captain had been nursing. I also retrieved a few bullets, their powder necessary for the working I had in mind, and making sure that I had my knife close, I strode to the edge of the boat and jumped to the shore.

Sadie and Amaya both hollered at me, rising to their feet, and I called back to them as I went into the trees. "Things need attending to. Stay here and keep watch."

A weariness passed over me as I stepped beneath the cypress, the crackling light from the whiskey boat already being swallowed by the night, calling back to them. "If I ain't back come morning, it means I'm dead."

If either woman protested, it was lost amidst the sounds of the croaking frogs and the river lapping against the shore.

I waded through the marsh, the darkness closing in tight. It was a night that I was familiar with, where a man stepped out of the real and across the threshold where no light could penetrate. The shadowed shapes of trees loomed out and I brushed across them, watching the bark twist, faces appearing and deforming in silent screams as I passed. Spirits or visions, I couldn't be sure.

The sounds of death surrounded me. I heard a hog squeal and a gator hiss, water splashing as the former was dragged beneath the surface.

The Gun whispered to me, guiding my steps. The ground grew firm, and I stared up at the shadow of a cross silhouetted against the stars. It was an old Spanish Mission, the walls sunk halfway into the swamp. I was standing amidst two dozen tombstones, black mold growing thick and obscuring the names of the dead.

I pulled the leeches from my arm, fat with my blood, and dropped them one by one into the jar, hearing the wet plops as they settled at the bottom of the glass beneath what remained of the dead woman.

I set aside my boots, draping them across a wet headstone, my sweat-stained shirt and hat following. I stood bare chested against the night, the thick mosquitoes flying close to suckle at the scraps the leeches had left behind.

Found plenty of driftwood, each log as black as the sky above, and piled it high before draping dry moss across the top. According to Hoyle, if one desired a meeting, one had to be inviting.

The bottle of alcohol sloshed in my hand as I retrieved it, I cut the bullets from their casings, sprinkling the gunpowder into the waiting bottle.

Didn't take much fishing before I found my matchbook, the tiny flame coming alive and driving the darkness back. Another splash on my right, another gator came creeping, couldn't see what else lay beyond the reach of the little light in my hand, struggling desperately to push at the shadows, crowded and hungry.

I tossed the match into moss, and despite the humidity, it caught quickly, flaring up.

I cut a groove across my arm and dripped my blood into the jar, making sure each leech was covered. I reached in and turned them over, coating them in the ash.

"By three things I call, by that which you devour. These I offer up to you, taken life burned to dust, stolen life in bellies full, and given life offered true."

The leech twisted between my fingers. Silhouetted against the burning flame, it looked like a shadow I had plucked from the darkness around me. Then I brought it close and swallowed it whole. Tasted the bitter ash, my own blood. The leech wriggled as it slid down my throat, as did the rest that followed.

Bile rose and I steadied myself, just as I'd been taught. There'd be a terrible consequence should I throw my attempted offering back into the mud. I managed to choke it back down, my vision swirling, my mouth slackening.

Lorelei cradled my head in her lap, the mourner's veil falling over me. I felt chills run down my spine. I'd made the calling, put myself in her power. The Lady of Mourning could consume me whole if the urge took her.

She lifted me as easily as an empty oat sack.

"Shut your eyes, Salem, unless you mean to part yourself from your flesh."

I did as she said, feeling the veil pass over me as she brought her lips to mine. The kiss was cold, one that conquered every mother's son that rode the trail of a bullet.

She inhaled and I felt the squirming things in my belly crawling, wriggling up my throat, and eager to heed her calling. Heard the squishing, the leeches crushed beneath her teeth, and she released me from her embrace. I stood, feeling the warmth of the fire behind me, a soft comfort for the cold that seeped deep into my bones.

I was quiet as she finished her meal, hearing the Gun's warning in my mind, my fingers dancing across its grip.

Her left hand disappeared beneath the veil, the other tapping at the heel of her own six-shooter. I heard a contented hum coming from beneath the fabric, and then her voice, clear as a crisp winter. "The night is mild, walk with me so I can remember what we shared."

I offered my arm, she took it, and together we strode through the old adobe of the mission, leaving the fire and my accoutrement behind.

We walked in silence for a time, the molded structure gale blew around us, sending the old and rusted bell tolling as we passed. My heart beat faster, and the dark stretched out before us, the bog and marsh fading away like imagined things in the desert.

I chanced a look at the woman walking with me. I could see the silhouette of her face, the one I had once known. I wasn't green when we'd first met, but Lorelei had been like a child, seeing beauty in the stone and water, her eyes wondering at the sun and life.

I imagined Granger had called her back into the world

the same way Virgil and I had all those years ago. Now she wasn't under some illusion that she would find some true love and create life instead of take it.

She'd had those dreams, had whispered them to me on a dark prairie while a campfire kept us warm, and had nearly swayed me from my revenge before Virgil had reminded me of why she was riding with us.

To obtain a weapon to ward off death, you had to kill death herself.

We'd made love, and in the restful calm of after, I'd cut her throat. She'd looked up to me with eyes pale blue as a clear mountain stream as her, and when she'd finally gone home, Virgil and I had taken her empty flesh and brought it to him that provided our Guns.

I remembered it clearly and wondered if Lorelei was eager to repay the deed that had been done to her. I was no longer in the world where I held jury over who lived and died. I'd committed my soul into her hands above stakes.

The swamp had petered away, the two of us now walking between great outcrops of rock adorned with black paintings of ancient hunts between men and beasts, others that caused pain simply to gaze on. I knew where we were. It was hard to forget the place where Virgil and I had bartered for our weapons, the place where I'd offered up the shell of the Lady of Mourning.

It was a grand pueblo village, stone and adobe mud carved into magnificent terraces and homes under a great red cliff. Things moved in the black windows. I heard growls, the screams of something being violated in the shadowed doorways.

Lorelei turned and made a sound like a catamount voicing its ire, and the screams inside the building quieted, the darkness silent again.

Thought I saw the hint of a smile beneath the veils. "They're waiting for you, eager to lay you raw and quivering across the stones, just like you've laid so many others."

She pointed a gloved hand to the horizon where a red sun struggled. The darkness of this world was illuminated by the sickly light, and stretched out under the sun was the entirety of my life. There were thousands of graves, each marked with wooden crosses dotting the landscape. It was everyone that I'd ever killed and squatting on the horizon at the center of them was Trail's End.

It sat like a fat buzzard over the dead plateau. I could almost see the buildings breathing, suckling at the rot beneath the ground. Lorelei traced its outline, finger dancing through the air. "I wonder if those that lived here felt betrayed at the end . . . living so long on the threshold of perdition, sure of themselves that the devil wasn't going to call them to account."

I stared at the distant windows, the crows and buzzards still feasting on them that I made sure wouldn't see the punishment of fire or kingdom come. "I've known plenty who thought their sins and sorceries would earn them a throne in hell. I just made sure they couldn't claim theirs."

Lorelei laughed, a sound like a breeze on a still winter's night. "They suffer there."

Felt the weapon at my side. I wasn't the only one remembering times gone by, or the want I still felt to hurt those that made me send my sister below the earth long before her time.

"I hear her weeping for you," Lorelei said quietly, her head cocked to the distant dusk as the leprous sun disappeared back into the dark.

I wanted to take my Gun, press it against Lorelei's head, and kill her a second time. But here, I might as well have been trying to spit up a rope.

"I didn't come here to relive old deaths, nor take a measure of everyone I've killed. I came with a purpose. With questions I mean to see answered."

Lorelei stared at my drawing hand, held tight around the Gun. She whispered, "You play as if you don't love me."

I wanted to curse her, damn her and the hell that

birthed her, tell her that every death on my head had been done to stave off the coals already pressed against my feet. But it wouldn't have been true; every foul deed, every drop of spilled blood, every bullet fired; I'd done it because I lusted for it.

Slowly, I lowered my hand. I couldn't see her eyes beneath the veil; she could easily go for her own pistol, instead, she rolled her head back to the adobe buildings. I left the monument to my sins behind me, following her through the sun-caked bricks.

Lorelei passed the pueblos and the cracks between the stones leaked blood, I felt it gripping my boots and saw it staining the fabric of her dress. There was only one place we could be going, only so many places in the world a man could go to sell his soul.

The kiva was a circle at the center of the village, a ritual place, its stairs leading down. Lorelei didn't turn from her path, disappearing into the black at the bottom of the steps. I followed close behind.

I liked to think that I'd walked every path of the other side, and I knew the risks. I'd already wandered far here and the currents of this place weren't always known to bring a man back to the land of the living.

As I trailed after her, I drew the Gun. I didn't think she'd kill me, but that didn't mean she was tempted to pay me back for her murder . . .

I reached the bottom of the stairs and stepped out into a memory. I recognized El Jardin, the mission laying at the end of the road, dingy cantina with a brown blanket covering the way inside. Run down pueblos where hopeless eyes stared out.

Lorelei was with Virgil and me, fresh in the white shirt she'd worn that day, staring in wonder at each set of sullen and hopeless eyes peeking out from behind drawn curtains. She examined things like a child, laughing as a dog crossed the street, even as it gnawed at the bloody remains of a chicken that it had managed to steal. This town was a shoreline for true sin, that was the whole reason why we'd come. All the knowledge we'd gathered had pointed to here.

Living downwind of hell itself had sapped the light and life from these wretches, just like it had the folks back home. I saw their hunger, sizing the three of us up as we rode into town. They wondered if we had money or food. If they could murder us and live just a bit longer.

Smoke drifted through the streets, carrying with it the aroma of cooked flesh. We found the source in the center square; a fountain ran thick with bright blood and El Jardin's newborns roasted on spits.

The land was dead, I'd seen it riding to this place forsaken by anything but the devil, these people could eat nothing but what they could create. Hunger could drive a man mad; it was at the root of all wants; hunger for women, hunger for money, hunger for killing . . . Hunger for flesh.

Three women screamed in the fountain, their swollen bellies quivering as they gave birth. Men waited, their ragged clothes drenched in the birth fluid, hands eager, and when the squalling infant was whisked into life, they took it to the spit and gave it back to death.

"My . . . god . . . " Virgil breathed beside me, his horse fidgeting, it didn't like the stench of blood. I reached out, taking the reins from my brother before he could go and do some fool thing that would get us killed.

Lorelei clutched at her gut, holding her own pale mount steady with her other hand, red tears streaming down her cheeks as she shook her head. "I can feel them. I . . . it hurts."

Her hollow eyes swallowed me, following the crimson currents into the dark where what Lorelei really was existed. I heard her whisper. "Promise me, Salem. You won't let these escape." I'd sworn that I would return and bring El Jardin to rights.

Then she changed, and the hazy midday of Mexico

disappeared as a rolling black thunderhead came over us like a wave. I watched Virgil's horse rot and disappear, its rider doing the same until he'd become nothing but dust and bone laying in the dirt. The buildings of the town peeled, wood and lacquer trimmed away, some disappearing completely into the dark.

And Lorelei sat atop her pale horse, stained cotton and trail pants replaced by the flowing ebony dress, the long veil covering the red tears and pallid beauty, her anger burning so that I could never see her face. Her bitter whisper came floating from beneath cloth. "You've lost yourself here."

I breathed hard. Trying to fight against the pull of the spirit realm as it tried to drown me in another memory

A fire burned between us, and Lorelei stoked it. "You kept your promise, you and Virgil both, except when you came back to El Jardin, you'd holstered your own sins worse than those that lived there."

Looking at her across the flames, I could only wonder what I looked like, a worn crow of a man with eyes burning hollow with their own cinders. "They were just breathing in the smoke from the pit. I was brought up in it." I ran my hands across the Gun's metal, and I looked to her. "It's coming for me too, sooner than I'd reckoned. But you know that."

She paused in her ministrations. "Mind Bertrand's shiny timepiece, he knew my comings and goings well enough."

I nodded, resisting the bitter laugh I could feel building. "Reckoned you would say that. Still, I came with other questions for you."

There was silence as shadows thrown by the fire twisted and danced, a dark tapestry of deaths playing out over the walls of the kiva: a man lost his head to an axe, another swung by a rope from a tree, a woman's shadow writhed, impaled.

Lorelei held up three fingers. "Three questions, for our

past times. If Granger hasn't bound my tongue, I'll answer it. In return, I've three questions of my own."

I nodded and went to tip my hat before I remembered it wasn't there, I'd left it with my body back in the world of the waking. I took a moment to gather my thoughts, shivering, and feeling sick in my guts. The ritual was wearing off and the barren dust of the real world was calling. Had to make this quick.

"What does Granger want with the women?" Seemed the easiest thing to ask, with an answer I feared.

Lorelei paused, long enough that the gooseflesh ran down my arms. "He aims to do what you did all those years ago. You made him feel small, he doesn't aim to ever be small again."

She sighed, like the last breeze of autumn before the cold set in. "If you cheat me, he will do what you once did, he'll offer his sacrifice of new life, then he will offer me. Your Gun will answer to him."

The veil parted, just a bit, and all the flame and vigor in me looked like dying sparks compared to the fury I saw in that eye. I recoiled, a cough of blood erupting out of my throat and spattering into the fire. I couldn't avert my eyes from that malignant gaze. Wiped my mouth, only to find my eyes stinging. I was weeping blood.

Lorelei whispered bitterly, "He cannot meet my gaze, none of them could; the two-faced deviant, that young man you've made sour, the burned woman, the mad warrior . . . but not you. You look at me like you aren't afraid."

Pain came like the edge of a knife scraping across my eyes, flaying the nerves. "Never . . . said I wasn't a-afraid. Just accepting . . . that the-there ain't ho-pe or rest whe-re . . . I'm headed."

She closed the veil, breaking the connection between us. Her hand came through the fire, the flames refusing to touch her gloves. Her fingers felt cool to the touch, and they danced across my cheeks, through the scruff of my cheek and chin, gathering my blood.

Her blood-stained glove disappeared under the veil and I heard the wet gasps as she suckled. I tried to ignore it as I focused, feeling the spasms up and down my arms and legs, my body revolting against the ritual offering I'd devoured.

"How many? How many can you bring back?" I let the Gun hang lazily over my knee

Lorelei unholstered her gun. She paused when she saw my own hand jump, clutching my weapon a little tighter. "You've become addicted, Salem. Jumping at every gun leaving its holster. But I know you don't fear, you can't be killed by a gun. You just thirst for death . . . for me."

She offered it to me, and I reached for her revolver, letting the cool metal grace my hand, and I heard it whisper . . .

Felt the sting, like a rattlesnake bite, my own weapon growling a warning to me. It wouldn't tolerate another, that wasn't the oath I had taken, and my debt had yet to be fulfilled.

Lorelei reached out and plucked her weapon from the kiva dust. She didn't have to answer, one touch of the weapon had been enough. Six chambers for six bullets, six lives able to be called back into the world again and again as long as these bullets from the grave rested in their flesh. All commanded by the Mourning Lady.

I had melted the bullet inside Gwendoline Bell; burning up the rest of her had just been the fixings on the meal, the punishment of the grave was all that was left for her.

I counted two left inside her pistol. That left three that I couldn't outright kill, but Granger Hyde didn't hold sway over my Gun, not yet, and there weren't any bullet dwelling in him keeping him above snakes. He could die the same as any man. Supposed that I had sown his fury, his desire to humble me, and time had come to reap that hate.

She still had those two shots, two more resurrections I wasn't biting at the bit to see performed. There were plenty of folks in graves strewn all over that I'd rather see stay beneath the ground.

"I know Granger is sitting pretty in my home, but where are the other three?"

Lorelei swept some of the salt from the floor, whispering to it before throwing it into the flame. The fire roared and in it, I saw Sagara Katsutomo and Thomas Grail riding, twelve Orphans trying to keep pace behind them.

Her trigger finger pointed at Thomas, drawing my own gaze to the hayseed's hardened look. "The boy and the warrior hunt for you. I feel them, their every thought. The boy hasn't stopped to think of the grave that awaits when his task is done. He hasn't stopped to think why he's off his feed, why he feels nothing but cold; his vengeance for his father the only thing that is warming him."

Her finger wavered, turning to Katsutomo. I could only see shadows under his strange helm, that blood-red armor with its strange, segmented plates, all of it reclaimed from where I had left it in Trail's End.

Lorelei leaned forward, the veil hanging down into the fire, illuminating the outline of her face underneath. "He reminds me of you. He kills, he rests, then he kills again. He doesn't speak, not since your daughter killed him in El Jardin. Unlike young Thomas, he knows what's waiting for him once this is done."

I remembered the New Orleans cemetery, and the time out in California before that. Katsutomo wasn't a man like the rest, didn't seem to be living when I had looked into his eyes, just my own reflection taking flight to escape whatever teeth he bared in his soul.

Lorelei caught my thoughts. I couldn't see the surprise on her face but knew it was there regardless. "You fear him, don't you?"

I looked straight into that black veil, unwavering, uncaring that the mortal coil wasn't strong, slipping away from me like water through a sieve. "I fear him the same way that I fear you."

"You didn't fear me enough, you murdered me," she replied.

I leaned forward, feeling the heat of the flame against my chin, uncaring of the agony licking at me, the vision of salt disappearing as I whispered, "As I said, I fear him like I fear you."

Her hand reached for me, stroking my cheek. "Good . . . that is not what I want from you. You taught me what this world was when I thought I saw the beauty in things."

I nearly reached for that hand, to hold or remove, I couldn't say, but Lorelei withdrew to her place on the other side of the fire. "Marland's passenger will know if I let you see him, will whisper it right into his head, then he would come looking for your empty shell. You would be like Katsutomo, a greater killer than you ever dreamed, but less than the lowest thing in light and life."

I thought of Marland's second face, skinned and hanging in Trail's End, and briefly wondered if he had reclaimed it like Katsutomo had reclaimed his accoutrement, and sewn it back on like some tattered wagon tarp.

"All of them are in Indian Territory. They'll be heading up into Kansas within the week. Granger thought they would be best utilized getting the last women needed for the ritual."

The flames were beginning to die, but I didn't avert my gaze from them, looking into the hot coals, letting the dull red glow seep into my soul. It'd be another two weeks before we'd make Missouri on the river, wouldn't be any way of catching up.

"They make for the Adler home." Simple words, but enough for me to feel comfort. Granger Hyde or any of the rest of them didn't know everything about me. Or the folks I'd met along the trail.

I made to stand, feeling the weakness in my knees, my vision blurring. For the blink of an eye, I saw the Spanish moss and impenetrable black sky of the swamp, Lorelei and her fire in the spiritual kiva overlaid.

I couldn't linger. From somewhere distant I heard

howling, great lowing barks as hell sent its wolves, catching the scent of me, close to death.

Lorelei stood and the fire died, drowning the room in deep blackness, with the mourning lady an even darker shadow against the kiva stone. Over the baying of the savage wolves, I heard it, faint at first, like the first drops of rain coming before the thunder.

The adobe walls were swept away, thick water washing in and leaving us on an island of swiftly disappearing muck. Lorelei stepped through the billowing haze of the dead fire's smoke; her hands placed on my chest. She leaned forward, and whispered, asking the questions that were her right, and offering me eternity.

"Think about it." Her last words before she pushed and sent me tumbling down into the churning waters.

I woke retching, chewed, and dead leeches joining my stomach juices and blood in the mud. Anyone came along now and they'd have seen a crippled bird, kept low on his knees, trying to find the strength to stand.

My accoutrement was stained with the early morning dew, damp to the touch as I wrapped myself in the folds of my coat. I came stumbling out of the dark trees just in time to see Dewey picking up his row pole, looked like he'd been front row at a peep show when he saw me totter out of the woods. I brushed past him without a word, Sadie Faro watching me close. Amaya slept soundly, slumped against the whiskey barrels with a worm-eaten trail blanket thrown over her. Once in the cabin, my own exhaustion began to take me.

I glanced at Sadie one more time, my eyes falling cold on Dewey as he stood like a dumb mule. "Get him rowing."

I didn't stay to make sure that he went about it, only managing to disrobe and fall exhausted onto a dead man's cot.

CHAPTER SEVENTEEN

IT WAS A dreamless sleep, an infinite black only broken by the sound of a paddle dipping into the river's unending flow. I smelled meat, could have been pork. A deck board creaked, hadn't realized the Gun was in my hand until I'd leaped from the bunk, aiming directly between the intruder's eyes.

Amaya stood, a steaming cup of Arbuckle's clutched tight in her hand, the other holding a plate of trail rations. I lowered the Gun, feeling the hunger I'd put off for a day and more come roaring.

I nodded my thanks as I ate, the coffee searing through me, the fog of weariness fading around me. Amaya leaned against the wall, quietly watching. I didn't apologize for nearly killing her, there wasn't a need. I hadn't a doubt that she'd let fly more than a few times coming out of a dead sleep.

Her eyes tracked over my bare chest, looking at the still-red circles from the leeches, scars from the knives that had found me, and a few bullet wounds from my youth. Her eyes came to rest on the brand, always a reminder, a marring of the flesh and the soul. She wasn't the first to stare; that was the way of folks, they were curious, wondering how it came there. If the stories were true. If their nightmares were too.

"It's strange, seeing you this way," she said quietly.

I scraped the last of the grits into my mouth, beginning my work on the bacon. "What way is that?"

"Like a man, a regular man. The scars tell a story, one you left behind. You could pass as a river man making honest work."

Both of us looked at each other. I searched for myself in her eyes, in the shape of her face, and wondered if she was doing the same, tracing the heritage she'd come to know only through her mother's telling.

"But that ain't you, is it?" she said, leaning back and staring at the small rays of light shining from underneath the cabin door.

I set the tin cup and empty plate by the bunk, leaning back and feeling the soreness in my muscles. The flavor of my own blood and the wet taste of the leech still treating my mouth. "Never been one for that life. My father put me to work hunting everything that walked or crawled, still remember the deer bleats, the cleavers cutting away the fur after they'd sent their heads rolling across the chopping block."

Amaya hung on my words. She had been born in El Jardin after Virgil and I had come, the village wickedness swallowed by us in a haze of blood and gunfire. She did not know a truly cruel life.

But El Jardin had just been desperate folks trying to live, Hell's waters flowing down and washing against the dusty hovels. Trail's End had been a font of such waters, and my father had made sure that the cup never ran dry for any who lived there.

"Wasn't always animals, neither. Had to venture farther every year; nothing grew out of the ground but poison and any animals we kept were sickly wretches, so we raided wagon trains heading out to Oregon Territory. Men, women, babes, and livestock . . . didn't matter. A man will eat when he's hungry, and our neighbors' bellies were never full."

I remembered the fathers, screaming as their children were taken one by one crying into my family barn that never smelled of anything but rot, remembered the meat of women hanging off the hooks, their hollowed-out skin given to Trail's End girls for the pleasures of its men. I told her this, told her the story of Trail's End, sin's kin and keep.

She paled, eyes staring daggers into my own, hoping that I was selling her a story, that it was all chiseling and bad medicine, only to find that she was barking at a knot.

I picked the Gun up from where I had laid it, closing my eyes and listening to bleeding lullabies closer than a mother or lover. "A taste of what I endured, and I promise you that my own sin has been greater than those."

She didn't speak, didn't go for her guns. Instead, she asked a question, one that cut me deeper. "Why are you telling me this?"

I knew why I told her, knew it because I could still hear Lorelei's words echoing in my head, and knew that I wanted to know the killer who was my child better before my timepiece ran dry.

I set the Gun down and went for my discarded shirt, pulling it over my head "Figured it was time for someone to know my story."

CHAPTER EIGHTEEN

WE TRAVELED ANOTHER WEEK, diverting off the Mississippi River, and heading west on the Arkansas River. Occasionally I'd look to the shore, watching Roux follow us through the trees.

We saw the smoke rising from Fort Smith long before we arrived. I looked over at Dewey, and saw him trembling, trying not to catch my gaze. "Take us over to the shore, Mr. Powell."

I said it quietly but still saw him freeze. Sadie stepped up close and whispered, "I didn't sign up for murder, Covington."

I glanced over at her. "It's exactly what you signed up for. He isn't innocent."

Sadie Faro wasn't one to shirk at killing a man, and her contraption on the Dixie Queen had proved she wasn't one for letting a man fight fair. Kill them quick and trade their blood for coin.

She went for a cigarette, the match flaring as she stared down at the deck, away from Dewey Powell. "I've seen what you do, but you promised that boy you'd make things quick."

I unholstered the Gun. "He's done his duty."

The boat rocked as we hit the shore, the boy's nerves failing him as he took in his last few minutes of life. I didn't chastise him for it; could never know until you were staring it down how you'd react.

Dewey looked back at me, and I gestured into the

inviting shadows of the trees. "A final courtesy. You walk until you're ready."

He took his first faltering step, then another, never comforted but sure of his steps all the same. Roux joined us as we entered the trees, the long hawthorns and hickory limbs welcoming us. The red wolf clutched to my heels, trotting along close as we walked.

He chose the clearest path, pushing his way through the undergrowth, great vines and shrubs twisting together thick into openings between the trees.

Heard the sound of rushing water, and it wasn't too long before we found a creek cutting its way through the woods, heading towards the river. The stream was a deep green, with old brown leaves and pine straw floating across its surface as it tumbled ten feet or so into a pool beneath. All of it was dotted with rocks that looked like stepping stones.

Dewey's breathing came a bit faster, trying to stay calm, knowing what was coming. He turned and looked up at the sunlight shining down through the leaves like water seeping through a fishing net. He stared down into the current's flow, "When I was barely knee-high, my mama would take us to a place like this with my brothers and sisters. Before the consumption took her."

I let him tell his story to me, the death of his folks, his siblings leaving for better lives, a nowhere pig farm left to the trees and Dewey Powell tending to it out of duty.

He left; children always did when home became too much to bear. Then he'd found those running the whiskey boat. The comfort of sin outweighed the struggle of righteousness. He sat at the edge of the waterfall, soaking in the cool water

I stepped down after him, listening to Roux's whines above me, watching the dirt and grime wash off the boy in front of me, just figure of pale flesh and sawdust hair beneath the torrent of the stream. But Dewey Powell had one more deed in my service, and I crouched down until I was level with his head. "Need you to do something for me, Mr. Powell."

He looked out from the water, eyes as lost as a motherless calf, and I gave him his instructions. "When you meet Lorelei, tell her I accept her offer."

Dewey nodded in a daze then I stood again feeling the splashing water against my coat. "You ready?"

Dewey opened his mouth, the water flooding in and he simply nodded. I pulled the hammer, then the trigger and my debt to Hell dwindled just a little more. Dewey slumped to the side, red brain and bone sliding out of his head. He was carried over the ledge by the falls and tumbled into the wading pool beneath. Minnows came, swallowing the tiny bites of floating red meat; a fat crawfish followed, trying in vain to reach for the bits of brain. I reached down, thumb and trigger finger folding around the hard shell, watching it curl as it attempted to wrap its claws around my skin.

I deposited it inside Dewey's head, where it followed the ragged trail of meat, scooping up the soup of his brain and gnawing greedily. Saw more coming, emerging from the rocks to follow the red water back to a new meal.

And Dewey Powell's eyes kept their serene hopelessness as I turned and gestured for Roux to follow me all the way back to the whiskey boat, and the rest of the killing that needed to be done.

CHAPTER NINETEEN

WE FOUND A livery on the outskirts of town that looked like it had seen the bad side of every storm pushing through this town. The paint peeled in great strips, ACKLE LIVERY AND STABLE barely visible in big bold letters beneath the cloud of dust.

Ackle himself had seen better days. He wandered out with sand-colored eyes and sun-bitten skin. I pegged him for a veteran. He spat a wad of tobacco into the dirt, a fat and thirsty tongue wiping at the juices around his mouth as he nodded. "Expect you come for horses. Ain't got but nags left."

Ackle looked at Sadie, taking in her rifle, Amaya with her pistols after. "Little late to be hitting the trails. I must've sold to fifty bounty hunters this week. All of them were chasing them Comanche that left the reservation and have been stealing women, you ain't gonna catch up to them riding these . . . no sir."

Most of my traveling coin had joined the Dixie Queen at the bottom of the river; we paid with the money we'd found on the whiskey boat.

"Reckon that'll settle it," I said. It was an offering far more than what they were worth.

Ackle laughed, a sound like a hawk laying crippled, and reached out with a hand that was missing two fingers. "Shit, I ain't turning down that, mister. Just get you to sign some papers and we'll be—"

I held tight to the last few dollars, watching the man

close. "You give us the horses, you keep the money, and you don't speak of seeing us to anyone." I didn't bother asking if he understood; a smart man knew a threat when he heard one.

Ackle stared then swiftly took the money, nodding his head, eyes fixed on the brand under my eye. "Sure, don't want no trouble. Just let me get in there and saddle them for you." We hadn't paid for saddles, and I saw Sadie go to correct him before Amaya shook her head, eyeing me close.

Killing Dewey Powell hadn't put me at ease. I felt something moving in this bustling city. Most towns I'd passed through had been small, with barely a hundred townsfolk, but Fort Smith bustled with people coming off the river, settlers heading out west to stake their claims, fur trappers selling their wares, and bounty hunters stalking the sheriff's board for new quarry.

There was something here, felt like fate stirring the soup, turning my thoughts round and round to drown me beneath the waves. I'd checked the timepiece twice already, but Lorelei's foretelling of my demise was still etched on some further day.

I watched muleskinners bringing their herds in, stagecoaches carrying swells, none of them catching my regard. Nothing to indicate this wasn't anything but a street full of ordinary folk.

Ackle brought the nags, three horses that were near the worst that I'd ever seen. He handed me the reins, thanked us for our money, and went back inside, closing the livery doors. I heard the heavy impact of a latch being locked.

Sadie immediately began checking the meager saddle bags, confirming each was empty. "I'm not keen on heading out without provisions." She rubbed the horse's neck, staring into the dark eyes that begged for sustenance. "Riding these, we won't even make it to Indian Territory."

The Gun whispered to me. My eyes danced across the rooftops searching for the glint of a rifle scope, the shadows for those eager to make a name for themselves. My weapon didn't wake blind for those carrying bullets crafted by men. And it was a fool who turned his back on his instincts.

I handed the reins of my horse to Amaya, the dapple brown animal looking sadly at the ground. Saw my daughter question it, but I gestured toward the west. "Head on out to the river. I'll be along short enough."

I handed Sadie the pack I'd taken from the riverboat. "Try to find my wolf when you make the river and catch him a fat rat if you see one swimming."

She nodded, eyes questioning. I didn't intend to enlighten her on the answers I was going to seek, already knowing what could have woken my Gun from sleep so soon. And it was a powerful temptation to those who knew.

The two women took count of our heading west, vanishing behind the livery as I began my walk of the town. I kept to the wooden porches, the shade cooling me as I watched folks' comings and goings. A crowd gathered at the gallows, shouting abuse at two men. The sheriff declared them cattle rustlers, and one of them shouted down at his son to remember him, to not take the same path.

The other spat at him and told him to grow a spine before the hoods came. A taste of the pitiless and endless void to come. I could hear their necks snap from my place under the porch awning, their bodies jumping and twitching like they were dancing a jig.

The crowd applauded, and the sheriff turned to pay the reward for them. Answered my unease when I saw the hand that took those dollars. Went for his weapon when he saw me. It was reflex, I could see it in his eyes, followed by a laugh for the sheriff, who probably claimed he was just fooling. But his eyes never left me.

It took everything I had to turn, hard measure given the manner of things, but he had an advantage here. This wasn't some trail town with only three steady gunhands, this was civilization's bastion on the edge of the wilderness. If he meant for real play, I didn't like my chances.

FOR A FEW SOULS MORE

There was a sin palace sitting pretty on the corner of the street, plenty of horses tied out front, cowhands and muleskinners looking to escape from the heat of the day and rustle up a card game. I breathed hard with every step, watching the dust cake to my boots as I walked across the street. Trying to resist the urge to turn and let fly. I'd been hunted before, through all manner of country; an old teacher had seen to it that Virgil and I knew what it was like to be prey, driven by the fear that the next breath could be our last.

I couldn't be killed by a gun, every day I woke with that certainty, but it wasn't all true when ground down to the seed of it. There was one out there, one weapon holding the bullet that would kill me one day. My brother's Gun.

And I'd just laid eyes on the man wielding it.

Didn't hear the shot as I crossed the street, didn't hear it as I mounted the steps and pushed into the saloon. A few doves danced with drunk men; their eyes heavy as they shoved money down their partners' corsets while a piano man played a bawdy tune.

I sat and ordered a whiskey, taking in the group of eight arguing around the poker table. Ordered another and told the bartender to leave the bottle. I thought back to our time riding together. It had started with my spur pressing hard on his throat. He'd gotten the measure of me; seen the vengeance I had poured out on them that had killed my teacher. And after all that, he kept riding with me even when released from the oath he'd sworn.

The saloon doors flung wide, a brief flash of sunlight shining through. Men looked up from their game to see if it was anyone worthy of notice before burying their heads back in their cards.

He walked up to the bar. "Mind if I bend an elbow?"

I shook my head and he took his seat. I passed him a glass and poured the whiskey, tipping my own glass as he uttered his thanks.

He took his drink, a bitter sigh escaping his lips. I kept

one eye on his free hand, hiding behind the folds of his deep blue coat. His drink empty, he stared into the whiskey glass. His eyes were older and hungrier. The hope for the future he'd carried when I'd met him cut out and left bleeding somewhere behind him.

He chuckled a bit. "I imagine this is that curse you told me about before you headed off."

I downed my own glass and reluctantly took my own free hand from my Gun, resisting its temptation that I could finally be clear of dying, reminding me of Lorelei's own promises. All I had to do was kill this man.

"No matter distance of time or bullet, we're all meant for the fire. Told you that too." I poured the man another round, watching his free hand leave his Gun. "It's good to see you, Jake."

Jake Howe had been faithful in the union with his Gun. I could see the hunger burning bright, could almost hear the soft murmurs in his own damn head. The early morning had fled before the afternoon sun as the crowd gathered to watch the two of us make our way down the street. Folks knew killers, Fort Smith had seen its fair share of gunmen come through. Their gazes hungered, wondering if the two of us would let fly.

Jake's eyes wandered over them, same as mine. His hand resting in easy reach of his Gun. He closed his eyes and breathed deeply, resisting the urge to create a slaughter. He hadn't given in fully, not yet. I would've seen wanted posters if that had been the square of it, but his Gun's thirst wasn't going unheeded. The blood hung over him like a barrel fever.

He spoke as if he could read my mind. "Didn't think it was all nonsense. I saw too much to not believe, but it's painful hard denying the urge." He said it reluctantly, eyes riveted on the church dominating the street, steepled crucifix shadowing the two of us. There wasn't salvation to be found in there; picking up that Gun had incurred a debt that would be repaid by blood or soul, whichever came first. But hope was a powerful thing to quell.

"Thought I'd be stronger," he finished.

We watched two boys run past, fighting with play sticks as their mothers forced them off the street, fearful eyes cast our way. Sooner or later I expected one of them would run to the sheriff or marshal. Then I could show Jake the measure of what he'd been burdened with.

"It isn't a question of strength. You could live and breathe the damn law, and that Gun would still worm its way under your soul. I know what it's like having it whisper to you when you're alone, dwelling on it and what it wants."

The two of us paused under the gallows looking at the dead men, reduced to nothing but empty husks. There was a time not so long ago when Jake had been on the drop board charged with desertion. I'd killed the marshal charging him, the deputies who'd tied the rope. Even allowed him to save one of the two others strung up with him. But death had declared its want and I wouldn't stand by and see it cheated. He'd chosen the Lakota man tied next to him, and saved the whore accused of killing paying men. A choice that had nearly seen the both of us dead.

I saw them like ghosts in my mind, but it wasn't that dead brave or the woman strung up. I saw my own eyes burning back at me and wondered if Jake saw the same.

Jake stared at the two dead outlaws. "The sheriff said he was surprised to see these two still breathing when I brought them in. Hardest thing there is nowadays, even strung up like a stuck pig, just want to watch their brains run from their skulls." He licked his lips and turned his eyes away from the scaffold. "My partners, they suspect I've waded through gunfights that would have killed any other man." He gave a look I recognized, the bitter smile. "Well, not every man."

A few deputies emerged from the sheriff's office,

leaning on the porch and keeping a close watch on the two of us. I looked to the afternoon light, ready for the cool night to come.

"I warned you, wasn't your intention or want to be wielding my brother's Gun, but like it or not, you won't set it aside." I tapped a finger against my own weapon. "Not until this finds you."

Jake looked down, admiring my Gun like an old friend. "Is that why you came here, to find me? Ready to be held to your account before the Good Lord?"

I leaned towards him. "You can shoot your mouth all day, Jake. Don't reckon you're going to shoot me when you finish."

Jake removed his hat, running a hand through his hair. "I expect they'll be calling me some moniker; I already killed too many, and it's starting to feel good."

Virgil had been the same. I'd tried to shelter him from the worst of our upbringing. I expect he'd thought we could lay down our weapons and accept damnation once it was finished, only for him to realize that any reluctance he'd had was swallowed by the killing.

It would be the same way with Jake and there wasn't any stopping it. Already he was like a prairie wolf looking for prey. he'd find one, then another, and another. A parade of killing that ended with him dead. By my hand, if fate was true.

But that was a day that I hoped was far off, and if I meant to heed Lorelei's offer, I didn't want Jake riding the same trail.

Six years had passed since we'd laid eyes on each other. Reckoned there was quite a story there. "I left you with plenty of comfort. I remember Catarina."

Jake's face fell at the mention of her name, eyes hardening. I could practically see the wound cut on his soul. He stared at the third noose the marshal had hung. "There was a huge storm the night it happened. I thought I was back. I can still feel that knife sometimes." I saw his hands trembling, remembering the man who'd killed my teacher, the man who I'd butchered in turn, but not before he'd had his chance to work his 'bloody craft' on Jake.

He reached down for his weapon and the trembling stopped; he let it speak its comfort to him. "I was seeing him everywhere that night. There was a ranch's worth of mud, that little spit of desert doesn't see rain. I was shooting at phantoms . . . "

He gritted his teeth, the grief coming faster than a train plowing across a prairie. "It wasn't the first time I'd had the nightmares, and this damn Gun has shown me worse than that. Catarina talked me out of it before, I could hear her yelling for me that night . . . "

He reached to brace himself against the gallows. I knew who he wished was swinging there now.

"I didn't even have time to bury her before the neighbors came. Seeing me in naught but my union suit and this damn thing still smoking."

He looked over to me, hoping I'd have some comfort for him, looking for assurances that it would grow easier with time. Maybe even hoping I'd take the opportunity to end things for him.

"They screamed, called me murderer . . . " He laughed, a light breeze blowing his regrets and bitterness away. "Suppose I am now, especially when they came for me, felt like I had no choice . . . "

Ah, a slaughter. When justice had come, he'd cast aside the righteous man and sank into the red killing that the Gun could give. Couldn't say whether it was true or if I had just been on the side of so many massacres that I knew what had happened. I saw it, like the visions I'd seen walking in the next world.

He had dug the grave with his own hands, tears like falling rain, and had laid Caterina down into the newly dug hole. Then her kin had come. I don't imagine they would have had anything but two rusty squirrel poppers between them, doubt Jake had even noticed them screaming until they'd laid their hands on him.

He'd already been reaching for the Gun, he just hadn't known it, and then he'd let the bullets take him, and he'd filled his beloved's grave with the blood of everyone she'd ever known.

And in the present his hand gripped the weapon, hard enough that his veins popped, and I knew that he was trying desperately to forget. "Mexico isn't so inviting with a price on your head, I imagine ."

Jake had fallen silent, a small shake of his head the only indication he'd heard my words at all. I realized where Jake Howe was on his journey. He was Virgil, fresh off his first murder . . . he was me after that first bloodbath. I couldn't say why I pitied him, maybe it was because of our time traveling together, the feeling that I owed him a debt, or maybe I just didn't want another thing like me roaming the world.

I gripped Jake's arm, pulling it away from the holster. He resisted before he saw the look in my eye and let go. I decided to give him the knowledge he'd need. "I know the pull it has on you, all its promises to let you cast off your guilt."

Already saw his hand drifting back, decided to warn him. "If you keep going to it, it'll feed your soul, fill it whole with every sin you can imagine, but when the sun finally goes down on your life, you won't be the same."

Jake's face darkened. "I ain't gonna start killing innocents. I'm not you."

I laughed, a low and bitter sound like the last crackling embers in a fire. "If you keep going as you are, you might as well kneel and accept it. When that happens, you'll take a peek at yourself through that looking glass and you won't see anything but me."

Jake glanced at the brand under my eye, matching the symbol on the hilt of his Gun, and the one that would sear him all the way down to the soul when the only thing left to crave was the lives of others.

I'd heard harsher truths in my time. Sometimes that

was what was needed, to hear the stone breaking the window of your make-believe life, to go out and find what threw it, and give it the fear of you. Sometimes you were what you were, until you weren't anymore.

The two of us stood there for a time. I had the sense he thought about trying to kill me there in the silence of the west wind, dust blowing straight through Fort Smith's now empty streets, fury burning when he realized that the things I had told him years ago were in motion. I wished he had killed me then. It might have even saved his soul. But Jake wasn't like me, he wouldn't kill a friend in cold blood for speaking nothing but God's honest.

But he only blew a weary sigh, the fight going out of him like water through a termite barrel. "Never wanted to admit you were right about it, it means that the number I know in my head is real. That I'm paying your brother's debt . . ." He shook his head. "Suppose I better get to it then, only so many years in a life, and only so many men who deserve a bullet."

He tipped his hat to me. "Appreciate it if you didn't kill anybody here. I don't want to explain to the sheriff that the biggest killer this side of the Rockies is a friend."

Almost felt amused. "That what we are, Jake? Friends?"

He chuckled. "I'd like to think so."

I thought about Lorelei's words, what she had promised me. If I had Jake tag along, he would be included in that obligation. Then I thought of Granger Hyde, sitting like a fat buzzard in my home, playing with powers he hadn't paid the price for. His double-faced oracle whispering my every move. Having another who couldn't be killed by a gun would put a spike in the wheel of whatever it was that the man had planned. Even if it meant that Jake and I ran the risk of killing each other.

"Reckon there is quite the reward for those that have been kidnapping women," I said.

Jake had begun to walk away but my words held him

tight like a rope around a trouble steer. He glanced back at me, chewing over what I said. "You know something about that?"

I nodded. "You traveled with me for a long time, Jake. What do you think?"

I gestured west towards the river. "What do you know of Trail's End?"

He snorted. "Gomorrah of the West? The town of ten-thousand sins? It's just a story."

I stared him down, trying to fight the urge to take my knife and cut off the other nipple that Sgt. Craft hadn't removed all those years back. Gradually his laugh died away and he nodded, his head cocked like he was listening to someone speaking that he couldn't hear. "Your home . . . should have reckoned that. That where these men are headed?"

Nodded in return. "Two different bands of them, cages loaded with working girls, daughters, wives. Some of them with child."

When Virgil and I had spent time in the Appalachians, our teacher had taught us to fish, and had told us that before we learned his magic. We had to learn the things that our father hadn't taught us; hunting for game, building our own shelter, what plants could heal and which could hurt. It'd been a pitiful effort catching that trout, hoping that it would bite the makeshift hook I'd crafted, but Azariah Stoltzfus had been patient and advised that drawing in a fish or a man wasn't hard. You just had to use the right bait.

Jake wanted to be a good man, and with his lover's murder, he wanted redemption. And in the end, that was all a good man wanted.

He nodded, eyes already considering the possibilities. "I'll have to warn my partners, riding with you is liable to kill a man."

I began to walk away. "Only if the need arises. Get your partners, meet me at the west river."

CHAPTER TWENTY

IT **WAS NEARING** nightfall when they came. Sadie had fed and watered our mounts, such as they were and was sleeping against a nearby log. My daughter looked up from the small campfire she had made, two gophers roasting over the flames. "Find what you were looking for?"

I stepped to the fire, finding a seat in the grass. Wasn't in the mood to answer questions. If Amaya's curiosity hungered she didn't satisfy it, settling into silence as she tended to our dinner.

The moon had just begun to poke through the gloaming when I heard the hoofbeats. I kept one hand on my Gun, readying myself should Jake come with murdering in mind.

Sadie had been lured by promises of coin, Amaya wanted to save her mother, and Jake wanted to play the hero. I couldn't be sure what he had used to entice his companions to come along this winding trail. The allure of money had corrupted more than one man.

Sadie barely moved, her hat pulled low over her face, a light snore echoing from under the fabric, but the hand on her rifle spoke a different tale. Amaya had unholstered her pistols when she'd heard the coming horses, standing with me as I waited for our company to announce themselves.

Three horses appeared from the gloom, Jake riding at their head, hauling up just short of the fire. "Didn't imagine I'd ever see you without that stage of yours," he said.

I gestured for Amaya to lower her guns. "Sunk on

Gwendoline Bell's account, just means I'm eyeing for a new one."

He dismounted, looking at my daughter and speaking to her. "Any other man talking about Gwendoline Bell I'd call a flannel mouth, but I've seen stranger things riding with him."

Amaya watched his approach with a cautious eye, his hand offered. She didn't take it. "My mother spoke stories too," she said. "But it didn't save her from his sins."

Jake's welcoming grin vanished his open hand closing. "You're spitting cinders, ma'am. Just trying to be friendly like."

One of Jake's partners spoke up. "Don't imagine you'll have too much luck, amigo. That's Amaya Shrike."

Pegged him as a Comanchero. He wore a faded blue cavalry jacket adorned with a few feathers and animal bones, holding a great knife; any shootist could have hit him from a quarter mile. His hair fell in two long dark braids, a large black poblano hat highlighting his grin under a thick handlebar mustache. He looked too damn clean. Like the trail dirt considered it blasphemy to touch him. I took stock of his nickel-plated, polished like he was gunning to win a county shooting contest. He carried a sword on his hip, a thin cavalry saber by the look of it.

It had been a long time since I'd traveled down through Mexico, but even I had to shake my head at the near ridiculousness of it. He jumped down from his horse. "Maybe we should give up, si? How much coin would the Black Magpie and the Shrike fetch us?"

Jake looked at Amaya with newfound curiosity. "Might be able to kill this one, but you'd be dead before the night was through for trying to kill Salem Covington."

One of Amaya's revolvers was pressed against Jake's temple faster than a diving hawk. The man's pretty pistols cleared their own holsters and the other man on his horse raised a rifle, both aiming at Amaya.

Jake chuckled, leaning into the barrel. "Go ahead, pull

that trigger. Traveling with him, thought you would have heard or seen a thing or two . . . " He took a breath, smiling. "I'm sure he's said it plenty, but I can't be killed by a gun either."

His partners laughed, and Jake grinned. Amaya's face burned red, her finger twitching against the trigger, and she looked at me as if I could wipe the egg from her face.

"He's not bluffing." I said. "Take a real hard look at that piece he's carrying on his hip."

Amaya took a quick glance. My brother's Gun wasn't any different from my own. Other than a few nicks the metal had taken over the years, it was the same all the way down to the symbol branded straight onto the handle.

She lowered her guns and Jake turned to his comrades. "Stand down, boys. I think that Mr. Covington here has a use for her and would be upset if he had to find a replacement."

The Comanchero holstered his pistol. "No call for trouble. Isn't that right, Nahum?"

He addressed the other man, a large figure wrapped in a dark brown coat lined with fur. His black skin mixed with the night. What I'd taken to be a rifle was in truth a shotgun, leveled at me.

I could smell the death drifting off him. His name, Nahum, was one I knew. His gaze broke with mine first, the shotgun never leaving me as he nodded at Sadie, still pretending to sleep. "What about that one? Ain't moved an inch since we rode up. You think she don't have a piece trained on us?"

He spat into the dirt, a bit of his saliva catching on his thick facial hair, gesturing to the Comanchero. "Check her." Jake looked about to protest, but Nahum turned his shotgun back to Amaya. "You and the Magpie might not fear a gun, Jake. But this one is killable just as any other. I'm not getting off this horse until I'm sure I ain't gonna be shot."

Thought about killing him, it would have been simple,

just one quick draw and the pull of the trigger, and he could make his pleas before the lake of fire took him.

But in his death twitches, he could kill Amaya; one trigger and her guts would spill over the dirt. He would kill my kin, take what was mine, and for that would deserve far worse than what an eternity of pain could offer.

I would chase his soul and drag it back pleading, and in that cool and annihilating dark, I would show him that hell didn't discriminate, all were equal before the throne of sin, but I would show his spirit a personal suffering.

The Comanchero looked at me as he reached Sadie, nudging her with his foot, "Did you give this one some-"

Sadie rose in one fluid motion and stuck a knife to the man's throat, her teeth barred. "Luis Paradis and Nahum Wallace, don't you know to never wake a lady?"

The Comanchero, Luis, laughed, holding his hands up to show that he wasn't going for his guns. "Apologies, senorita Faro."

Nahum lowered the shotgun, a grin stretching across his face as he hopped from his horse. He walked past the fire and offered his hand while Sadie lowered her knife. They shook, then Nahum wrapped the bounty hunter up in a silent hug like a large bear falling on its prey.

When he finally retreated, she looked at Jake who shook his head slowly. "How the hell are ya?"

Sadie chuckled, reaching down for her discarded hat. "A damn sight better than the Crogan brothers."

Jake cocked his head, smiling. "Got a telegram from Luther Moon down in Louisiana saying they were headed this way. You kill them on the trail?"

It was Amaya who could see the threads, the words I'd told Luther to write, and where to send them. "He did this, he sent for you." She said it quietly, but in the still night, her words hit with all the force of a cannon.

Jake turned to me. "You?"

Nodded. "Wasn't a lie that there are outlaws riding the trail. I just didn't think you'd come if I asked for help."

Jake didn't respond, didn't have to, I knew his heart.

I gestured to where our mounts grazed. "Hitch your horses and find a patch of grass, then I'll tell you who we're hunting."

If these men were going to ride with me, they needed the truth. I told them what I had visited on Granger Hyde in Lawrence, Kansas so many years ago. I told them how I had hung Charles Marland from a tree and carried his flayed face on my saddle. How I'd condemned Sagara Katsutomo to a life toiling on the railroad, his arms and armor taken with me for a trophy. And finally, I spoke of Thomas Grail.

Jake remembered him. I saw his mouth draw into a thin line as he traced a crude drawing of a bison into the dirt.

I did not speak of Lorelei. I left each of them to believe that it was Granger and his newfound sorcery that kept these men alive. But mostly I spoke of Trail's End and what they would experience. I tried to take the measure of each of them as I spoke, curious as to what my home would dig out that they so wished to remain buried.

"When I was a boy, my father led the flock, and through his wickedness, he spilled enough blood to satiate even the strongest thirst for death. Every sin partaken, and every want indulged." I remembered the lusting hands as I spoke, roving over my siblings and me, my own hand holding a stone knife, carving into a boy barely older than me. A burning rod held in my other, ready to put out the eyes of his mother so it would be the last thing she'd see.

"Doing things like this, killing like this, it does things to the land, creates places with ties halfway here, and halfway in the next world. And it festers, rots away at the roots until any living there aren't but shells devoted to slaking their sins."

Jake stared into the fire while Sadie counted her ammunition, listening but uncaring. Amaya looked enraptured by the tale, while Luis Paradis heard my story with a large grin. It was only Nahum Wallace who shook his head.

I regarded him, hands clutching the shotgun tense as a polecat, and I knew what he felt. I'd heard the stories of this man, hunting those that had fled to the west or to their decrepit homes in southern marshlands, all of them wanted for their deeds during the war, and what they had done before it. And here was another in front of him who'd fought on the side of those that had aimed to keep him toiling in the dirt.

I fought against those in blue for the same reason I had everything in those days. My brother fought for the other side, and the Yankees hadn't looked kindly upon my deeds. And here I was telling Nahum Wallace that his given liberty and righteous fury wouldn't help him when tempted by the place we were going. He thought himself blameless, striking back at the wicked world, and in due time he'd learn the only truth of men. We labored in life, and in the end, we died.

"You're a flannel mouth, Covington. I've killed men drinking blood in back alleys, feral men living with wolves, and every former 'master' who thought it right to own a man. Seen needless cruelty, and this ain't nothing more than that." He spit into the dirt as he glared at me. "Jake's just lucky, that's all. There ain't some devil's curse keeping him above ground."

A nervousness came around the fire, Jake watching me and my hand. The rest were similarly clutching their weapons tighter than a rich woman clutching her jewels. I stared at Nahum through the flames, his eyes barely living, and I wondered if he could see what was lit in mine.

"If you really believe that, Mr. Wallace, take your shot," I said. "Let fly with that cannon and in your last bit of life, you'll feel the fear you threw away all those years ago."

FOR A FEW SOULS MORE

Nahum bristled, he looked like a bear with its hackles raised and rearing to tear out my heart. If he stood, would be just another drop in that part of me that would never be full. Just like the marks I knew marred Nahum Wallace's back would never match the rest of his skin; time scarred all wounds, but men never healed from them.

I heard the Gun whisper to me, and I wondered what Jake would do when I killed his friend. He declared himself mine, but if that were true, he didn't realize what a friendship with me entailed. Or that I had buried plenty of friends.

The tension washed over us like a wave and Nahum's hands twitched, but his gaze broke in the inferno of mine, and he looked away. "A town of hell, bullshit."

I took my place next to Amaya, seeing her smug grin. Luis's laugh split the night, looking at me. "You do not disappoint, hombre, and you do not speak lies." He looked between Nahum and Jake, then smiled ruefully at Sadie. "We have tracked together before, but what do we know about each other truly? Other than we are all wonderful killers." He gestured to Jake. "He lives under a curse. Nahum? His hate keeps him strong. And you? Senora Faro? What sin have you indulged in other than murder?"

Jake interrupted before he could continue. "Friend, if I were you, all of you, I'd quit talking while you were ahead." He glanced back at me, unable to disguise the warning in his voice. "You don't want to see what happens when this one gets his fill of your lives."

Silence descended on them again and I leaned back against the log that Sadie had been resting against.

"Get some rest. We ride hard tomorrow, and when you get where I aim to take us, you all can decide for yourselves what you can endure."

I whistled once, and in the night, I heard Roux's howl. The three bounty hunters twitched, weapons aiming into the dark. But Jake and Amaya never moved, both already making their place to rest.

CHAPTER TWENTY-ONE

WE TRACKED THEM for two weeks, riding hard through the day and into the night, only stopping to walk the horses when they were sure to fall.

We came upon our prey in the evening, three plumes of smoke floated upwards from the horizon. We watched from a rise, dust blowing across the prairie. It carried screams with it.

My companions squirmed in their saddles, a few casting glances around at the barren scrubland like we were being watched. There wasn't anything around for miles, nowhere to hide, nothing but the long and endless sky under the bloodred sun. We couldn't shake the feeling that there was someone there, and there was, even if we couldn't see him, or know when his eye was watching.

I reckoned it was Marland, his blasphemous face watching us from the shadows of the next world. I wanted to turn to where I thought that he watched, tell him that his whispering would fall on ears as dead as he was. In the end, I ignored his eye and stared out across the prairie at the smoke and wondered what people were being murdered.

"Should we do something?" Amaya asked.

Below the smoke, figures appeared, a caravan leaving and heading north, their destination fixed the same us. I knew they were heading to the Adler home, and had questions about why they had chosen that as their rendezvous.

FOR A FEW SOULS MORE

I looked over at Jake and he slowly nodded, realizing my intent. I kicked the scrawny thing under me forward. "Let's ride."

There were no war cries, no shouts to let those before us know that they would soon meet she who rode the pale horse through the hollows of night.

I counted twenty or so, about half turning their horses to meet us when they saw us coming. There were five wagons, full up with women behind the bars, all of them sobbing over freshly removed hands.

The men were still too far away to be accurate, no matter how well they placed their shots. The same couldn't be said for Sadie Faro. Her hat had fallen back as she rode, tumbling behind her long platinum hair as she shouldered the rolling block in the saddle. The crack of the shot was louder than the thunder of hooves and a rider's neck exploded in a shower of gore, his head falling away. It bounced once, twice, and then was crushed under a horse's hoof like splattered squash. The headless corpse bobbed in its saddle, a charnel general bidding the rest of the riders to come and join him, and By the time he fell, death had found the others.

Sadie had managed to kill two more before we drew near, Jake and I riding high, our Guns united in their purpose again. Bullets bit into the dirt around us while some guns failed to fire. I saw a woman scream when her pistol exploded, the misfire sending the shards of burning metal scorching into her hand. She didn't have long to contemplate her maimed state before my shot fountained her heart's blood out her back.

All of them wore those red masks covering their faces, my wonderful Orphans, left to wallow like a pig in slop, all of them lured with promises of death. And that was a promise I kept to them. Murderers they may have been, but pistoleers they weren't. I guessed they'd spent their time picking on those who hadn't seen them coming, taking their fill of women and children that couldn't fight back.

Their horses boiled over as we rode among them, tossing them to the ground and making for the distant hills. Luis hollered a declaration of death in his own tongue as he drew his saber. A red-masked man had barely clambered to his feet, digging for his cannon when the blade stabbed him through the mouth. He didn't die quickly, his hands scrabbling up even as Luis continued his ride, the steel bend on the sword pulling tight through the back of his neck and sending him sprawling into the ground as it pulled his throat out.

The caravan wasn't so far, my eyes fixed on the leader, a man standing like a statue backlit by the sun, firing desperately at us. His gun ran dry, his shots having gone wild, and I leveled my gun to send him to his permanent reward.

I heard the crack of a rifle, the warning from the Gun that came a breath too late. The horse under me died, the bullet chewing through its heart and sending me flying. I barely had time to curl into myself before I hit the ground.

I hit the dirt, rolling. But luck had been on my side; the wretched animal's strength had been all but spent driving it across the plains and it had barely been living, only collapsing under its own weight. I came up firing, killing two more men. Both collapsed as little more than twitching meat against the wagon wheels.

There weren't more than twelve left now, firing as they could, taking cover behind the wagon, hoping that we wouldn't fire on their captives. Nahum scrambled from his horse. He ran around the wagon, and I watched as he took a bullet from two men who'd been aiming for him. There was a flash of blood and the big man screamed as he fired. The shotgun near cleared the man out of his boots before he fell into a puddle of his innards.

The other tried to flee before Nahum's hands wrapped around his skull, squeezing tight. The man writhed, digging his nails into Nahum's skin, screaming for mercy. Nahum's thumbs dug underneath the gunhand's eyes, and the man's already hoarse screams reached a new pitch. It didn't take long before they popped, and over the gunshots, I heard the wet slurping as Nahum dug his thumbs deeper, working away until they dug through brains.

The women in the cages hollered keening war cries, a sound that had been the last thing that many a white man had heard before an arrow had lodged itself in their chest. For a moment, I thought that I was back with the Comanche, raiding an Arapaho settlement. It wasn't Jake but Virgil, and this was our first test under the banner of the People.

I cursed myself for a fool when I turned and saw another man charging straight at me, his gun discarded for a long Bowie Knife, his eyes fixed on me like a bull's. The man's already stained and decrepit vest acquired a new injury, and he fell to his knees a hands-length from me. He reached towards me, barely grasping at the edges of my coat, coughing. I saw the desperation in his eyes, the want. He stretched his hands, his knife aiming for my legs. Blood dribbled onto his chin as he struggled to breathe. I watched him until Amaya stepped up and shot him through the head, spitting venom as she did. "Cabron."

I gave her an approving nod, then I looked down at the dead man. Sadie rode close looking down at the body. "Those who aren't dead are running."

It took an effort to take my eyes off the dead man, imagining the feel of the knife cutting through my leg. But I drew my gaze back up at Sadie and her sweat-stained brow. "Take Luis and ride them down."

She nodded, gathering up the reins of her horse and hefting her rifle, reloading as she galloped off. The woman was a crack shot to the manner born, and those left wouldn't escape.

Jake fired another shot and the lock from the prison wagon fell into the dirt, he offered his hand to the women inside. A few tottered out, sobbing around the blackened stumps where their hands used to be. He gathered them in a circle, all of them huddled together. There wasn't a child amongst them, and I knew that they were lying dead back in the smoldering remains of their village. I figured they were Cherokee by the look of them, what markings and tokens they'd been allowed to keep speaking to their tribe. Most were with child. Those that visibly weren't, were of age.

Hair that had been done up in braids had been pulled at and brought down around them. Each woman looked like a pond of darkness, a mourner's veil for their lost lives. They weren't my people, and I hadn't learned at their men's feet, but their tale was the same. their homes taken, confined to a land not their own. And fate had conspired to take more from them; their children dead, their men dead, taken to a place to be gutted like pigs for what was growing inside them. I knew it plain because I had done the same once.

Jake tried to speak to them, but they ignored him. They shirked away as Nahum appeared, his face smeared with blood, looking over the crop of women. "Ain't no reward for redskins, Jake."

Jake glared at him. "Not everything can be measured in coin."

Nahum snorted, his eyes alighting on one of the younger Cherokee girls, barely in her maidenhood. "Everything has a price."

I came between them, staring down the oldest woman who acknowledged me with a nod. "Neither of you is speaking truth." I squatted down, the Gun showing "The only thing a man can be measured by is how many bullets it takes to kill him."

I spoke to the Cherokee woman. I hadn't learned the tongue as well as I had those of Comanche enemies, but it was enough that she would understand my words. We spoke together and she told me her story, the stories of the other women, and the history of her entire band. When it was done, I asked her if she wanted to continue living.

She held up the blackened stumps of her hands, sores oozing. Without a sawbones, it wouldn't be long before infection set in. "Our men are dead. We cannot hunt. We will starve." She took a shuddering breath, tears in her eyes falling. "I did not understand their tongue, but I heard the sickness in their words. Just like I hear the iron in yours. Your word of death has spoken for them, just as it has spoken for us." I nodded. She began to speak to the others, some twenty or more, and a few began to sob fresh tears when they realized that their shattered lives were about to end.

I wiped the blood from my nose, bloodied from my tumble, looking at it smeared across the leather of my glove. "Mr. Wallace, why don't you secure the horses? Jake, you keep an eye on the horizon, just in case they have friends. Miss Shrike and I will lay these down."

Nahum nodded, lowering his shotgun and moving away. Jake paused, looking over the women before cursing under his breath. He looked the lead woman in the eye. "I'm sorry it came to this."

She couldn't understand him, but it seemed that she received his sentiment, pausing her death song to nod to him. Jake took a deep breath before he forced himself to turn away.

I caught his arm before he left. "Keep walking, Jake. When the shooting starts, your weapon is going to be just as hungry as mine."

He gave a slight nod, more an acknowledgment of my truth rather than an agreement before he turned away.

Amaya watched him go. "You really mean to kill them, don't you?

The hammer was already pulled. I had set the table well, and now it was time to invite my daughter to the feast. "Have you wondered, little bird, if you're strong enough to rescue your mother? That she might be wallowing and with child, just like these?"

Wetness stained the bottom of her eyelids, and her

hands gripped tight around her pistols. I twisted the knife deeper.

"They might've even taken her feet by now if she had the sand to try escaping. Course, all of them have raped her by now, seen what that can do to a woman. Might not be much left by the time we catch up . . . "

"Bastard . . . " She was quivering with rage. The tears made ravines down her cheeks, and she spoke in a choked whisper. "Why do you say these things? What fucking right do you have?"

I reached out with my off hand, grasping her wrist, and pulled it until the barrel of her gun was pressed against the head of a girl no older than her. The Cherokee woman paused for only a moment before continuing her song, then I scarred the wound in Amaya's soul that I had made. "What will you do if you find her like that? Going to leave her to suffer? Killing like this will give you strength, even if it's a strength born in blood."

I released her wrist and pulled her thumb back for her, the Cherokee girl breathing hard when she heard the click of the bullet coming into the chamber. I leaned and whispered into her ear. "A slow death is coming to gnaw at them who did this to you over the next few days, the hole in their stomachs eating them until there is nothing left but skin for the buzzards."

There was a shot and the Cherokee girl's brains splattered against her neighbor.

"You might have the strength to fly yet, Miss Shrike."

I killed the oldest, the leader, the one that asked for their deaths. I made it quick, feasting on their souls, even if I took no pleasure in the killing.

I figured Amaya would leave me to the work, one death was all that she needed. I felt satisfaction when I heard her next shot. My Gun and her two pistols waltzed together like partners in a dancing hall, and for a moment, I felt a bond between us. I could almost imagine a different future than the one that haunted my dreams.

One of blood stained all the way to the sea.

Amaya was breathing hard staring down at her last victim, a woman who had been in the late months of pregnancy. My daughter didn't break, didn't fall to her knees because of what she had done. What she had joined me in doing.

I holstered the Gun, and I began to arrange the women into an eternal repose. There was no time to create a proper platform, a cairn, anything to mark that they had lived. They weren't my people; the Comanche did not mourn nor make rites for those they fought or killed, but their deaths had come because of my sins.

I lay them out row after row, wrapping the stumps of their hands across their bellies, cupping the life they had failed to bring into the world by no fault of their own. After a moment, Amaya began to help. Together we arranged them in a circle. Better for the dying day to recognize its own reflection and take their souls up to the heavens.

I heard the hoofbeats behind me before Luis and Sadie emerged out of the gloaming edge of the night. Sadie dismounted from her horse, standing close and staring into the faces of the women. We'd closed the eyes of those that the bullets had not marred.

"Damn you for causing this, Covington," she said quietly, her voice a whisper.

"Don't burden yourself, Miss Faro. My soul was forfeit plenty of years ago," I said as I knelt in the grass, running my hands through the rivulets of blood that the thirsty ground already began to drink.

I began to sing a Comanche song to let the next world know that there were new arrivals coming soon. And when it was finished, I stood and didn't look back, listening to the wet pounding of the rain and the thunder overhead, washing away every bit of blood that coated the dead, the world beginning to bring them back to what they once were.

Dust to dust.

CHAPTER TWENTY-TWO

WE PUSHED AHEAD through the driving rain, the lightning cutting across the sky like the edge of a knife. The riders' destination hadn't been difficult to discern. There was only one place they could be heading out here, the same place we were heading.

It had been a hard drive through the elements, but the Adler home wasn't far off, and soon the lanterns rattling against its porch and barn shone as the only light in the wet darkness. Shadows moved across the porch, Hyde's men no doubt wondering what was taking their companions so long to arrive. The rain washed away the smell of blood that came from not eight miles away.

I trusted my daughter and Sadie to keep any of these that escaped what was coming from getting far. Any that ran would find themselves face down and bleeding, fodder for the worms in the churning mud of some ditch.

This house was a stop along the trail for those settlers heading up to Oregon. It had seen its fair share of travelers and its fair share of death. I'd known them and anyone else who did the devil's work.

I reckoned those here now knew it was an empty haven, but I bet they didn't know of all the ways a man could enter the house. I knew it because there wasn't a guard waiting at the trapdoor a quarter mile out.

It took some time to find the rain running through the ground. I pressed an ear to the wet dirt, listening to the water splattering against the stone below. It didn't take long to find the hidden ring and a sharp pull to reveal the dark hollow beneath. I didn't bother to feel for the ladder, the old wood had rotted away. I jumped down and pulled my Gun as I landed, brandishing it against the blackness. The Adlers had built a labyrinth straight out of some story, and I wasn't sure of what might be lurking in it.

Jake followed, his boots splashing into the pooling water. I ran my hand across the stone, the roots overhead, feeling the echoes of long-gone fear and agony. Things had been done down here in the dark, unspeakable torments visited on those who'd thought they'd found a safe and warm place to rest.

My old friend's eyes narrowed in the gloom before Nahum and Luis joined us in the pit. I watched him relive it, the last time the two of us had ventured under the earth. He'd been mutilated, but that was before the Gun had found him before he'd been made strong.

I could hear my brother's weapon whispering to him now, driving away the fear, feeding his soul that killing lust. "What is this place?"

I nodded to the darkness in both directions. "Place of suffering."

There wasn't any use telling them to follow as I plunged forward, none wanted to be the one left standing under the wet torrent. I let my eyes adjust, taking the twists and turns my memory brought me, trying to find that chamber at the center where the old clan had done their work.

We crept silently, but the voices of those ahead echoed through the tunnels; hushed whispers, warbling ululations uttered in a foreign tongue, piercing shrieks.

Above us, the earth was replaced with the house floor, shafts of light drifting down between the planks, and before us was end of the tunnel. We emerged into a large room that had once been the cellar. The shadows spun from the flickering light, dozens of them swinging and dancing.

The fireplace burned, irons glowing as they rested in it. I could smell the haze of something familiar, burning herbs that could bend the senses. Birds hung from the ceiling, wings splayed, feet bound by twine to the boards above us. Black ravens and crows, brown hawks, black magpies. Some still lived, cawing and protesting as they wiggled in their bonds, flapping around the room in a mad flight. The rest bled, their bellies slit and dripping.

Sagara Katsutomo stood under the birds, his mouth open, drinking in the life, staining his armor with every new slice from his sword. A song came from his throat, a deep and guttural toning.

I marveled how he could make any noise with three blades shoved so far in his guts. Counted three of them; could see the scarred and gouged plates of his armor where he had drug them, ritual punishments for himself, letting that hurt drive his hate like a trail hand pushing a herd.

Jake pulled the hammer back on his Gun. Katsutomo heard the same. The man froze from his feast, his grip tightening on his blade, the guttural song ceasing.

The birds cried, life clinging to him as old leaves clung to a tree in winter.

I held my hand out to keep Jake from shooting the man dead, stepping out of the tunnel and into the burning warmth coming from the hearth. I wondered if Katsutomo could even feel it.

I pointed the Gun at him as he pressed his blade flat against the plates of armor on his arm, the sword point aimed at my heart. Katsutomo's eyes wavered over the dark as Jake came, Nahum behind him holding the scatter gun level with the man's chest.

I circled him. "This time, I won't be delivering you into chains." I cocked my head back down the tunnel to the rainy night. "Can you hear it? That pine box calling? Hell's yawning and waiting for you." The blood-soaked warrior glared back, empty eyes watching me, utterly uncaring of my words.

He lashed with his blade, cutting the twine keeping his sacrificial coop bound. The birds' cries mixed with the scent of gunfire as we let fly. We couldn't see anything in the onslaught of birds. Our shots killed a fair share, carcasses littered the floor. Tufts of black feathers fell in spirals into the fire.

And Katsutomo was gone, vanished into the dark catacombs beneath the Adler home. I cursed as I heard the commotion above us in the main home, chairs being pushed back in the dining room, voices raised.

There was a trail of blood on the floor leading to the tunnel across from the fire, the telltale signs of Katsutomo's retreat. Jake tried to make for it before I stopped him, gesturing to the only other tunnel open to us. "There's a ladder that leads up into the main house."

He nodded, not questioning me. What was waiting down here in the dark wouldn't satisfy the hunger filling him. I nodded to Luis and Nahum as they passed, both men staring with curious eyes at the dead birds.

I turned to the black tunnel and followed the trail of blood left for me.

Above me, I heard the gunshots and the screams, footsteps running across the floorboards as Granger's riders, my Orphans, tried to cling to life despite the ending that had come for them.

I reloaded my Gun, expecting that a man given over to savagery of the mind wasn't going to let himself be brought low by one shot. The tunnel forked and I crouched low, running my hand along the stone and earth until I felt the still-warm blood splattered against the dirt. I followed it down the tunnel, guided by what little light came filtering through the floor above me.

Shadows danced as I heard the roar of a shotgun firing, crashing silverware following along with panicked shouts.

I looked up and realized that I was under the dining room where Herr Adler had hosted many an unwary traveler.

I was familiar enough with this place that I knew its workings. I felt along the wall until I found the lever, pulling hard and listening to the grinding pulleys give way . . .

The floor opened and the two men above it fell; there was a crack as one set of legs broke against the stone, bones shattering like ice melting in spring. I put a bullet in the head of the other, decorating the floor with his brains.

The living one screamed as the floor began to close above us, the light disappearing like it was being swallowed. Then the floor shut, and in the dark, the man looked up at me, hands grasping at his twisted legs as if they could pull the agony out. I wondered if this was how the wicked found themselves when fate folded their hands, left to hurt in the dark as they came face to face with the devil.

"Long time, Mr. Berger," I said, but didn't give him a chance to answer before whipping my fist, catching him full on, and dazing him. I stepped over him and made my way further. I knew now where Katsutomo was leading me, could smell it, near overpowering, and I could hear the flies.

The tunnel ended in a charnel pit that had been dug into the floor. A solitary lantern burned some thirty feet from me, and I watched as the flies lit from the remains. The rain came in from overhead, filling the pit, and lifting the old bones in water nearly stained black from the rot.

I moved around the room, looking at all the places that he could be hiding . . .

Heard the bones move at the last moment, the water splashing. I threw myself to the ground, and the knife sailed over me, sparking off the stone. I twisted around to see Katsutomo drenched in the offal of the long dead, water and blood running off him, pulling back for another shot at my head. I fired twice, seeing the spray as the bullets entered him.

I rolled away from the stone and into the gore-soaked waters, he waded after me. I floundered to the other end of the pool, firing again, the bullet tearing away the shoulder piece of his armor, blowing a hole clean through him.

I saw the stroke coming, his hands grasping tight around the hilt of his blade but I wasn't quick enough to dodge the thrust. I felt the pain as the blade entered my wrist, my fingers going numb and the Gun fell into the water at my feet. Katsutomo twisted the blade, and I gritted my teeth, drawing blood as he leaned forward. His eyes weren't empty, the hate that filled them danced.

The dance died as I struck quick with my other hand, wrapping around one of the blades he'd stuck in himself, and wrenching it out, opening his guts and letting the old decay flood into his bowels. He staggered back, taking the blade with him, a dry gasp erupting from his throat.

I reached with my uninjured hand. It was a foolish man who couldn't fire with both hands. I emptied the last three shots, watching them tear into his neck, chest, and forehead. He fell to his knees, eyes going hollow before sinking into the pit, the flies descending on him like waiting buzzards.

I looked at my ruined hand. I knew plenty of workings to heal it but that would take time and gathering ingredients. I holstered the Gun as I staggered out of the water, grabbing at Katsutomo's dead arm.

Then I dragged him away from the sight of the dead.

I tied Katsutomo and Anton Berger to the chairs, using my teeth for the knots in lieu of my right hand, wrapping my wrist tight in cloth torn from Berger's shirt.

Footsteps came from behind me. Jake appeared, breathing easy, splattered in the innards of some soul who'd spent his last moments wondering why the man coming for him wouldn't die. He gazed at Katsutomo's corpse, eyes wandering over the wounds I'd given him, and I wondered if he knew the working nestled somewhere in Katsutomo's skin was rocking the dead man in Lorelei's cradle. "Few of them made it out. Ran straight into the rain. Not sure if Sadie or the pretty miss stopped them."

He took a place by the fire, staring into the dying coals. "Wondered if you would live going after that one yourself. I remembered our predicament back in Deadwood."

I showed my wrist as I joined him. "Drew more from me than Craft did from you." I thrust my hand close to the flame, feeling the bite as it ate into my mangled flesh. "Man like that is only capable of drawing pain," I said, pulling my hand away, fabric wilting, a few sparks fluttering to die. "But there are other things that steal into the world, Jake. Growing the seeds planted in your bones. You and I are carrying that."

Something moved through the air, a working silencing Anton Berger's whimperings and bringing Katsutomo back to the world of the living. He gasped, focusing as he tested his bonds, glare focusing on me.

"Watch them," I said, heading to the tunnel and the ladder beyond it. Jake took ready in case there was any more savagery Katsutomo could conjure.

It took time to climb the ladder, my hand nestled against my chest before I emerged into what had once been Frau Adler's drawing room. Three dead lay on the floor, two men and a woman, their blood running into the grooves of the wood, the furniture destroyed.

I found my way to the front door, grabbing a lantern from its hook and waving it out into the dark like an island man signaled for boats to come back home. It didn't take long for my daughter to appear, Sadie following, the two of them leading our horses. The tip of Sadie's rifle was still smoking.

Sadie shouldered her rifle when she saw me. "Two of them tried to make for the barn. Made sure they won't see another sun."

The rain had not let up, the raging storm was still moving its way across the plains, visiting its fury.

Amaya joined me on the porch, staring at my arm clutched tight. "Your hand . . . "

I looked down at the stained cloth. I couldn't feel anything now.

"With a wound like that, I hope you're just as dead eye with your other," Sadie said, shaking her head.

"Leave my wounds to me and take the horses to the barn, get them situated. We have questions that need answering."

Sadie had already turned away, lit against the night by nothing but a few scant lanterns. I returned to the house, Amaya following in my wake. When we stepped inside, I smelled the blood of our slaughter. Nahum had made himself busy, piling the gun hands outside through the scullery entrance.

My stomach rumbled; I could still smell the last meal that these men and women were served, rich stew and fresh bread cooked in long forgotten ovens.

Luis had propped his boots on the table, the smart blue of his jacket coated with flecks of blood, his hair sopping wet with sweat from the exertion of his duel. He'd taken the head seat, and the man he'd killed slumped across the table. He reached for a loaf of bread. As I passed through, he called out, "A moment."

He smiled when I turned, pointing at his two table mates with the tip of his saber. "My curiosity demands to know, they are after all leaving this land because of you?"

I watched the Comanchero's grin widen, stabbing at my past. I briefly wondered if he thought this weighed on me. He was mistaken.

Amaya watched from the entry as I went to the one on the left. It was a woman. Her black and grey hair flowed across her place at the table like dark rivers. I wound my good hand through her hair and pulled her head up to stare into dead eyes where life had once made its home.

"Her name was Matilda Fuller. She and her husband wanted to make a life with their children, but they settled on land that did not belong to them. My teacher and his people, my people, we dragged them from their sleep. Her youngest daughter, barely more than a babe, was shepherded away under a Comanche Moon. Her husband we stretched out under that hot sun the next day until he blistered. When they began to weep, we poured ants into the sores . . . "

Luis' eyes followed my finger, his grin disappearing when I began my tale. I pointed to the tattoos on her cheeks and chin, the stylized lines and symbols. "This is what she was worth when we sold her to another in the tribe, three blankets and a horse. And in that time, she had to watch her little girl raised by another."

I let Matilda's head fall back to the table, splashing into a bowl of soup she'd laid out. I looked at Luis, letting him know that this old wickedness hadn't been coerced from me, but one that I had participated in with pleasure.

"I'd assume she was freed when Quanah finally surrendered right before Mr. Howe and I met." I let the musing hang in the air as I approached the other dead dinner guest. His head hung back; mouth open. Surprised that death had finally found him.

"And this one was a farmer, Claud Stokes. I offered to hear his story over a hot meal during a gully washer. He pulled his rifle, and claimed that he would have no business with outlaws. I offered him the same again . . . "

I looked at his skinny frame. Even in death, his eyes were still fixed on the meal he'd prepared. "Waited in the dark until the rain stopped, and when the mist was thickest, I took a torch to his crops."

I walked around until I was behind the dead man, bending until I could whisper into Claud's ear. "Can you hear me? Did you think of me when you were hungry? When you shivered in the cold and your empty belly screamed for anything to relieve your hunger, did you curse my name?"

FOR A FEW SOULS MORE

I rose and ran a finger through Claud's blood, tracing the dark path until I found the bullet hole over his heart that killed him. "I would look in on him from time to time, borrowing eyes that drift on hot winds to watch him eat the leather of his own shoe before Granger must have found him." I took my hand away from the wound, smearing the blood inside the bowl of soup on the placement in front of the dead man.

Luis' fingers clacked against the tabletop, pointing at me. "Just as death will find you someday."

He said it with such certainty, and I inclined my head to him. "Seem mighty sure of yourself, Mr. Paradis, especially when you've seen a man take a bullet to the chest and rise up strong as the day."

Luis shrugged. "I did not say I don't believe in the spirits. God, or the devil, they all make play with the lives of us weak and mortal men . . . " He gestured towards himself. "I just remember that I am a man, unlike you, Mr. Covington."

It had been a long trail, and not many had the gall to speak their thoughts. He was so certain that I thought of myself as some glorious outlaw, trying to outdo Hell itself on pouring out the cup of suffering.

But there wasn't some grand purpose. I didn't ride and collect all that I had because I believed that Hell would accept all my gatherings like an offering. I didn't believe I was above men at all, just believed that I had thrown off what chained one.

I was the furthest depths of what men could be, an ending for them that decided to throw off the yoke they'd been living under. They came to me, asking how they too could kill and rove forfeit of what made them decent men. And with one pulled trigger, I gave them what it was to live like me.

Claud Stokes had chosen that bullet, Matilda Fuller too, and August Lamb many years back. Granger Hyde and his ilk had chosen the bullets from my Gun twice. Even when offered an escape, they couldn't fathom it, craving the shot and the ending, wishing for that strength.

All who picked up their weapons and came for me desired an ending, all who traveled with me desired an ending. Luis Paradis had an ending coming too, even if the dawn of that reckoning hadn't yet graced the world.

But the Comanchero wouldn't have understood that yet, just like my child wouldn't have understood. I left him there, busying himself with finishing what food wasn't stained by the dead.

Amaya followed me as I made my way to the trapdoor that would lead down into the dark beneath the Adler house, eager to attend to my business with Katsutomo. He had an ending waiting for him too.

CHAPTER TWENTY-THREE

JAKE WAS WAITING for me, standing vigil over Katsutomo. The fire had been stoked and threw its light across the face of the twice dead man.

My daughter glanced over the Adlers' ancient instruments of agony, the pokers, and pincers, blades and chains that hung from the ceiling to elicit the secrets from reluctant tongues before they were entombed behind stitched mouths.

"This place has seen evil," she said.

Jake looked down at a desiccated body that lay with the stab wound still in her skull. "Seen justice too by the look of it."

I knew the body and knew the story of how it came to be there. "The woman was a killer. Her family robbed and killed those who came here. I dined with them more than a time or two."

Anton Berger nearly choked on a bitter laugh. "Don't surprise me at all, you son of a bitch. Horseshit and flies stick together."

I crouched in front of the two bound men, tilting my head as I examined Katsutomo. His eyes seemed empty.

Katsutomo was nothing now besides his hatred of me. I was a talisman that he could etch all of his sufferings onto; maybe I always had been.

Anton decided to speak for both of them. "Granger's already sending some to rescue us. The only reason you're still standing, Covington, is cause you got the drop on us. Came through the damn basement . . . "

He spit, grinning wide. "But Marland is watching. They're not leaving the two of us down here and they won't come with guns, they'll come with a rope for you."

He spoke with certainty, like a preacher so sure of his piety. He'd been blessed to see the workings of this land, he had seen "Mumbling" Marland speak of things not yet passed, or things that had happened a long time ago.

I finally spoke to him. "Do you believe me invincible, Mr. Berger?"

Anton laughed. "You're just a man, Covington. The Black Magpie ain't nothing but a man."

I reached out and traced a finger across Katsutomo's forehead. The bullet wound that I'd given him weeks ago had healed, but I knew that it still rested in his brain. He tried to pull away as I touched his armor, tracing the tears where so many shots had frayed the material. "The same applies to you, Mr. Berger. I've never claimed to be anything else."

Anton ignored me, looking at Jake. "You're a bounty hunter, right? Go on and stick this asshole with your knife and you'll be sitting finer than any man from here to the Pacific."

I glanced up at Jake. I could see the memories of those he'd helped me usher into the next world flickering through his thoughts like a pretty picture show. "You've killed plenty yourself, sir."

Anton laughed at Jake's words, shaking his head. "Just Injuns and Mexicans, occasional whore if she couldn't bear no more children. No God-loving folk had anything to fear from us; even Sagara here restrained himself from hurting innocents."

He shook his head, the short shock of dirty brown hair already beginning to go grey at the roots, the effect of chasing vengeance. I could have sworn he was a decade older than he was.

"Course you may be an Injun lover, like this one here," He nodded his head towards me, his smile disappearing.

"Maybe a fool as well as a little squaw lover? He'll do worse to you no matter what he paid you. Put the hate in me when I was seventeen. He killed my Pa for being in his way, then left him there rotting on the gallows in Littlecreek. Killed him to save some deserter!" Anton shouted his words, rocking in his bonds.

"And now you . . . you and that little Mexican bitch are helping him!? And you say that my killing of some savages makes me the same? You listen to your own bullshit or do you—"

Jake stepped forward, drew his Gun, and struck him. Two of his teeth rattled across the floor, blood running down his chin. Anton whimpered, "Fucking idiot, you don't care about who he hurt, who else he's going to kill."

Jake grasped Anton's face and whispered, "Don't care for Indians, but I loved a woman, loved her so hard I killed her. And don't tell me about them he's hurt, I know it better than most. After all, I helped kill your Pa."

Anton's spirit drained from him, the silence only broken by his short breaths before he roared something that only the devil could have understood, base and animal, struggling hard in his bonds and gnashing his teeth as he tried to reach Jake's throat.

I turned to Katsutomo, stained an even deeper red from the blood he had soaked himself in.

"Reckon I'll keep this again, your sword too."

Katsutomo did not answer me, his eyes did not rove to my hand or my Gun, they just stared, and I reckoned that he could read my story and my intentions like a cheap dime story.

"Wish that you could understand our words, truly. I sought my answers to you in the next world when you first came for me, and I listened to what they knew. But isn't the same as hearing a man's story from his own lips."

I looked at the design etched into his armor, etched into his sword, the same one burned into the skin below my eye.

Katsutomo did not respond, did not speak even as Anton continued to hurl his guff at Jake, at me, at what he perceived as the injustice that had fallen on him.

"Enough," I said standing, and motioning to Jake. "Kill him when you're ready."

My friend nodded; his Gun still grasped tight. I saw Anton's blood coating Jake's bare hand from where he had struck him. Didn't admonish, Anton would die more painful than most, but until then . . .

Well, a man of no importance, no harm in punishing him for what he'd done.

"Amaya? Your assistance?"

She nodded and together, we carried a bound and struggling Katsutomo deeper into the dark.

The tunnels beneath the house were a mystery to them that hadn't walked their trails. The Adler family had been meticulous in their labors, trip wires strung to release implements that would spill a man's guts over the stones. We passed iron doors and cells, the small gaps in the metal showing nothing but the gloom of dirt and roots within. The Adlers hadn't been ones to waste good suffering; when the time had been short, they'd always saved room to dine on agony, their victims left to smoke to perfection.

Through the earth, I could hear the thunder of the storm, rain running through the ground and dropping to the floor under us. Katsutomo remained silent as we dragged him, unafraid of what was coming. I aimed to cure him of that.

The last room was simple all things considered, nestled under the barn, decorated with old farming implements from traveling sodbusters that had met their end here.

We tossed Katsutomo down. He groaned as he hit the dirt and rolled to a stop, squirming like a maggot. Pulling hard at his bonds, rubbing his skin raw.

FOR A FEW SOULS MORE

There was one thing here that I had seen on my last visit, a prize of mahogany, and the meal of worms. Behind old casks and barrels full of rotten fruit, behind the stacks of pilfered moonshine, there was a coffin. The corpse of a woman hung out of it, old, rusted chains holding the bones clad in a wedding dress.

I pulled at the chains and the woman came with them, barely heavier than a saddle bag. I laid her as gently as I could on the floor, placing a hand against where her heart would have beat.

Amaya watched as I leaned forward and whispered, "I apologize for taking your resting bed from you. I have need of it, to put another to rest who desires to be where you are now."

I didn't believe in robbing the dead of what they deserved, another sin marked on my soul. But needs must, and my Gun ever hungered.

I angled the coffin to the floor next to Katsutomo, turning to Amaya. "Watch him. If he gets loose, kill him."

I climbed the distant stairs and pushed through the trap door that led into the barn. Our horses were stabled, Sadie doing their work before taking refuge back inside the house. I found our saddles piled neatly and reached into my trail bag, retrieving the four filled jars. Our path along the prairie had yielded their occupants, stinging and crawling servants of pain, they built their cities of sand beneath the earth. Now they would build their nest in flesh.

I paused before I returned to Katsutomo. There were plenty of horses packed tight in the stables, the animals staring from the gloom of the stalls, their eyes gleaming from the glow of the solitary lantern burning at the edge of the door.

There was a stage sequestered here. The caged wagons had been left outside to rust in the storm, but inside, carved from blackwood, was a replacement for what sat on the bottom of the river. The inside had yet to be hollowed out, both seats still intact for travelers. There was nothing but the paneling, the blinds were drawn tight, no sigils or signs, nothing like my traveling home. But I knew that Anton Berger and the other Orphans had brought it here, that he had sat on the driver's seat pining for his father, thinking that his skill with a persuader, his newfound savagery, an anger he'd spent half a life tending, that all of it made him like me. They saw the surface, the horns of me, and all of them thought that gave them the grit to outdraw eternal damnation.

I left the stage, returning to Amaya and the bound warrior, cradling the jars as I laid them into the damp soil around the coffin. Katsutomo eyed the jars, lying to himself that everything was still above his bend, that Granger Hyde's promises ended in things other than agony. That there was nothing but deathless oblivion waiting.

I took his armor from him, piling it until Sagara was left with nothing but his undergarments. Then I gestured for Amaya to take his legs and together we hoisted him into the coffin. He dropped to the padding and rolled for a moment, like a piece of meat on a spit, and I unsheathed my knife, ready to begin.

Katsutomo tried to resist, squirming as I dug the knife into his wrist, cutting down to the bone, slicing the muscle, savoring the smell of his old and clotted blood as it stained the coffin red. He took everything in an agonized silence, baring his teeth, barely a grunt escaping him.

Amaya helped me roll him over onto his back, a fresh snarl escaping him as his ruined wrists were crushed under his weight. She reached out and clasped his jaw in her grip while I angled my knife close to his eye. I felt him try to flinch and get away as I brought the tip just shy of cutting.

Katsutomo's breathing came quicker, finally beginning to lose himself to the fear. I let the knife point trail across his lower eyelid, and I listened to his breathing come faster than a gallop. "By the time the sun rises on your ruin tomorrow, they'll have stopped worrying what became of you. You can't die, but you can be hurt. You've felt the pain of every shot entering you, every cut . . . " Fury rose in me, riding up the slope of my intent like a man on horseback trying to reach a peak, and I whispered the final lamentation to a dead man. "And it's not often I dole out killing on a man who can't die."

I wormed the blade underneath his eye, my mangled arm pressed firm on his chest to keep him still as he writhed, he made noises like a trapped animal. I felt the pressure of his skull against my blade, and as his howling reached a crescendo, I pushed on the hilt and burst the left eye. A fresh helping of blood ran out of the hole, and I could see the ragged meat and nerve underneath. The eye rolled to a stop in the corner of the box. I reached down to pick it up, feeling the tension underneath my hand, barely bigger than an egg, and showed it to my daughter.

"Take a man's sight, and you take the peace from his soul. He'll wander the next world blind, in the same darkness, and the same pain."

She smiled, watching me squeeze until the thick white fluid rolled down my glove. Then I offered her the knife. "Time to teach you how."

She didn't hesitate, taking the blade from me. "I've taken the eyes from a man before."

Katsutomo's remaining eye widened as Amaya crouched over him, then the cutting began anew. I watched my daughter work, experienced but not skilled; her knife left great cuts in his eyelid, and when his eye came free, it looked like he had thrown down with a wolf and had come out wanting. He gasped, unable to even weep, his tear ducts reduced to nothing but ragged ruins. He would bleed out soon, minutes until the end took him, and then we'd wait. Wait for him to come back, expecting to see the colors of the world, only to find that he'd left one oblivion for another.

I saw his tongue licking his lips, devoid of color, tasting his own blood as it ran down his cheeks.

I reached for one of the jars, removing the lid and

smelling the bitter scent of dirt. I took a small twig from the ground, sticking it in and twirling until the jar's occupants had got their back up. They roiled over the inside the jar, looking for whoever had disturbed their home. I tipped it over Katsutomo's empty socket, and the swarm of ants fell in. I filled the hollow to the brim and the ants dug into the moist flesh inside his skull. And he began to scream.

"Hold his head." I said.

My daughter moved to follow my request, wrapping her hands around his chin and head, holding him tight. She nodded when I tipped the second jar, watching the biting insects fall into the wet darkness. His screams reached a fever pitch, and the third jar was poured down his throat, silencing him. He struggled to breathe, little geysers of dust spouting into the air. Then the sputtering died away, the heaving of his chest slowing, the soft oblivion of death a respite from the pain that would resume when the hitch in his chest pulled him back to this life.

Amaya wiped the ants clinging to her hands back onto his body as I poured the last jar across his chest, watching as the ants gravitated towards the dry blood and the entryways to his flesh. I reached up and closed the coffin lid, one of the discarded locks from the prison wagons securing it tightly.

Amaya and took it back through the tunnels, to an empty cell. Katsutomo returned, back to the darkness, back to his new torment. The ants would reach his brain eventually, and eat their fill. I wondered if he would feel himself slip away and if Lorelei's bullet would keep him coming back. Soft in the head, forever dying, until the bullet didn't have anywhere to nestle in him.

CHAPTER TWENTY-FOUR

AMAYA BEDDED DOWN in the upper room. Luis told me that Sadie had already headed for some shut eye herself, taking a cold bowl of stew with her. He and Nahum had since departed to their own lodgings, leaving just Jake and me to sit by the dying fire, the only source of light besides the thunderbolts flashing like blue flame outside.

Jake stared at the flames. "Take it that the Chinaman isn't among the living?"

If had a few weeks of leisure been available to me, I'm sure I would have waited and made sure Katsutomo suffered. But time was short, and my traveling companions would accompany me home tomorrow. I planned to visit my father, planned to visit my mother, my sister, Granger Hyde, Charles Marland . . . and Lorelei.

She waited for me and I pondered on if young Dewey had told her that I'd accepted her words before I'd ushered him from this life. I supposed that those things could be answered in time.

"You'd be right," I said, sipping on a cup of Arbuckle's that I'd found stowed away in a long disused pantry.

Jake leaned back. "What exactly do you aim to do? You heard that gun hand, Marland has already made for Trail's End—" He paused. "Truth of the matter is I have a hard time believing it's real, even if you say it."

I leaned back in my own chair, staring out at the storm. "Believe it. Those that lived there wanted a place hidden from God's eye, where every sin and want was met and indulged. Everything permitted."

I went on. "That was the gospel they preached, they gave sacraments to the devil in all the ways that a man could offer, then they went further." I couldn't remember the last time I'd been this loose-tongued, but this wasn't some settler, soldier, or rancher just trying to scrape out a living amongst the dirt. Jake knew the wages of what Virgil and I had done better than any. He deserved to know where his own damnation came from.

I sipped the bitter coffee. "Learned to ride there, learned to shoot there, learned to kill there . . . and when we left, my brother and I rode far and wide trying to find a means of killing everyone who lived there."

Jake glanced at his Gun. "Imagine you found it," he said.

My hand drifted to my own weapon, and I saw the shot in my mind that had killed my father, one of the first that had ever tasted a bullet from the Gun. I didn't smile at the memory, all the tribulations and pain that I wanted to dole out on him had been reduced to just a bullet.

"Yeah, imagine we did." I replied.

Lightning illuminated the windows and the silhouettes of endless storm clouds stretching to eternity, and Jake threw another log onto the fire. "Expect they'll be waiting for us. I would be."

I nodded. "Yeah, they'll know we've killed Katsutomo and his men when the sun rises and wipes away this storm. Marland's passenger is going to start telling our moves."

"Why don't you and I just ride in alone? They can't kill us. We can take the rifles, maybe have Sadie grab a perch, and shoot from far off. Luis and Nahum can hang back and come riding in if we run into trouble."

It was a good plan; Jake's time in the cavalry and his time killing after hadn't been wasted, but it wasn't according to my design, or what Lorelei wanted from me.

"You know more than most, Jake, enough to know that there are ways and arts that could drive a man to murder or madness. Trust me when I tell you that on this trail, you and the rest are going to experience new knowledge and that we will enter Trail's End unseen."

Jake knew better than to ask. His time spent riding the shotgun seat on my stage had left him with the sense not to ask questions that he didn't want the answers to, even if his curiosity pricked at him like a horsefly. Instead, he asked a different question. "The girl . . . who is she to you? She get a spur pressed to her throat too? Or did I just rub your bonnet strings wrong?"

He said it with a laugh, eliciting a small smirk from me, and for a moment the echoes of past times with my brother lived again.

"She's my daughter." Took a sip and watched Jake's eyes widen just a bit, the bullets fitted into the chambers of his mind. "Her mother's been taken."

Jake sighed, falling back in his chair. "Shit . . . "

I raised my nearly empty cup, Olivia Verganza was likely dead, or soon to be, and at the very least, she had been raped. That was the nature of folk when it came to sinning; those taken from positions of strength could be made low, could be broken just like any horse, until they were willing to serve.

"You remember her mother?" Jake asked.

I nodded. "Remember most everyone I meet."

Jake sipped the last of his drink from the tin cup, looking like he already regretted riding with me again, but knowing better than to go back on a bargain made. He sighed and stoked the fire, sending a wave of sparks rustling up the brickwork of the chimney.

Regarded the sparks. "It's a new feeling, Jake. Having a child, blood of my blood."

He slipped a flask from his boot and I could smell the whiskey. He took a long drink, wiping the edge of his mouth with his sleeve, offering the flask to me.

I accepted it with a nod. He spoke as I drank. "Do right by her then."

Left him there by the fire to stew in his own thoughts. I bedded down in the cell beneath us, right next to the coffin where I'd laid Katsutomo. I listened to his muffled gasping, the life entering him again, and again, and again . . .

Round and round like a wagon wheel.

CHAPTER TWENTY-FIVE

I **WAS** **UNAWARE** of the time that passed as I lay in that dark; wasn't often I received the gift of this kind of killing. Couldn't say I had spent six days laboring over my creation, but I was content to listen to it suffer inside the pine. The weariness took me.

The Gun was still clutched in my hand, a habit that I hadn't indulged in since my first days carrying it. In that quiet, its voice could become full on desires, and you wouldn't always wake where you had decided to lay your head.

In my dream, I saw myself as it did. I was drenched in blood, gathering bullets, discarded and water-logged books, and tender newborn babes. All of them offered to a worn and weary stage, its door open and accepting my offerings.

I awoke on the tide of pain, my off hand jumping to my eye, nearly scratching the skin raw with my blood-caked glove. It took me a moment to realize I wasn't gracing the stone cell beneath the Adler home. I stood on the plains outside the home, a fire burning in front of me.

I stepped forward, aiming the Gun at the waxen skin of the man sitting there. I caught myself before I pulled the trigger. It wouldn't have done much anyhow.

He was clad in a coat made from the skin of those unfortunates he'd built coffins for. Sickly black hair grew like plague roots from his head. His skin was yellow like he'd been abusing his forty rods, matching teeth in a rictus grin.

"Long time," I said.

The only color in this man's eyes matched the hue of his flesh and stared pointedly at the barrel of my Gun. I took it away, holstering it slowly, and sat down across the flame. Felt the caress across my mind like a lover's lips, the warning that the searing sting I felt on my cheek was just the early fixings for what could come if I wasn't careful. After all, this was the man who'd prepared a place for me.

He finally spoke. "You've done some mighty things on this drive, that's for damn sure."

I leaned back, keeping my off hand free. "Only thing I know, ain't a mighty thing, killing folk."

The man's smile never wavered, but his eyes changed. I'd seen the look in a hundred men who'd decided to try for real play. "Your companions would disagree."

"Most of them haven't felt the fire as close as I have," I said.

The old coffin-maker laughed, sounding like gallows rope swaying. "Truth in that sentiment, but that long trail that has me making pine for all your killing, that's coming to an end, isn't it? You won't be owing the house your soul anymore. I suppose if you wanted to go soft, you could get that back at a bargain."

Both of us took shelter in the silence, letting his implication hang. I wondered if he really thought I would go running to the altar, begging for forgiveness, or if he just feared me slipping his yoke.

I broke the silence first. "Come to speak your mind, then get to it. Reckon you and I are soon to be clear of each other."

His grin disappeared quick as a blowing tumbleweed. I saw his fingers twitch; he wasn't heeled, but I didn't know if that would even matter to him.

He leaned forward eagerly. "To put it plain, you came to me once willing to pay whatever was needed. Put plenty in the ground before you stood in front of me. Weren't green, even then. You'd betrayed the trust them that taught you had invested, and all that blood, fire, and sin produced that weapon for you. You've worked your wicked intent up and down this country. Now I'm asking if there is anything else you want."

It was a tempting offer, wasn't often the powers and principalities strove for you so clearly, and there was much that he could give me. I could bargain to shed my flesh, could become a bird, a wolf, could learn to walk in all manner of skin. I wasn't looking for the power to put someone under, had that strapped to my hip, but there were darker sorceries yet that I coveted, and my desire gnawed at me.

Come the sun on a not-too-distant day, my debt would be paid. And I knew I could pay again. What was another lifetime of blood?

Then I thought of Lorelei. She'd made me a promise, named her price, and it was an offer that would see me forsake both Kingdom come and the fire.

I denied him. "Been entertaining other propositions. Ones that don't end with me burning."

The frown on his face deepened. I'd seen a man in a traveling show once that had been able to stretch and contort, that's what he looked like now like his skin didn't fit. "Limiting for a man like you."

He reached out lightning quick and took my maimed hand, reigniting the agony as I gritted my teeth, the pain escaping from me in a pathetic snarl as my flesh burned.

He spoke in a hoarse whisper. "Imagine it, eating fear and drinking the sulfur, the saints and all the law trembling on Judgment Day when you crawl out to let fly." He released my hand and I found that he'd healed my flesh, the skin only marred by a dark sunburn.

He grinned, staring out at the scrubland still wet from the passing storm. "I could seal it, give you more than just a lick and a promise. Assure you a place as my best gun."

He tapped his fingers quickly across his knees, reminding me of young'uns ready to take their first knife or weapon, excited at what they could kill. "Just imagine it . . . " His voice deepened like a bellows working on a furnace. "Hunting down them that couldn't pay back what they owed. Stringing them up, taking the rope to them, or maybe nailing them out and peeling them raw, one cut at a time . . . "

The thing about hell is that it doesn't come offering terror. It would be my Pa, them that had followed his word, my brother . . . put up like prize pigs, and I could feast forever. A And all I had to do was listen to the Gun in my holster, hungry to go home and bring me to do the devil's work.

I raised my hand and the old coffin maker did the same. He had a knife that he stabbed into his palm. A smile stretched to reveal black gums.

"For once and all time, Salem Covington. That last gasping breath by rope or blade, you come home."

I took it from him, hand trembling, raising the blade high, listening to my Gun croon victory.

The door to the Adler home opened, and Jake stood silhouetted against the rattling lamp on the porch.

"Salem?" His voice was like a crack of lightning, bringing me back from the cusp of whatever cliffside of the next world the Gun had brought me. I felt Jake's presence, his hand reaching for me. I stood and looked down at the charred logs from some past flame, my own blade held in my hand.

Stood right, watching my companion's hand drop away. "What are you doing out here?" he asked.

I sheathed my blade, and looked at my healed hand as I spoke. "They say it takes forty days for the devil to come calling, and he offers you things, Jake . . . "

I passed him, heading back to the merciful stone where I could listen to man and death come closer. "Might want to return to the soft arms of your bed, lest he comes offering something to you."

CHAPTER TWENTY-SIX

LIGHT WAS BEGINNING to peek through the drapes we'd drawn. Nahum still slumbered, wrapped up in his coat like he was alone on the cold flats. Amaya and Sadie were sitting quietly, heating coffee in the fireplace.

I didn't know if Jake could hear my thoughts from his place at the table, the connection between our weapons feeding him little scraps of my intent, but he stepped close, whispering to me. "What happened out there last night?"

I looked to Luis who had pulled the curtains and was staring out into the dawn sun. "Just a sour dream."

He didn't believe me, would have been a fool if he had. There'd been a time when he would have left it there, but he'd carried his Gun for too long. "Never seen you like that," he said, speaking low.

"Caterina saw you that way, Jake saw you that way right before you fed that weapon so it'd break your chains."

I saw a cool calm wash over him, the same frozen hate that had driven me, driven everyone who had lived and died in violence. "I'm not the same man you left in that little spit of desert, haven't been ever since I picked up this damn thing. Never understood it when I watched you, traveling or talking to that dead Comanche. But you can hear it, and I can hear mine, and it shows me things."

The cool hatred drained from him as he spoke, and I saw ghosts of something else, the guilt that he was carrying.

I felt the same from time to time, I reached out to grasp

211

my old companion's shoulder. "You're going to kill that guilt in the days ahead; you, me, our companions, my daughter . . . we're going to feast."

The Gun spoke whispering comfort.

I saw Virgil's face overlaid upon Jake's as I made him a promise. "We're going to fill the mountains with their dead. The hills, the valleys, and the streams, we will fill them with their dead. We're going to make them desolate forever. Then they will know who we are."

I left him to ponder those things as I went to saddle my horse. Pondering the entire way whether I'd gone soft. Those were the same things I'd once promised my brother. Old words, said when we had set out to kill everyone who lived in Trail's End. This land had already suffered at our hands; now I had returned promising another wound. I thought I sensed the edge of something across my mind, the soft touch of fingers forged in metal hellfire.

My fingers drifted to the Gun. I mused if it fed me things unaware, in my dreams, in my thoughts. An old teacher had told me once when he'd heard my deeds that it was only a matter of time until I wasn't the master of my own desires. That I wouldn't be anything but an extension of the hate that burned in the chambers of my weapon.

I'd resisted the urge to laugh when he'd told me. After all, I'd been raised to be a tool of the devil.

CHAPTER TWENTY-SEVEN

THE SUN ROSE like a corpse being pulled from a grave, dull red and bloated. Underneath and around the Adler house, the corpses of the slain had begun to sour, I could smell it through the floor as I walked the length of the home, and flies had come from near and far to this holy land of rancid flesh.

Nahum had positioned himself on the porch, abandoning the tart rot of the inside for the cool air of the field. Even still, flies made their way about him trying to find an opening to the sweet feast inside.

Luis dunked his head into a watering trough, dark hair falling around him like a fisher's net. He smiled widely at my approach. "I do not think others will find this place very welcoming anymore."

I looked back to the house as Sadie and Amaya emerged, and for a moment, I imagined that I could see the ghosts of this place. Those that had died, those that had killed. I looked at Sadie and her arm brace and imagined her in a red dress, just like the woman who had killed the Adlers, suspected she came from the same place.

"Was never meant to be welcoming, Mr. Paradis. Only inviting," I said.

Amaya waved away the flies as she stepped down from the porch. She came to me. "Does he suffer?"

I nodded. "Slept after he couldn't do anything but moan. His tongue is gone now."

Jake emerged from the barn, his horse behind him,

saddled and ready. He stared at the rising sun. "I prepared the horses. I'd like to put this place behind me."

I made sure that each man and woman of my outfit had taken their fill of the dead's ammunition. Couldn't say how many Granger Hyde had seduced to his cause.

Then we left the Adler home behind. There were only two riders left now, then Granger Hyde, and her . . .

We rode west for a week, heading across the plains into the corner where Colorado met Indian Territory and Texas, going until the grass began to wilt, baking under the sun, barely clinging to life even with the storms that had passed through.

I knew what I was looking for when the weeds stopped securing themselves in the earth, unable to live in a place where death itself had purchase in this world.

At dawn on our ninth day, we stood at the edge of a large cliffside, staring down at a blighted trail of sand, half covering a railroad, buttresses, and rails rusted by the passage of years. Beside it was a station.

We were some two miles from town, but I could see it, even with the pale light of the sun struggling to rise behind us. Trail's End squatted like a gaping wound, its buildings gashes, and the small crosses marking graves spread out around it in all directions were sutures keeping it rooted halfway in this world.

I found the path leading down the cliff wall; it wasn't the way I usually returned, but it was familiar to me all the same. From here, we could come home unseen.

I kept my eyes on the old station, occasionally glancing up the cliffside running behind us. Looking for the glint of sunlight off a gun. Wouldn't do to be ambushed here, not when we were this close.

A breeze came from the east, blowing dust across the nearly rotted platform boards. They creaked underneath our weight, and the old station windows rattled.

FOR A FEW SOULS MORE

A rock tumbled from the top of the cliff. I glanced up in time to see the red wolf staring. Roux, following true. He disappeared as I stepped onto the old platform, listening to the wind.

I stared into the shadows of the old railway station and discerned the two dead men sitting rigid in their seats.

They were nothing but bones now. The buzzards had eaten well after I'd put a pair of bullets in them. I remembered their faces, eager as kids looking for sweets, with knives at the ready to dig into us as Virgil and I had dismounted from the train.

I also recalled their pleading as we'd drawn on them, their begging when we took them back inside, and their screams as we killed them. It had been a hell of a homecoming.

The corpses of those we'd left weren't alone. I saw the flick of a match, a lantern's slow glow, and three men slowly shuffled out. The one with the lantern had a red mask hanging around his neck, though it looked more like a rag now.

His eyes hadn't adjusted to the dark. "That you, Albert? Thought you weren't coming in 'til sunset."

"I'm sure he is, Mr. Bray. I'll give him your regards," I said calmly, feeling the anticipation of spilling blood.

He dropped the lantern as all three went for their guns and found their insides decorating the platform. I put the first shot directly through Cleveland Bray's neck. A shot from the second man winged Nahum. He winced as he fired the shotgun, blowing the man's leg into powder and gore.

The last one hadn't even made his holster before Jake and Amaya killed him. His head peeled, nose and skull caving in as the shots made their home in him. I spared a look for him as I walked past, replacing the spent bullet. Looked like a small pond of blood had filled the cavern of his skull.

I crouched down next to Bray, listening to the sweet

gurgles as he drowned in his own life, his eyes looking up at me with hate and sorrow. I rested my hand on him, coating my glove in his blood. "Safe travels, Mr. Bray. You'll be with that wife of yours soon. She'll be proud you fought, proud you tried."

Small bit of comfort for him; it's hard on a man to travel this long, fill himself with purpose, only to find the world had taken its eyes from him long ago. Saw his eyes flick to the brand on my cheek as his eyes slowly went dark, it was the last thing he had seen when he first began his journey, and the last thing he saw as it ended.

The other man caterwauled as he clutched the bloody stump of his leg, trying to staunch the flow of blood; it looked like water running through a sieve. He pleaded for his mother, to the Good Lord, anyone who'd help him. Anyone who'd save him.

Luis unsheathed his sword and strode forward until he was standing over him. He looked down on the man coldly, then he sunk his saber deep into the man's guts, a small crying whine escaping from the man as Luis twisted the blade deeper; the Comanchero gritted his teeth as the man died.

Nahum clasped Luis' shoulder, nodding once. It was a gesture that the Comanchero didn't return when he pulled his blade in one wet slice from the dead man's guts.

Looked down at the corpse, but I couldn't place his face or his name.

I would bury them later, create a working and reach for their stories in the next world, and they'd take their place in the ever-growing bone orchard that surrounded my home.

Sadie scanned the land between us, looking at the crosses. "No cover between here and the town limits. You're sure they're in there?"

I couldn't see any torches or lanterns burning in the windows, but I could almost hear her, same as the Gun could whisper, the voice of the Mourning Lady calling.

I licked my lips and drew the Gun. "Yeah, we've made it this far. Imagine that Marland crying hell."

"So, how're we going?" Jake asked.

I looked at the steeple, wondering if Hyde had removed the corpse I'd nailed there years ago. "Mr. Paradis, Mr. Wallace, and I will go straight in, follow the thickest flock of graves. Jake? Take Amaya and follow the tracks. There are gulches north of here, it will take you to the other side of town. They'll bring you in unseen. And Miss Faro . . . "

I pointed to the steeple, the highest point in the town. It was built on the mound my family had found when they'd settled here. "Circle around to the south and kill any in the church. Imagine you'll have plenty more to shoot once you reach that roost."

Jake and Amaya headed left, following the directions I'd set. Sadie headed in the opposite direction. I watched until they had vanished into the black, the early morning mist swallowing them like the tide took sand.

I began my own journey, stepping off the platform and feeling the rough dirt beneath my boot. A calm washed over me. This wasn't some town on the wrong side of my Gun. This was home.

But I'd scarcely made it a hundred yards before I was struck dumb, my gait slowing like a man mired in thick mud. I heard a sound, small, but powerful enough to send my blood running cold. Gooseflesh raced up and down my arms, and I reached into my pocket.

Only ever heard old Bertrand's timepiece in the scant few seconds that its previous owner in Silver Creek had spent begging before I'd put the bullet in him. It had remained frozen in my stage since I'd taken it. And now it was ticking in my hand.

"What is it?" Luis asked.

I tried to keep him from seeing my trembling hand as I put the timepiece back into the folds of my coat. "Nothing," I replied, fixing my eyes ahead and going to meet what was prepared for me.

CHAPTER TWENTY-EIGHT

WASN'T SURE THAT Luis and Nahum had gone to following me, not until I heard the crunching footsteps, pebbles shifting under their boots, afraid to be left behind in the purgatory between the station and field of crosses around Trail's End.

The ones furthest out were the freshest; wouldn't have been surprised to see Dewey Powell's name scoured into dead wood. This is where they all ended up when they were planted; didn't matter what boot hill they'd lain in, all paths finished here. Especially when I'd had a hand in it.

I let my hand drift across one of the crosses, tracing the name with my fingers. I looked hard between the graves, just in case any of my Orphans lurked amongst the dead.

"You kill all these, Covington?" Nahum whispered behind me.

I nodded as I glanced at the nearest one, bearing the name of a man named Clifford Fleming. "Every single one."

Luis gave a disbelieving laugh. "That is some high-grade chisel. There are more than I can count here."

"I've seen the cemetery in Graverange, the folks you and Jake planted were still there unless you're a damned resurrectionist too," Nahum said.

I wrapped my hand around a clump of dirt, letting it trickle through my fingers, the dark soil like a bleeding wound. "Said I killed them all, Mr. Wallace. Never said I was the one out here burying them."

I rose and began the final leg of the journey, keeping

to the road heading down to my left, heading for the nearest building that had once been a livery. It looked like they had taken the bones from the horses that Virgil and I had killed and stacked them into several piles strewn around the pen. Saw their horses in various states of rest around the pen, watching the three of us come, eyes reflecting the gleam of the dawn sun.

"Mr. Paradis, why don't you make sure none of these have a chance to go riding off?"

He drew his saber, muttering some prayer, and then I heard the scream of a horse as he plunged the metal deep into the beast's neck.

I should have kept going, but the horse's death cry stopped me cold, and I turned around, leaning across the fence to watch the Comanchero work his craft. There were two others in the pen. The horses stamped in the dust at the smell of their fallen brother's blood perfuming the dawn.

The second animal watched Luis come with cavern eyes, a long shudder passing through its lips that could have passed for pleading, then Luis swiped his blade across the nape of the stallion's neck. The dark brown skin peeled back, and I heard the clicking of the blade against the horse's spine. The beast collapsed in a throaty bellow of suffering, blood pouring out like thick trail soup into the rest of the pen.

Luis turned, noticing Nahum and I staring, and he flashed a devil's grin, flourishing the blade and bringing it down through the animal's eye, ceasing its swift breathing.

I forced myself to leave, giving Luis his time to converse with the emptiness that had pooled inside him. The sun had finally crested the horizon behind us, stretching the shadows from every building lining the main road. I pressed myself tight against what had once been Croaker's Dry Goods. I remembered old Eli Croaker and his lecherous hands; they had roamed free across the children he had kept chained in the cellar underneath the shop.

Hugged the building wall, listening to the porch boards creak as someone wandered out. I determined there was another with him as he muttered, "Those horses sound like Morgan's been out there beating them again."

The other man grunted. "Probably smell a coyote. Them and the damn crows are the only things living out here."

I crept closer, one hand urging Nahum to hold his ground, then I went silent as an owl in flight over the railings, the creak of the old rotting wood barely giving the two men a warning.

One man was standing, eyes rooted on the west that was still clutching to its necklace of night. The other sat in an old rocking chair holding his coffee. His eyes widened when he saw me clamber over the railing, voicing something between a scream and a warning as he went for the pistol laid on the ground in front of him.

I threw my knife and heard it swim through the air, embedding itself in the hollow of the man's neck. His blood spilled out his throat, running over his white union suit.

His friend turned to look, before dropping his coffee, fumbling for the peacemaker holstered tight against his pants, and turning to find the Gun pressed against his forehead.

I recognized him. "Long time, Mr. Jenkins."

Horace Jenkins looked at me with all the regard of a man who'd found a snake in his coop. "Go to hell, Covington."

I leaned in so I could look into his eyes. "Where do you think I took your brother when I killed him? Now drop that gun of yours, you know it can't kill me leastways."

I turned Horace with my other hand and we watched the other man die. I recognized him too, a younger man named Michael Dillon; his father had been a sheriff who'd clung to his belief that the law of his town overrode fate and damnation. Michael had curled in on himself, reminding me of a spider after meeting the underside of a boot. He gnashed his teeth, trying to draw breath and only choking on his blood as it painted the old floorboards. It wasn't the first time a man had bled out here. The ground drank the blood in lieu of the water that had long disappeared from this place.

Horace dropped his weapon, closing his eyes as Michael Dillon let out his last rattling gasp. "We've been waiting for you. Ol' Granger, he's got a plan, and you're going to regret all the good folk you've killed."

I let him speak; this wasn't one who had sold his soul direct, he was just a man consumed by his grief. He'd come a long way only to find death waiting. I leaned forward until my voice slithered across his ear, letting that fantasy fill him before I twisted the knife into the truth of his deeds. "Suppose all of them women weren't nothing to you, whores and sinners all. That why you rape them?"

He tensed under my grip, his breathing coming faster. "Go on, end it. I ain't explaining shit to you. If you'd cared about these redskins, whores, and nigger lovers, you shouldn't have gone killing better people. It's your sins, YOUR SINS! YOUR-"

I twisted his neck, feeling the bones snap under my fingertips, his spine cracking like a water reed. I watched him crumple, his ruin falling wet in Michael Dillon's blood. I reached down and retrieved my knife and then whistled for Nahum. He emerged from the shadows I'd left him in, then the two of us headed across the center of town, making for the saloon.

My eyes were drawn to the church at the end of town, and I knew what was waiting up there. She'd been punished for the sin of me, and now was nothing but a womb for the blackest depravities.

Jake and Amaya emerged from the other end of the street, coming up the road that led down to the barren lake that had long since gone dry.

The four of us crept up on opposite sides of the road. There wasn't any light shining inside the old saloon. If there were any waiting, they saw our shadows flash across the smashed windows.

I didn't waste time waiting, pushing through the doors and into the dark, holding the Gun forward like a shield, eager to taste the blood of any fool waiting. Turned out that the only fool was me.

Granger had anticipated my moves, had taken account of my lust for killing, that he'd known my eagerness to shake the yoke from around my soul. Truth be told, I was afraid. The timepiece in my pocket had been counting down, reminding me of the near end, and I was trying my hand at outpacing death itself. Either way, I came through the door and saw the match strike, the small flame illuminating a face full of wrinkles . . . and one sightless eye encased in lead.

Granger Hyde rolled his words like he was rolling a thick wad of tobacco. "Hello, Covington. It's been a while."

The match drifted down until it drew light from a lantern, painting the rest of the saloon in its glow. I saw the bones of those I'd killed long ago, and a company's worth of men and women, each of them wearing the same damned crimson mask.

The light reflected the unabashed hate they harbored, gleaming eyes all around, like wolves surrounding a deer.

Or a magpie.

Charles Marland rapped his knuckles behind the bar, the men and women parting like the sea as he laughed. "Almost had us, Salem. Moving on the Chinaman in the rain, passing from my sight with your little magics. But you forgot we've known the day and the hour since she came."

Her scent came drifting from the upper level, the smell of mistletoe and Jerusalem cherries, intoxicating, and with a sigh like a dead man's last desperate breath, Lorelei came from the dark. She drifted down the stairs. With the collective breathing and muffled shuffles of all them packed tight into this bar, I could only hear my own heartbeat, her steps as she came, and the ticking of the timepiece I was carrying. It seemed to grow louder as she drew closer.

She took her place next to Granger Hyde, and the old man smiled, reaching out to grasp the glove of her hand, "Magnificent, isn't she? I see why hell spit her out when I asked for something to end you."

I heard footsteps behind me. Shadows crept across the windows, and a quick glance confirmed my fear. Each building was giving up its occupants, another thirty or so Orphans spreading out across the square, two of them dragging a bloodied Luis Paradis between them.

Granger leaned forward, he reminded me of a few men I'd known playing cards. When they had a winning hand, they weren't shy in letting all creation know it. "There isn't any retreat, Magpie. I've done my work; I've laid the rails of your ending and you followed it like the damned thing you are." He gestured with the stump of his hand, the one that I'd cut and left rotting somewhere in Lawrence. "Followed the trail of your life, learned everything that you learned, ate up every scrap of magic from those willing to teach it. Learned more when I came here—"

Let my Gun sing, and one of the Orphans stepped between Hyde and the bullet that was meant for him. A spray of blood coated the old buzzard's face as the man's brains fountained out of the back of his skull, and the saloon came alive.

I dove backward, rolling across the porch and coming up firing, killing two of the Orphans. Neither one had gone for their guns, they wielded blades instead.

Nahum fired and a man flew apart as the shotgun hollowed him, bits of intestine slopping out as the corpse toppled. I couldn't make Granger in the haze of gunfire, but I saw Marland striding through the din, reloading, his damned eyes fixed on Nahum.

The bear of a man turned just in time for a bullet to catch him in the shoulder. Nahum stumbled back, bracing himself against the wall of the saloon. His shot caught Marland and

\blasted him back and over a table. He rolled and came to rest, his hair parting just enough for me to see his passenger. The second face chittered and hissed, three small teeth chewing as it whispered things to its slack jawed host.

Then the Orphans were spilling out into the street after me, blades raised and eager, uncaring whether they met their own deaths so long as they could lay me low.

I saw more of them coming from behind me. They came sprinting from the empty buildings around me. I heard the distant crack of a rifle, and the lead fell, her head bobbing on the edge of a string of skin.

Could see the distant gleam of Sadie's scope, and the measure of her killing. She looked over Trail's End, and she acted in the angel of death's stead; where her gaze fell, another went into death.

I brought myself to my feet, firing from the hip, and taking a woman through the stomach as she threw herself at me. Killed two more before I started running. I headed towards the church, letting Sadie cover my retreat, even as the sun finally crested the distant east, and cast the inverted cross down on me.

I was running towards my own damnation and I knew it. There was no more gunfire behind me, wasn't sure if Amaya still lived, or Jake. He and I couldn't be killed by any gun, but that didn't seem to matter with Hyde and his army. I recognized the working that Granger had them under. His magic had driven away their fear, their thoughts of anything but killing me.

To them, no price was too high, the big jump wasn't something to be feared. It didn't matter how many of them I killed. They'd throw themselves forward like a stampede to see me bite the dirt. Felt that finality come round my heart, the certainty of what was coming, and I heard the timepiece winding to a close, my time come round at last, within spitting distance of paying off my debt.

I was almost to the church doors, hearing the shouts and the pursuit behind. Seemed fitting that I should end things here, in the house where the people of this town had offered up their wickedness. Now it had come time for me to worship, and with the only god I'd ever glorified gripped tight, we would kill until the charnel house of hell was full.

I came through the doors running, pulling the beam to block the door behind me.

My pursuers began to pound on the doors as I backed away. I glanced at the windows around me, the old stained glass shattered from Virgil's and my rampage all those years ago, too high for any to climb through. I reloaded, my fear driven away. Only had to kill so many, and they were so eager to die.

The door creaked as the men and women threw themselves against it, testing themselves against the rotten wood. Sadie climbed down the ladder from the steeple, frowning like she was facing down a noose. She looked up at the inverted cross looking down on us from the pulpit. A westward wind swayed the old bones nailed to it, tattered rags fluttering like an old battle standard.

"Thought you were more, Covington," Sadie said, shaking her head as she slid a round into her rifle, pulling her pistol and checking the ammunition.

With my off hand, I unsheathed my knife, watching a crack split down the middle of the beam. It wouldn't be long now.

I walked to where Sadie had upended a pew, taking aim at the door. She sighed and removed her hat, the crisp white hair tumbling. "They weighed and measured you. Did you think you'd kill them all?"

I kneeled next to her, taking my own hat off and thinking about my next move, the only move I had left. Lorelei's offer, what she had whispered in my ears as we'd met in the next world, the one I had sent Dewey Powell to accept on my behalf, the one I'd tried to outrun since the beginning. The thing every man tried to outrun and fell short, be it by bullet or time.

Her price had been set, one easier and harder to pay.

What were six souls to ten thousand? If fate was kind, the others still lived. I hoped that Granger would want to feast on the rotten scraps of our humiliation, the defeat that he thought he'd dealt me.

"Before they come, I'd like to hear your story," I said, looking at the scar running down the length of her cheek, the eye patch covering the exposed socket, and letting my curiosity run.

She shook her head, shoulders shaking in a bitter laugh. "Lived in a place that was made to train women to kill those who needed killing, but I failed, and the Silent Room wouldn't have me."

The beam barely held, more cracks appearing, the door opening just enough to see the crowd gathered outside. I thought I saw a few carrying ropes.

"Figured I could do the same as my sisters. Fight any badness we found." A soft bitter laugh escaped her, and she looked over at the door. "Suppose I'll die doing just that."

I picked up my knife again, clutching the Gun tight, and nodding at her. "Thank you for the tale, Miss Faro."

She looked back at the door, firing once, and pulping the head of the closest who'd deigned to stare at us through the gap. She fed her rifle another bullet. "Reckon we have maybe thirty seconds before they're in. What about you, what is your story?"

I leaned down behind her. "This is my story, beginning to end." I slit her throat and watched her blood run. She clutched her throat with her right hand, and with her left, she tried to kill me.

The blade jumped from the brace around her wrist. The noise was near overpowering. The shouts outside, the splintering wood, and the steady drip of her blood.

I felt a measure of respect when I saw that she had ceased trying to stop the flow, and focused entirely on killing me. She stabbed at me, and I stepped back, weaving away as I counted down the seconds until her life finally emptied. Old Bertrand would have been proud.

She sprang, fast as a scorpion's flicking tail, and I found I wasn't quick enough. She missed my throat, but I felt the blade go through my shoulder, deep into the bone of my firing arm. I grunted, relishing the pain flooding through me, and I stared into the deep well of hatred that pooled in Sadie's eyes, and I watched that hatred drain away like someone had pulled a cork on everything. Supposed I had when I'd traced death across her neck.

"Good, Miss Faro. A good blow. Reckon I'll be seeing you soon."

Sadie sank into death, sliding down against the support of the pew she'd uplifted to guard against the mob outside, not Orphans anymore but mayflies thinking they had importance and weren't just a passing thing in the stories of those I'd collected.

The beam behind me gave one final effort to keep the crowd at bay then the doors to the church gave way.

They came in slow. They might have been nothing but puppets of Granger's magic, but it didn't mean that they were eager to court death. They lingered at the foyer, staring up at the massive symbol that had replaced the cross in here long ago. The same symbol that was branded underneath my eye.

I aimed the Gun, looking at their gleaming eyes underneath the masks. "I've killed your own with the sword, and with hunger, and with death, and with the beasts of the earth. Their suffering tongues proclaimed their stories, and I remember them all, so why don't all of you come? Unmask yourselves and spill your lives for me . . . "

I gave myself over to the Gun and fired, killing a woman who'd been standing with her knife drawn high. They didn't break, didn't come running towards me.

Felt a chill despite the heat, then the men and women moved like they were in a trance, the spell moving them. I could smell the working in the air, strong; wasn't often you could perceive the art at work.

Then she came, Lorelei, passing through them, on the stub of Granger's arm, the old man grinning.

My rage burned white hot, and I pulled the trigger on the Gun, firing at Granger until it had spent every bullet and was as empty as the space where my soul should have lived.

But there was no rush, the familiar feeling of killing a man that my weapon gave me was absent. He gestured to the thing that looked like a woman on his arm. His lead encased eye rolled towards her like it could see. "Can't kill me like that, Salem. Not with her to ward it off. She exists to end men like us."

I said nothing in response, just stared back at him, at his limp, the crippled stump, the unseeing eye . . . And the Navy Colt he had holstered.

He saw my gaze and nodded. "Aye, came prepared, should Jake Howe decide he isn't willing to help."

Reloaded as Granger snapped a finger. The Orphans filed in around me utterly silent, soldiers for the magic put on them.

Granger chuckled. "If I'd known that trick back when you greybacks came riding through, don't think you'd have maimed me . . . or killed my boy."

He didn't realize that his son wouldn't have recognized the man in front of me. I'd only flayed his body, scarred his soul. But Granger had done his own mutilation and had gone about his damnation like it was his duty.

I felt an odd manner of pride come to me. It was like looking in a mirror. I expected that Granger Hyde was what my soul looked like if it could look back at me. And by the gun on his hip, he aimed to make himself more than just a reflection of me. He aimed to be me.

I decided to speak truth to him. "All the sorcery in the world couldn't have saved Jackson. He made his play and he paid for it, same as you. Only death didn't find you that day. But I promise you, Granger, today it will."

I looked at Lorelei, feeling my heart beat faster as I asked her, "Is it the time you designed?"

She nodded. "Yes, these are your pallbearers."

Granger snapped again, and the Orphans surrounding me lunged. I managed to slash one's throat, and gut another before I was on my back. I remembered pain as it came; it was an old friend that came calling every so often.

The blows rained down, an agonized grunt escaping me as a foot jabbed hard into the wound that Sadie had given me. Felt the sharp pain as they slit both of my hamstrings.

My hand still clutched the Gun, screaming for me to move, get up and walk, to kill. I heard cries of protest.

They'd brought my companions and my daughter. Granger released Lorelei from him, and she drifted to me, the chill of her hand like sharp ice driven into my wounds.

Granger hobbled between my friends, jabbing with the stub of his arm at me. "Look at him, he ain't one to fear, he ain't one to love. Look at your partner!"

He pointed to Sadie, her blood running through the grooves of wood, face slack and accusing. He lumbered to me, painfully lowering himself until he sat beside me. I tried to kill him there, tried to turn the Gun and pull the trigger and plant a bullet in his fat heart. But I felt nothing but the cold fire in my wounds. My strength gone like a lame horse trying to rest its weight.

Granger leaned in close. "When you rode down from those hills with the rest of those butchers when you and that beautiful Gun cut me down, I thought you were the Devil himself . . . "

He reached and tapped a finger against his lead encrusted eye. "Last thing this saw was you. The thing every rebel and blue coat whispered about; the thing babes woke screaming cause they had seen your bullets killing their fathers in their dreams." I watched him point to the sun. "And that fear dies today, and all the folk you've hurt are getting their justice."

I watched him stroke his own feathers, and preach on about his own self-righteousness without realizing the chains he was forging for his soul.

A man could fool himself into thinking he was a hero. But I had broken that self-claimed virtue on the blackness of my heart and the certainty that my nature had been birthed from blood and ash. I had been born amidst slaughter and I had come so others would drink from a cup of sorrow.

Granger thought himself to be more than me and couldn't even grasp that bitter cup.

Granger Hyde's face transformed, fury seizing him. "Those here, know at heart you're just a ten-cent man. You lost as soon as I found this place, Covington. You burned, cut, and did your damned best to make me suffer, but you were just forging your death. You could have stayed away; you would have lived longer before I'd come looking for you. We've taken so many women for the ritual and I was ready to scrape my soul over those coals like butter if it meant taking everything from you . . . "

He laughed. "Suppose Marland can have his way with them now that they don't have a use. Why draw this out when I can just kill you and take that pretty pistol? Can't think of anything better than you dying whimpering on your side. And when I leave here, I'll make sure your name is buried in some unnamed dirt."

I didn't beg him, didn't feel the need. I was eager to feel the dark. Instead, I whispered to him, "Do it, if you've got the nerve."

I stared down the lead eye, but Granger shook his head. "Too easy. You think after all them years riding and reaping, you'd get a bullet simple as any other man? Don't deserve it. That ain't justice."

He waved his arm and I saw Marland haul Amaya from the crowd. She fought against him, expected that of her. She drew blood when she cracked her head against his nose, expected that too. In the end, without her weapons, the Shrike didn't have her thorns.

They put her on her knees before me, close enough that I was sure she could smell the blood. Granger put his blade back to my throat, looking over his shoulder at his partner. "Don't pull the trigger, Marland. Unless this piece of belly to the ground shit decides he cares more about his pride than his child."

He leaned forward, his cheeks quivering as he spoke. "Beg . . . beg to live, beg me not to kill her, beg as I did!"

I saw his tears. Wouldn't take long before grief and guilt felt like a memory for him, and I knew his pain. Only now it didn't feed the thing that had kept me sated, it just felt empty, pointless . . .

Granger pressed his knife to me, just enough to nick the skin. "Beg . . . you beg and she lives. That's more than you gave Jackson, more than you left me . . . fucking BEG!"

I stared up at him and felt empty, clutched the feeling tight, and waited to die.

Jake was shouting. I looked at him. Thomas Grail was holding a blade under his throat, a clean mirror of me. I wondered if he had words of comfort, or maybe he hoped I had some last shred of working that I could produce.

"You bastard." Jake's words should have bled me, but I nodded at him. He knew me better than these. Knew I wouldn't plead, or beg, not even for my child.

Then the world slowed to a crawl, Granger and the rest going still as statues in a garden. I felt a chill enter my bones, driving the cutting pain to the back of my mind until it wasn't but a dead soreness. I looked up and saw deepest black, like a piece of night's firmament had been ripped away and held in something too pale and weak to contain it.

Lorelei knelt next to me, the shroud of her mourning veil flapping as a dry wind blew through the windows, showing me the outline of her unearthly face. Her voice drifted from beneath it like a sigh. "I won't let it end like this for you."

She traced my eye with the tip of her gloved finger. It felt like cold fire stitching my tattered skin.

"We made a pact. You promised me an escape and named your price," I said.

I opened my eye and looked over to those that were going to consume the lives of my friend and my daughter. "I wasn't able to pay. I leaned on my own sand to escape that bullet you set for me."

It was a hard thing for a man to accept. I'd sacrificed, killed, and given away to damnation everything. I'd fed the Gun and let it feed me in turn until I could barely see the boy I'd started off as.

Her breath felt bitter on me as she leaned down cupping my face, so close I could feel the cool pale of her skin as she whispered in my ear. "Do not fret, Salem. My price will be paid in this world. The night comes for the day, and you will be born again in blasphemous conception."

It was cold comfort, but comfort all the same. The dead fire in my heart which had reduced my soul to ash sparked, and a small tenacious flame blazed forth again.

I felt the veil part, scarlet lips that could suck the life from a man brushing against my ear as her hands wrapped around me. "All you must do is endure death."

She pulled me close, past the veil, the cloth insulating us like the roof of a cathedral. I saw her face, her white unblemished skin, dead as a headstone or a long prairie of snow. Her lips were like blood, and her hair looked as if it had been pulled from the ether of the evening sky. But it was her eyes that pierced me, infinite and dragging me down into the vast of night, and I saw things there.

I saw dark stone obelisks etched with unfamiliar names, a long dust coated wilderness where children struggled with cracked hands, and seas of blood filled with things that swam in coagulating dances of birth and death . . .

So many Hells, and in her gaze, I was thrown through each as her lips locked around mine, and the kiss froze me. Agony cut through my veins, freezing my bones, unraveling my being, and stitching me back together into something that only resembled what I had been My soul made to fit into the fleeting meat that would rot beneath the ground.

It seemed like there was just the two of us, the only real

things that existed, just us and the faint cry of the weapon both yards and an eternity away. The kiss broke and the cool nothingness was replaced by the oppressive heat, the dark given way to the bleeding morning.

And I was strong again.

The world returned to normal, and I saw Granger fall back, stumbling over Sadie's corpse. Supposed it would be startling to see a man bleeding such as me. It rolled from my eyes, ears, some of it even bubbled out of my mouth, fresh and red. Everywhere Lorelei had touched, my life drawn up by her lips. A feast for a woman like her.

Granger recovered quickly, standing and offering his hand to Lorelei and she left me. I saw his smile return, wrinkling around the edges, his bald and liver spotted head seeming to age just by touching her.

Couldn't feel my feet anymore, the strength Lorelei had given me was just enough to do what I had to. I rose onto my knees, hearing the panic come from my enemies like sweet fixings, as I aimed.

I had six shots and I saw the way that could save me.

I turned the barrel on Amaya, and I pulled the trigger. Her eyes became round and dark, wondering why her father had killed her.

The twisted grasp of sorrow wrapped around my heart. Heard Jake screaming, hollering curses at the world, at Granger and Grail, at me . . .

I wanted to crow my pain, but I let the emptiness in me feast, and I looked into Granger Hyde's damned face. Then I killed Luis and Nahum, both quick and clean shots to the heart, both looking confused at their deaths come calling early.

Then I turned the barrel on Jake. Fate had seen to it this would happen.

I saw his hand jump, not giving a damn about the blade at his throat, finally gone cold at the thought of me.

But he had to clear his holster, and my weapon was already aimed. The Gun sang death for my old friend. I emptied the chambers, three shots, and Jake's insides ran as he clenched his teeth. He tried to aim, tried to fight, and I saw Lorelei inhale as he slumped forward, my brother's piece skittering across the floor as his soul untethered from this place.

Lorelei kneeled, wrapping her hand around Jake's fallen weapon. It wouldn't bind to her, wasn't nothing resembling a soul nestling inside her flesh, but that wasn't the purpose. She'd set my ending and meant to see it through.

I threw down the Gun and looked at Granger's bewildered face. "Take what you won. I'll be seeing you."

Then Lorelei pulled the trigger.

CHAPTER TWENTY-NINE

RISE UP DEAD MAN.
In the dark, I clawed through gnashing teeth and wailing despair, feeling the desperate hands rake across me. I savored life again, swirling shapes and figures of darkness dancing before virgin eyes that had never seen light. I tumbled to the ground, feeling the old and rotted wood, the taste of salt on my lips and tongue.

Naked, I shivered and heard the voice above me.

"God in heaven . . . "

I recognized it like a fleeting memory. It seemed so long since I'd heard something that didn't weave its patterns of pain.

Words . . . speech . . . I knew these things. I touched my neck, feeling smooth skin.

"Salem . . . Salem, get up."

I knew my name. And when it was spoken, the living world came stampeding back. The light solidified; a lantern was held against the blackness.

Two faces hovered over me, a man and a woman, and I knew them both.

"Jake . . . " My voice croaked, unsure. I had the impression I hadn't used it to do anything but scream for a long time.

"Yeah, it's me you bastard."

I looked up at him from the floor, trying to recall when we'd last parted. We'd been hunting a man who'd summoned the oldest wound, had wanted my Gun, had wanted to live free from fear.

"Had a dream, Jake. Dreamed we lost, dreamed we killed, but there was no coffin this time, there was just hell . . . "

I gathered my bearings and knew that my dream of death hadn't been some nightmare after all.

"Thought you'd do what he did, that old Indian you carted when we met. Thought the grave couldn't hold you down . . . "

He practically spat the words, shaking his head as he looked down at me, and I saw tears there. "You killed her, Amaya. Killed Sadie, killed my partners, and then you fucking killed me."

I remembered it, through the fog of dirt that clouded my memories. I also remembered her face that had tormented me across perdition's winds, the despair marking my soul deeper than the brand that had burned me.

Tears came trailing from Jake, slow drops reminding me of a funeral march, and the boy grown into a killer gritted his teeth to keep the sobs buried. "I would've killed all of them. Your daughter could have lived, I would have made that oath on the Gun. You and I both know you don't make that promise 'less you aim to keep it."

Outside in the dark, I could see flickering light from the lanterns that had been hung on the street, figures chasing others between the buildings, none of them casting an eye towards the church.

I climbed to my knees, breathing deep and spitting out the salt in my mouth, feeling damp confusion give way to the cold, the anger fueled by the black void I'd passed through. And I knew this church, I'd been witness to the wicked things done to appease gluttonous appetites, and I knew what could be done if a man knew the rites. I turned away from him and beheld the woman lying on the altar, her belly empty like a cavern, salt falling into the hollow where hands had dug.

My mother, twice over.

"But you didn't give up that pride, didn't belly up. You were dead no matter what, you and I both know it. But Amaya, she could have lived. I could have gotten her out. You didn't have to kill us."

I looked at the eyes of my mother, still squinted in pain from when the curse had finally taken her, and asked calmly, "What could you have done with that knife to your throat, Jake?"

I could feel him behind me. "I soldiered just fine before you came and put that spur against my neck. I've killed more since then, ain't a stranger to such things."

After all my time digging knives into the spirits of men, I shouldn't have been surprised when those same blades were stuck back into me.

"But it looks like they broke you, you were afraid, lacked the faith we couldn't end them for you. And because of it, Granger and Thomas, our Guns, and the rest are dead," Jake finished.

I wasn't going to deny it. I felt alone in my thoughts, I realized the depths of Lorelei's treachery towards Granger and his notions. When he'd summoned her up, she'd set my death, and I'd played my part on the strings of fate. He hadn't realized the escape she'd set for me, and the power to overcome the Gun stolen from me.

Killing me, he'd claimed my pistol; no need from that point to enact the blasphemous ritual, no need to spill Lorelei's blood. There could only be one man who killed the Mourning Lady, her beloved murderer, and I aimed to see to it that her affection wasn't misplaced.

"Not broken, Jake. My bones burn with fever." I stood, the coat that Jake had clothed me in falling away, and I stared down into the womb I'd been summoned from, still stained with the blood of the sacrifice offered.

I asked the question that raked over me. "Who'd you kill, Jake? How many women did you cut open until you found a boy?"

He was quiet for a moment. "Didn't have to murder anybody, Salem. She brought her, your last victim."

I closed my eyes. The female face that had been looming over me when I'd come back to this world was now familiar, and the pain burned hotter.

I looked into Olivia Verganza's lifeless eyes, and at the gashing hole in her belly. I felt the rage against Granger Hyde and knew the violent pleasures I'd rain on him, from bullet and boot.

Lorelei stood over her, the obsidian blade clutched in her hands, blood already drying on her gloves.

Jake went to stand next to her, taking Lorelei's hand from Olivia's corpse. "There . . . there was pain, in hell after you killed me, in the heat and the darkness. They promised to release me, wore Earnest Craft's face, but I told them that you had something, some bullet, some magic, you wouldn't leave me there . . . "

His fingers held the Mourning Lady's flesh tight, but I saw them tense, then begin to tremble as the memories came. "You didn't come, but Lorelei did, and she told me how to do it, how to release myself from the hooks wound under my muscle and flesh. And I told her to go to hell. That I'd sinned enough for twenty men since picking up that damned Gun. That you'd find a way to slip the noose she'd set for you."

He reached out and pulled Olivia's hair back from her face, looking into her dead gaze. "But I was the way. Amaya told me about your trip into the dark after you killed Gwendoline. I remember those trips, your communion with some evil spirit or other. Guess this time you set me up to be that escape."

He wrenched open his shirt and I saw the three wounds I'd put there, but there was a fourth, the shot that had returned him to life. And fired from the pistol in Lorelei's holster.

I thought of her words, her offer, and could already feel the weight bearing down on me, the timepiece ticking down to the moment she came to drag me back through the blasphemous womb behind me; she was eager for our eternity of killing.

I hadn't wanted Amaya to die but made my bargain knowing the cost, and I could bear it. Dead friend, dead kin, it was all the same in the end. Those who revealed here would not live to see the light again. It seemed right, I'd begun their stories, supposed it was time I finished writing them.

Jake glanced at the pistol in her hand, the seed of his un-life. "Expect you're going to kill all of them with that pretty piece. I'm going to help you. Going to get revenge for Amaya, for Sadie, for Luis, and Nahum. And after, I never want to see your face again."

I looked back at him, didn't feel the hurt of his words. Jake would play his part that Lorelei had set for him tonight, and then he would walk the path I'd prepared for him all those years ago when he'd taken up the Gun. But I wanted one last confession from him.

"If you're so keen on severing our ties, Jake, hating me because of your death, then why'd you undertake this working? The darkest magic?"

Jake looked down, a hard flash of loathing for himself coming strong. "Those bullets that have looked for me for near six years wouldn't have to look long to find me now. Don't know any killer of men baptized in heathen things better than you . . . "

He looked up at me, mouth set firm. "Didn't need some gun hand. I needed the Black Magpie."

Lorelei released Jake's hand, letting him sink into one of the old pews as she joined me, both of us regarding him as he tried to feel anything other than the blasphemous life beating in him.

Lorelei watched him longer than the rest. "He reminds me of Virgil. After you severed your brotherhood, he sat alone letting his weapon whisper to him. Couldn't overcome his guilt at what he made you into."

She pulled my head to her, and I stared into the canyon of her gaze under the veil, threatening to swallow the whole damn world.

She handed me her pistol, and it whispered sweetly to me.

I looked at the pale gun in my hand, ivory grip carved with the visages of weeping men and women. Engraved filings that looked like farming scythes stretched over the white metal in silver paths. And it was loaded with new bullets crafted by her. I knew this because she whispered it to me, words in my head, her words. I tightened my grip and felt hands unclad from their gloves wrap around my soul, and she whispered a bullet's lullaby.

"Now, oh killer mine, I have delivered them into your hands, but Granger still has me in his. Send me to wait for them, just as I'll wait for you."

She handed me the obsidian blade and I pulled her close. She didn't fight, just let the cherry red wine from her veins pour out into the dirt. I saw the moment that her essence left the shell of flesh, that slight slump of the shoulders. I sent her off to her home in midnight oblivion, then I went to Jake, and together we went out into the night, ready to shed blood.

CHAPTER THIRTY

IT **WASNT A** natural dark that blanketed Trail's End; a white halo of light sparked and danced around the black circle staring down on the world. An eclipse. Powerful craft could be worked at a time like this. The veil split, the tombs emptied, and every soul and devil that walked discarded my first flesh and clothed myself in the sacrifice of life that never was.

I heard laughter coming from the saloon.

A few of Granger's boys wandered the streets, deep in their cups, naked as me, clad only in the fucking red masks they thought made them something terrible, something feared.

Jake and I let the shadows of the unnatural night in day clothe us, watching, and waiting. Three emerged from a nearby house, all of them roostered, holding onto each other for fear of falling, singing some bawdy saloon tune, off key from the distant piano. My only interest in them was the clothes they hadn't seen fit to discard like their comrades.

The one furthest from me stopped, his hand drifting down, hollering, "FUCK ALL! Got to take a piss!"

His two friends cried after him to hurry, that the women they'd robbed from all over the territory wouldn't keep with every pecker in the town having their turn, and I watched him stagger towards the darkness.

I crept from the shadows, letting the wet drip of his relief disguise my steps. He sighed and looked up transfixed at the sky's white halo. Wondered what he was thinking when I wrapped my arms around his neck and twisted.

I felt his flesh stretch, the drunken squeal of surprise, and the satisfying snap as his bones gave up the fight.

I removed his clothes quickly, his brown coat, the black tie he wore, shirt as red as fancy wine. I'd just retrieved his pants when his friends began calling asking, what kind of piss took this long.

Called on one of my other skills, recalling this man's voice as I'd heard it, mimicking it as best I could. "Might have to go on without me, boys. Think me and the jakes are going to have to get better acquainted."

Listened to their laughter, their promise to save a woman who'd fit his peter true, and their drunken flight towards the hotel. Satisfied, I took in the face of the man I'd killed. I didn't know him from Adam, supposed I had killed a loved one sometime past. I took his gun, bullets, and the knife he had strapped to his hip. With the latter, I cut into the flesh of his back, coating my hand in the still-warm life.

My new flesh was unmarred beneath my eye, free of blemishes or marks.

I drew the symbol in the dead man's blood. Then I went looking for those I'd come here with.

I found my daughter on the edge of town, facing the west, towards the dry lake and the barren waste it watched over. They'd stripped her of her adornments, her six shooters gone, her dignity trampled and left like refuse. They'd impaled her on a pole, letting her corpse slide naked until it couldn't move further.

Felt the fury in me as we brought her down off of the pole, looking at her ruined form. I fired a shot that was lost amongst the flurry of others outside in Trail's End, but I reckon a chill passed through them, a knoll to let them know that the hourglass had tipped, and their tombstone was calling.

I crouched down over Amaya, my hand closing over the new wound that didn't bleed, and I whispered, "Your dead shall live. Together with the others, they shall rise. Awake and sing, you who dwell in dust, the earth has cast out its dead."

I spoke my litany to death, Lorelei's words light on my tongue, and when the last one left my mouth, my daughter took a deep and desperate breath.

I smiled down at the eyes that focused again, blinked again, and spilt fresh tears when they saw what had been done to her. I patted her cheek and the confusion and desperation disappeared, replaced by hate when she saw my face and I whispered to her, "Welcome back, Miss Shrike."

She drew herself to her knees, uncaring of her state, looking up at me with new tears. I saw the same fog that had clouded my mind when I'd come back from my journey.

"How . . . how did you both escape?" She spoke in a hoarse whisper.

Jake wrapped his hands around hers. I saw him hesitate; I knew my daughter's skin was cold as stone. He looked out into the black. "We died. " Saw his hands shaking "But death's been overturned, Amaya. It made a sacrifice of your mother."

He hesitated before finishing, but I heard the hate in his voice as he nodded toward me. "The child in her belly brought him back."

She gritted her teeth, glaring up at me and wondering if it was worth it to send me back, to try to kill Granger on her own. There were still two shots left, enough to suit the purpose of any that went looking for revenge. Jake saw me check the shots, but it was Amaya who spoke. "Will I be whole again? Like you?"

I shook my head. "Unborn flesh and blood were used to bring me back to true life. Not the life this shot forced on you." I stepped over them, resuming the search and calling back to them both. "Gather yourselves, bury your grief, and come with me."

We made our way through the streets, listening to distant sins, and the screams that followed. I'd warned Jake, had warned all of them. To stay here pulled it from you, your deepest depravities. I wondered how many of these that I'd wronged had been righteous in their worship every Sunday.

A glance through the window of a home that had once been a laundry revealed two men and a woman all naked and surrounding a man tied to a frame. I saw the tin star punctured through his skin, blood dribbling down his bare chest, the naked woman on her knees and licking up the running life, her face stained red. Her companions were busy taking blades to his balls.

Must've been a lawman they'd caught, come to rescue the women like some white knight. He had been welcomed with a bullet, though; this place was never short on pain.

This whole place stitched a painting of my soul, my childhood. I knew the ritual these three were enacting, remembered when my father had done it. Geld the flesh, sear the wounds, feed them the right things, and watch their mind slip into the black. They'd send him out to tend what little grew, corn and wheat, to raise the animals to be eaten, and for Trail's End's boys to murder as a rite of manhood.

It was Granger's work, setting up a new Sodom on the bones of me and mine. Almost felt flattered; the old buzzard wanted more than my name, my Gun, and my power. He'd gone further, the whole figure of it, my life and boyhood taken in blasphemy.

I left them to their work. I had my own tasks to undertake, small steps that would lead to a landslide. Call their chips soon enough.

I glanced up at the sky again as I made my way to the stables, looking at the baleful dark moon like it was an eye, her eye, watching me. Jake and Amaya hadn't followed yet, but I was not alone.

From the dark between the distant homes, I saw him come. He had followed me all this way and had waited when I'd gone under. Roux came, dogging my heels as I moved on.

The stables loomed up like silhouettes from the distant mountains. The doors yawned open, inviting me to come and see. I could smell the death that had taken place, the weapon I'd heeled myself with stoking the fires of my intent, the dead man I sought. I moved among the stalls, listening to the beasts.

The corrals were on the other side. I didn't recall them ever containing anything more than famine-starved cows not fit enough to eat, but Granger had made sure that was no longer true.

A massive bull roamed the pen. Horns that could have been the envy of the devil stretched from its head. Luis Paradis hung from them.

The Comanchero's eyes were dull, the confident smile slack, blood running from it. They'd let his corpse keep his threads; the blue fighting attire stained with its owner's insides.

The black-furred monstrosity carrying his corpse like a fine prize bore its own marks of suffering. Red gashes ran along its flanks, deep wounds that still bled, and the ragged hole that stared at me from the depths of its skull mirrored its master with his own missing eye.

In the humid blood, Roux bared his teeth at the animal, and the bull snorted, a lowing bellow echoing out of its torn lips, hooves stamping the ground.

I uttered a harsh word to the wolf, and the two of us withdrew into the shadows of the stables, waiting.

I felt the new beat of my heart. The black sun above us

wouldn't last forever, and Lorelei's love stretched only so far past the final breath.

I let that drive me when I found one of the Orphans, a woman I recognized. Her name was Edna Bullock and her husband had been the owner of the Bullock and Jones Mining Corporation. I'd killed him on his journey between San Francisco and Yuma and had left her wet in her husband's blood. I remembered her as a rich woman, a civilized woman. It was a miracle she had even survived the wilderness I'd left her in. She looked hardened now.

I took her into the dark and opened her throat, my heart racing at the spray of blood coating the wooden relics of my past, listening to the rattling scream claw its way from her open windpipe. Her eyes were confused, dismayed when she saw it was me.

I took her back to the stable, found the stacks of hay, and dipped them in her blood. Then I took it to the bull.

The corral gate opened in a long groan; the bull turned, bellowing a warning. I laid the offering down, the scrap of Edna's shirt adorned with the name I had chosen for the beast.

"Apis, Apis, Apis." I whispered the name and held still, hoping that Granger's sorceries on the beast hadn't included the binding of a name, just its growth and ferocity for killing. The bull lowered its head, Luis' body sliding down the horns, and it began to chew the hay and the scrap of cloth.

I rose, wrapping my hands around Luis, pulling slowly, and watching the man's corpse slide free, leaving the bull's horns stained with his blood. I laid him down in the dirt, turning back to the bull and patting the animal across the neck. "I promise this will be quick, Apis . . . "

It made a contented grunt as it chewed, barely acknowledging my oath to it. Just as it barely felt the blade enter its neck. I kept the pressure on it as the animal fell to its knees, its side, then fled this world with one final sighing breath.

I left a hand on the great corpse, asking for the spirits to receive it on the journey, and thanking it for the gift of flesh that would be a kiln for blacker magic, the knowledge I had gained from my last teacher, the one who'd marked me.

I'd made a vow once. Virgil and I would never ask for anything more from the Hell that had taught our hands to murder. A vow I was going to break. I could already feel the things that took their sanctuary in the dark around me laughing.

I waited for the next distant shot, then decided to bring the Comanchero back to the land of the living. I placed the bullet in his heart and let Lorelei's magic begin to do its work, as I began to do mine.

I removed the knife from the bull's neck, crouched between its legs, and began to open its belly. The blood pooled out slow, its stomach and intestines flopping on the ground, food for the ants. I could smell the feces and the coppery blood that covered me, as I hollowed out the animal.

There was a great inhale of breath behind me, but I didn't turn to acknowledge him, just kept staring at the dark hole I'd created, steeling myself for what I had to do next.

"Welcome back, Mr. Paradis," I said.

"Dios, dios, dios . . . " He whimpered it like a hand would come stretching down from the dark eye of night and scoop him right up to heaven. I glanced back at him and watched him fumble at his broken ribs, his marks of death that would not close.

"I . . . it does not heal."

I shook my head. "You aren't truly living, just bound to this world a little while longer. Here until I decide to cut the cord binding you."

He found his footing, taking hesitant footsteps, laying his hand against the bull carcass. His tanned flesh seemed paler, no blood pumped through him.

He stared out into the dark and I knew that he was trying to recall his time on the other side. He worried if, when the sleep came for him again, he'd lay in the cold earth at peace.

The weapon given to me whispered, and I knew that it was time. I whistled and heard panting breaths, paws padding across the dust toward me. Roux came close, and I allowed him time to eat. The dead bull's organs provided a fitting feast. My heart wrenched in my chest; my hands trembled . . . I did not want to do this.

"What are you doing?" Luis asked.

I wrapped my hands around Roux's head, stroking his fur. "There are two Guns out there that rival the one I'm carrying now. I could barely live against one in the past life, now both are in new hands. My new flesh ain't any stronger . . . " I tightened my grip around Roux's head. "But the fire that forged them, that can't be killed easy."

I felt my tears as the wolf began to struggle, paws pushing against me. I heard his choked whimpering, almost like words begging me not to kill him. He scratched at me, trying to bite, but I kept applying pressure, the death that I had saved him from those months ago come back for him. Roux foamed at the mouth, one last choked whine coming from him before his paws went still.

I wiped away my tears and conveyed the dead wolf into the remains of the bull, making sure that he was squared away tightly before I spoke to him one more time. "Rest for a moment, you won't be asleep long."

I turned to Luis. "Time to wake the others. There's killing to be done."

CHAPTER THIRTY-ONE

I **FOUND NAHUM** right where I thought he'd be. My kin that had founded this place had taken pleasure in making their captives suffer.

The whipping post had seen the agony of countless men and women. When I took the time to come home, I would sit on the porch of the saloon, listening to the winds and hearing the echoes of that long-lost agony. It'd been something of a town event; I'd hung a whip there from my collection. I'd taken it from a prophet obsessed with piety, and felt that he was shedding his own corruption with every new gash etched into a sinner's back. He'd thought himself a man of devotion, carving tableaux dedicated to the Good Lord in flesh.

When I'd come for him, I'd taken the brush of his painting, adorning it on the monument built for pain.

They'd clearly used it on Nahum. A lazy eye wouldn't have known that the ragged and shredded meat in front of me had been a man. They'd stripped him of his clothes and hadn't been picky in their choosing of pain.

"God in heaven . . . " Luis whispered beside me.

The lash had licked the man's face, biting deep and tearing the skin from his cheek. The same blow had taken his eye, popping the orb and sending the juice dripping down his slackened features. His back was flayed open, and I could see the curve of his ribs, his spine bared.

They hadn't cared that he was dead when they'd done this, working on his arms and legs. I felt the chill rise in me when I saw that they'd ripped open his manhood, the white testicles holding on by the nerves.

Luis moved forward, knife in hand, and I didn't stop him as he cut the man down. Nahum's slack eye didn't see Luis, and the man looked back up at me. "Fix him, bring him back, like you did for me."

"There isn't any fixing you, or him, Mr. Paradis."

I put a bullet into the soup of meat and didn't have to wait long before I heard the shuddering gasp, and the wet movement as Nahum Wallace sat up.

"Nahum . . . Nahum, my friend . . . " Luis said, crouching next to him, one hand holding his guts in, the other grasping his friend's shoulder.

The man coughed, looking up at me, with an eye emptier than the dark of a dry well. Death had broken him. But what had been buried and taken apart, could be unearthed, reloaded, and shot at the heart of this decadent imitation of my life.

I crouched next to him and looked into the one eye still staring empty. "Did you see the sin, Mr. Wallace? Was the cup poured out on you in the fire, did the punishment stop when the flog stopped scouring your skin here in this world? Or did that anointing with the cup of pain put the chains back on your soul?"

He blinked, his slack mouth moved, and words crawled from it in a tongue that no man living could have deciphered.

"They weren't bigger men, Mr. Wallace. They'd just locked away the things that made them weak. Granger Hyde doesn't care about money, doesn't care about the next poke. For near fifteen years he's thought nothing but pure hate. Thrown that away too, now he thinks he's won the prize."

I reached into one of the gashes on his chest, feeling the thick and congealed blood, lathering my fingers with it.

"The unfortunates they've gathered won't sate them.

Any righteousness they had is gone, eaten up by this place, and those they let live are going to walk and sow dead fields. I know you remember those shackles, Mr. Wallace. I know your old master dipped his toe in things unseen, that his scourge tore more than just flesh. They won't stop here . . ."

I painted his ruined chest with symbols of war I'd learned from my time with the Comanche, layering his black skin with his blood, transfiguring his soul. "Black, white, don't matter the color of flesh, they'll eat pain. It's what a man learns here, to dine on the pain of others. They could have all walked away swells; there is money I have gathered here. But instead, they fed their hate and let their hate feed them. They've left the pleasures of regular men behind."

I had ornamented him with bloody handprints, giving him success in the coming killing. Lines of lightning etched down his calves to give his worn legs speed, circles around the sockets of his eyes, the working letting him truly see. "And you've left the light of this world behind. Your lungs aren't but shreds, but you breathe because you remember what it was like. You can hear those baying hounds out there in the sand, waiting until that beating bullet in your chest ceases. Then they'll be ready to drag you back to hook, nail, and dark. But will you go alone, Mr. Wallace?"

I finished my working, a crooked arrow drawn directly on his forehead, an arrow that would embed itself into the souls of Nahum's enemies and transfer their power to him. There was meaning and power in this rite.

Nahum stirred and looked to Luis, then to me, and spoke in rasping hate that could have sent a mountain quivering. "Bring me to them, Black Magpie."

A man met his end in the jakes. He stumbled out of the back of the hotel, deep in his drink, fumbling with the belt of his pants, his pecker flapping in the wind and already pissing. He opened the door and found Nahum waiting for him. Hands adorned in symbols of war wrapped around the kid, cutting off his scream. The door closed and Luis and I listened to the gurgled sobbing as Nahum wrung the life from him.

The kid's body thumped into the dirt, a black ring forming on his neck, a bloody foam leaking from the edges of his mouth. Nahum stepped out and picked the boy up, his crushed bones sifting like sand.

We hid his body in the hollow beneath the outhouse, letting the shit swallow him naked. Then we went looking for Sadie.

They'd brought her corpse to the Trail's End mortuary. It was the furthest building from the saloon; seemed to recall that had been the intent when they'd raised it. The door to the cellar was already flung open, a flickering lantern burning inside.

I turned to say something to Jake, reminded of our first journey, and the yawning void that had seen his flesh torn, before remembering that I'd left him on the edge of town with my daughter. I was left with only Nahum and Luis, and both had their gaze firmly rooted in the yawning black before us.

"Follow me closely," I whispered. I took the steps slow remembering each one from distant days, the memory coming back easy. I reached the bottom, keeping my hand on the shooting iron I'd taken.

Lorelei whispered through her gun, reminding me of what I had lost, that a bullet could find me now. I felt a twinge of fear race through my nerves and wondered if my draw was still as fast as when I had first picked up the Gun.

I passed through the cobwebs, touching the wooden beams, and feeling the floorboards of the home overhead. I could hear squeaking springs ahead and knew what was happening, even before we came into the lantern light.

A woman lay under Charles Marland, steam from his

sweat coming from him as he exerted himself on her corpse. I raised a hand to keep Nahum from walking forward and ending the man's life.

Women were piled in the corners, the choice dead. Reckoned this man had gone to wherever they were keeping those they'd kidnapped and dragged them back. They were caked in dust, flies dancing on unseeing eyes, and in torn-open wombs. They'd been sorted, those waiting to receive a poke, and those that had already spent their time on the bed.

Marland spilled his seed, croaking like a fat toad. His tongue lolled out of his mouth like he was trying to catch the swarming flies buzzing around his head.

"Oh . . . oh, you're a regular calico," Marland wheezed with his eyes shut, finger wiggling in the gashed and torn belly, soaking himself on old blood and his own emission. A contented sigh escaped from the misshapen lump beneath his hair.

That was a weakness of his traveler, once he filled himself on pleasures, all manner of foresight fell away. He figured it a safe bet that I rested in hell, my soul gnawed and gone eternally.

Nahum and Luis both bristled, aching to kill this man, boiling for more blood, but he would last until I found Sadie Faro's corpse. The cellar stank with death, and I strained my eyes against the blackness and took in each face, the hollow cavern of their empty heads, some of them leaking Marland's fluids. But I found one still clothed and huddled in the dark, wreathed in blood-stained white hair.

Marland stood, his pecker wobbling as he rolled the naked corpse from the bed, letting it topple into a pile of others that had suffered his attentions. He breathed hard as he laid against the soiled mattress, basking in the silence that only sex could create.

He stiffened when he heard the click of the chamber being pulled, his eyes jumping open like they'd just seen bare flesh eager to please. "No, no, no . . . you're dead! You

. . . you can't . . . " "Hello, Mr. Marland. See your tastes haven't changed," I said and pressed the barrel of the pistol I'd stolen to his head.

"You've come back, Magpie?" He cocked his head, listening. I heard the speech coming from the back of him, words that sounded like the droning buzz of locusts.

Marland nodded, like a pastor hearing his god speak. "Wasn't right last time, you killing us. You and I both serve the same Hell, and your place has been assured at the left hand of sin."

He knelt on the floor, clasping his hands. "Please, I will help you. Don't send me back. Down there I'm helpless."

He licked his lips, a tremble running through him.

"It is not like other sufferings. I can't indulge my wants, can't move, I can only watch them take the flesh off suicides and murderers. That is my eternity, to watch but never indulge, but now . . . "

He bowed, black traces of hair tumbling wild and letting me catch a glimpse of the face pressing from the back of his skull like a misshapen boil. Its distorted teeth jutted out like grave markers as it jabbered in a tongue that man had never been made to hear.

"Now, we're both free from death, thanks to her."

I disabused him of the notion. "You're not free from it, Mr. Marland. You're enslaved to it."

Saw his confidence fade, the certainty that he and his passenger would live fading away as I leaned in. "Allow me to emancipate you from it."

He whimpered, clutching at the fouled mattress, bravado dissolving into pleas. I shook my head, feeling the rage simmer in my bones, and I looked at Luis, "Use your sword."

Unspoken things are understood between wolves, just like they're understood between killers. The Comanchero knew that I wasn't asking for a quick death for Marland, but for a bloody dance. Luis nodded and unsheathed his saber, twirling it and stepping to take my place as I gestured for Nahum to help me attend to Sadie.

"Please, sir. Please . . . " Marland whispered it, defeated.

Luis chuckled darkly. "Your squealing offends my ears." He flicked his sword and opened a gash along the side of Marland's belly. The man tried to roll away, pained squalls coming one after the other from both mouths occupying his head.

He looked like a pig being sliced open. Marland crawled, howling at every new wound. Luis drove the wretched thing that would soon cease to live, carving new pain when the man slowed to nurse his injuries, the blood painting designs of suffering across the cellar floor.

They came close, Marland dragging himself forward, leaving a trail like a battered slug. He paused when he reached me, earning himself a slice from the saber across his forehead. He bowed, prostrating himself like he'd been called to task before the devil. More mercy would have been granted had he found himself in that fire.

"For the love of God, Covington! Please!" He raised his head, and I watched the blood run down like tears across his sweaty and reddened cheeks.

I met his eyes and pointed to one of the dead women he'd propped against the beams and banisters, preparing for his touch. "Mercy isn't mine to give, Mr. Marland. Beg them, maybe they'll stand for you."

Luis stabbed deep into the meat of the man's ass, causing him to crawl on, dragging his leg like a limp dog, all while Nahum and I laid Sadie in repose.

I didn't whisper my words or ruminate on her being. time was short and death was long. I fired the shot into her belly and sat next to her.

Luis was mutilating the man's other cheek when Sadie returned. She sat up coughing, her windpipe whistling with each retch. She shouldn't have been able to speak, but such things didn't matter to the working in the bullet; the flesh was nothing when compared to spirit.

"Where am I?" Her voice wasn't low anymore, coming

out in a trilling whistle. Her hands drifted to her neck, feeling her death wound.

I spoke. "Still in Trail's End. Brought you back."

Her eyes stared at Nahum, looking at the open wounds that should have seen him resting in a maggot bed, before resting on me and I saw the rage kindle in her.

I caught her hand where the brace was hidden, easing it back down, and staring into the pale grey of her eyes, the sheen of life lost from them. "Spared you a worse fate; look to Mr. Paradis and Mr. Wallace if you don't believe. You were a down payment for this . . . "

I produced the pale revolver, the inlays gleaming from the power pumping life into her bones.

I finished. "So that when the name was erased from my headstone, the earth would stir and spit out killers ready to attend me and honor her." Stood and offered my hand. "You claim you punish wicked men, Ms. Faro. Look around and realize you're standing on Hell's foundation."

Her eyes settled on each dead woman, dead eyes staring straight through her and calling for justice beyond the veil. A solitary tear raced away from her.

It was Nahum who answered. "He was in Hell with the rest of us, Sadie. Saw him down there burning . . . " He pointed at the sobbing wretch, huddled in his own blood, still inching away into the dark. Luis stood over him, Marland's demon falling victim to the thirsty blade. "It was that one, his hands have sinned."

Sadie stood, hesitating, trying to remember what it was to move. But I heard the spring snap, and the blade took its place back under her wrist.

Luis bowed his head to her as she passed. "Welcome back, senorita."

She nodded to him, squatted next to Marland, and rolled him to face her. "You . . . you came back, lovely lady. To help me? To love me?"

He howled the scream of the damned when she shoved the blade through his cherries. I watched them both pop, thick blood running as she split his pecker from tip to tail. There's an art in killing a man slowly, but Sadie Faro didn't care about his punishment, the cost of the working placed on her. The empty grave called like an empty stomach, demanded to be filled.

She sank the blade until "Mumbling" Charles Marland's whimpers ceased, and when she stood, she rose hungry for more, the bullet Lorelei had put in him clutched tight in her hand.

"Where are they, Salem?" Sadie asked.

CHAPTER THIRTY-TWO

AMAYA AND JAKE had killed two Orphans who'd passed close to the edge of town. Jake holstered his stolen pistol, and offered his hand to Nahum and Luis, staring at the wounds that would never heal while they walked in this world.

Jake broke his gaze and found mine waiting. I was standing on a nearby porch, meeting each gaze and seeing the hopeless hate in those that were dead. Playing at life was a pain all its own. "Death flees from you now. No blade, no bullet, no working is going to change that."

I looked up at the eclipse, the sun still sleeping behind the dark. I stepped down and headed for the stables, didn't cast a look, and didn't spare pity for those I'd brought back. They would follow; the murder promised was the only thing that could break through the haze of pain.

There were more waiting for their second birth.

We returned to the stables and the corral where the slaughtered bull nursed the dead wolf. The darkness had hidden us, not that we'd had need. There weren't many left, these men and women Granger had charmed. Reckoned those that were left drank and fucked in every dark corner of town.

I traced designs into the wet dirt around the bull, secret names, invocations, entreating for the powers that walked the next world to hear me. And when I was done, I went and found a lantern, letting its flame bite an oil licked rag, my makeshift torch blazing to life.

Jake worked his hands, the needle and thread he'd brought from the church sewing Luis' and Sadie's wounds closed. There was nothing to be done for Nahum; he'd bear his ravaged body until the bullet in him was taken away.

I stepped up to the bull, staring into the torn belly where I'd placed Roux, and I stuck the torch inside. The hollow lit like perdition itself opened. I smelled the searing meat and the burning hair from the wolf inside.

I pressed my hand against the bloody symbol on the ground. "Rise. Eat the flesh from sons and the bones of daughters."

I'd sent Roux to the devil, but now he'd sent him back.

The hellhound growled at me. I had never performed this working. It was black magic that most of my teachers had shied away from.

Roux bared his fangs, sparks coming with every breath. I half worried he would latch onto my hand and drag me back into the flame inside the carcass.

I tried to suppress the sigh of relief that came from me when my hand remained my own, the fur running through my fingers feeling as hot as rocks left to bake under the sun. Then I drew the pale gun in my other hand.

It felt right.

We went to the empty street, staring at the dark windows of the empty livery, the laundry, the sheriff's office, and its cells. Only the hotel and the saloon burned with light in the unnatural dark.

Nahum marched straight through the dust; single eye fixed on the hotel. Luis danced his saber through the air. Sadie walked across the porch of the old general store, her pistol making sure that the old and dust-ridden places remained empty. Amaya and Jake walked close, and Roux padded ahead, each print in the dust charring the sand into glass.

I pointed to the hotel. Nahum turned towards it without saying a word and Luis trailed in his wake, knowing the task that had been set for them. Sadie stepped into the street, coming to me and hoarsely whispering. "If there's a rifle in that hotel, don't worry about the ones that run."

I nodded, watching her neck contort around the stitches. I turned to the saloon, watching the shadows reveling inside, then looked to Jake and Amaya, nodding to the alley. "You'll know the time."

Jake kept his gaze fixed on the doors, watching the people move inside. "You don't have the Gun anymore, Salem. They'll be shooting as soon as you walk in."

I raised the pale gun. "A cousin to ours. Death won't find me." A lie, but one that he would believe, and I fed myself the belief that fate would stay any hand itching to pull a trigger.

There was no hate, sand, or sorcery strong enough to keep them from their deaths. I would not be denied what had come due.

Turned my eyes on my flesh and blood. "I'm sorry about your mother."

She raised a hand and pressed it to my cheek. I saw my features in her face. "She was right about you, Father. The nightmares of you were true."

Didn't answer her. That was the way with the truth, didn't need answering.

She pulled away and they went into the dark. I watched until it swallowed them both, leaving me alone with my grit, and the reminder of Hell nipping at my heels.

My spurs clicked against the dirt, mixing with the laughter ahead of me, the muffled gunshot from the hotel behind me, and the creak as my feet met the steps. Then I was there, pushing through the swinging doors. Meeting my killers eye to eye again.

A piano had been playing, but its tune ceased as soon as I walked in. The drinks poured behind the bar were left full, and the desecration of my body left undone.

They'd propped my corpse up like a choice game, and they'd taken their turns wringing their satisfaction from my dead flesh. A dozen wounds perforated my corpse, my head wearing the wound that killed me like a crown. Three knives were stuck tight inside my guts.

Granger Hyde stared, his hand holding his whiskey tight, and the Gun holstered far away. Looked for Grail among the faces but the younger man wasn't there. I thought I knew where he was, though: sitting in the dark somewhere, worshiping the weapon he'd bargained for, had killed for. I knew the taste of the meal it offered all too well.

And I was eager to savor it again.

The silence that reigned was broken by Roux's growls as he stepped up beside me.

"She . . . she's death, she's your death, there isn't any escaping her. YOU CAN'T BE BREATHING!" Granger screamed the words, hand shaking, his nerve failing him. He couldn't be killed by a gun, but that was small comfort when death itself seemed to have been overturned.

I pointed Lorelei's gun at the old buzzard. "Grave couldn't hold me, Granger. The black pit was my cradle long before I picked up what you've stolen from me. And my hours spent in the flame were spent preparing a place for you."

Granger flinched, dropping his whiskey. It was a hard thing for a man to realize, that bullets couldn't touch him. I remembered the first shots that had missed me. That slow certainty granted a man freedom from death and consequence.

But now a slow smile spread over his face and his hand dropped to the Gun at his side. "Can't be killed by a gun now, Covington. But I reckon you can."

He drew slowly, cherishing the moment. It wasn't often

a man got to kill the object of his hate twice. But that was the trick of hating something; it could blind you to everything.

I whistled once and Roux leaped from the shadows of the door. I dove to the side, avoiding the shot that could have killed me. I watched Granger scream as he was brought down, his skin charring where Roux's paws dug in.

The spell of fear that had kept the Orphans frozen broke, and most made for real play. The wood splintered as their bullets chewed the old floor.

I kicked over a table, ducking behind it and firing twice with my plain revolver at a brave woman running forward with a double barrel. I caught her twice in the stomach before she fell. She was brave, but the same couldn't be said for those making for the back. A woman in her skirts was ushered forward by a man cradling his lever action like it could save him. Amaya was waiting for them both.

Four shots rang out as Amaya fired. The woman screamed as she lost her outstretched fingers, the second shot taking her straight through the head. The man crumpled in on himself, the bullets taking him in the gut; he clutched at the bar and dropped the lever action to the floor.

Jake was waiting, stepping across the dying man and taking his rifle, beginning the quick dance of hands that lead to men dying.

Three ran for the saloon doors. Two of them found Luis's saber waiting for them, their throats opened and spilling their intestines.

The third found Nahum. He wrapped his hands around the man's skull, slinging him like a bear threw its kill. The man hit the nearest wall, the wood splintering as his back broke. The corpse fell in a plume of dust.

They killed the rest, and I left my shelter, my want shining to one thing. Granger struggled desperately against the wolf. I called Roux off, stepping over the man. The stub of his arm that I had taken from him all those years ago couldn't raise him from the floor as he tried to aim. The lead eye almost seemed desperate despite its long-ago death, and his living one looked afraid as my shadow fell over him and I reached for what was mine.

I curled my hands around his fingers, listening to his pleas. "No, no, no . . . " They weren't the screaming appeals of a man who'd lost, just a man denying that his last hour had come. I pried his fingers away from the metal, and for a second, I could hear it whispering to us both.

Through me, there is power, Grrraannnggerr.

Your gift, your burden, your heritage. BURY YOUR SOUL, SALEM!

And I heard her words, urging me on as I broke the old man's fingers. I felt the bones under my grip as I twisted, his fresh screams a choir song, and the Gun tumbled to the saloon floor.

He looked up at me, head rolling like a stone dislodged. "You should see how you look behind your flesh."

I didn't have to discern what he saw; I knew what I looked like to those who could see the truth. Knew what my daughter looked like . . . Sadie, Nahum, and Luis as well. Only Jake still had something resembling a good spirit, and that was hanging on thinner than a trickle through a dry creek.

"It will not be so simple, Granger. Hell is an escape, and I won't let you have that. I have one shot left in Lorelei's pistol, who do you think it's meant for?"

There were no words left for him. He stared blankly, his mind trying to rationalize, some secret that he had learned that could have him escape. That's why I would take his tongue from him.

Then I plunged the knife that I had brought into his chest, burying it in his heart, watching the blood pool up. Simple thing really, to untether a man from a weapon that he didn't deserve.

Amaya drifted over to me, discarding her empty guns, and spat into the dead man's eye.

"COVINGTON!"

My daughter jumped at the sudden sound and instinctively grabbed the nearest weapon. A white-hot fury washed over me when I saw the Gun now held in her hand.

"COVINGTON!" My name echoed from the night as Grail emerged from whatever hole he'd been hiding in. Eager to try killing me just as I had his father. And holding the Gun made as a brother to the one clasped in my daughter's hand.

I felt tired as I stood and looked at Jake and Amaya. "Go out the back, get behind him. Kill him if you get the chance . . . "

They didn't pause, vanishing into the saloon interior. "Mr. Paradis, Mr. Wallace? Keep a watch on Mr. Hyde, and don't let him speak."

The men nodded, moving without speaking.

"COVINGTON! COME AND FACE ME!"

Grail ceased his shouting and I turned to Roux. "Come on."

We went to the saloon doors. I was sure that Grail would speak his peace, rather than just killing me straight off.

We stepped out into the dark, I saw the onrushing light of sunlight in the distance, the eclipse coming to an end.

Grail was standing in the middle of the square, directly in front of the fountain that had gone dry.

He raised his Gun and aimed at me, I stared him down. He licked his lips as he spoke. "You were quiet when you killed my Pa. I'd prefer you blubbered, but I'll settle for just killing you. Got this Gun, but I reckon your soul is worth ten times what I owe."

I didn't answer him, and it only seemed to stoke his hate. "Have to know, Covington, how did you do it? How did you slip out of death's noose? How are you living?"

I didn't answer him.

Grail walked forward, pressing my brother's Gun to my head. I could see the tears prickling out of his eyes as he shouted. "TELL ME! TELL ME HOW YOU KEEP LIVING YOU SON OF A BITCH."

"Why don't you let fly? Or are you afraid I've got the edge on you?" I said.

Grail's nerves failed him. His finger twitched on the trigger. Afraid that the Gun he was holding wasn't enough to keep me dead. "You brought yourself to this. I gave you the chance to go and live your life six years ago, but you came and tasted deathless life. But that weapon you picked up burned her bullet from your chest; when I plant you this time . . . there ain't no coming back."

There was a shot, and the ground exploded beside him. It was Sadie, taking her chance against a man who couldn't be killed by a gun. But it was nothing more than a distraction, an opening for me to bring Thomas the ending he'd been seeking.

I dodged to the side, jumping into the dry fountain, Grail fired and the stone shattered. I holstered Lorelei's gun and drew the knife I'd taken, waiting for the right moment.

I peeked over the side of the fountain, watching Grail turn and shout at the hotel, the saloon, everywhere. "SHOOT ALL YOU WANT, I CAN'T BE KILLED, I CAN'T—"

I leapt over the fountain and ran, feeling the dirt under me. Grail stumbled back, firing once, twice . . .

I felt both shots draw blood from me. Right shoulder and left arm, but both passed through.

Then I was on him, pressing the blade deep into his forearm, watching the Gun tumble from his weak grip and into Jake's waiting hand. I wrenched the knife out and he stumbled back towards the saloon. I whistled once.

Roux emerged from the dark beneath the porch, snarling as he streaked towards Grail, deprived of the Gun and bleeding from his arm. He screamed once as the hell wolf took him to the ground, molten iron teeth sinking into his leg.

There was only one place left for Grail, and that was the inside of the bull, still flickering with fire. Roux had the desire to go back home with a new bit of meat for the devil.

Amaya came from the dark, and along with Jake, we followed as Roux dragged the man towards the stables. Grail dug with his hands at the dirt, clawing and leaving fingernails and fresh blood, looking up at Jake and screaming for help, trying to appeal to his honor. When he managed to catch the edge of the stable door, Jake walked forward and kicked the younger man's fingers until they broke.

Grail twisted around, kicking at Roux, but wrapped in Hell's flame, the wolf didn't flinch as he dragged the man through the stable and out into the corral.

We could see the fire. The smoke billowed from the eye sockets of the dead bull, and I saw its belly open, black hands widening the gap. Grail's uninjured grip caught the rusted iron of the pen, and he looked up to find Amaya standing over him.

She didn't hesitate as she pulled the Gun and fired into his arm, decorating the ground with bone and offal. Grail screamed, losing his grip, then he was before the burning interior of the bull. He might've breathed easier when the wolf paused, head turning to look back at me.

I said my farewell. "Go on . . . sure I'll be joining you before long."

The teeth sank again into Grail's leg and dragged the kid inside. His screams reached a high-pitched keening as the fire licked at his feet, racing up his legs. I could smell the meat curl from his bones, and before he vanished into the red interior, I saw his skin begin to run like candle wax, eyes popping with new screams.

Those wails kept echoing even as the fire inside the bull died and left nothing but rotting flesh, waiting for the flies.

CHAPTER THIRTY-THREE

THE DAY HAD come for Granger Hyde. The eclipse had left, just leaving the fire of the day, a sun that seemed to burn hotter than any that had come before it.

According to the good book, Christ had hauled his own tree to the place of death. Reckoned that I could milk more agony from Granger, even if he was currently enjoying the cup of pain poured for him in Hell.

There was a hill outside of town. A little nest of boulders that looked over the halo of graves that stretched across the sands of Trail's End. It was a place to look and listen to the wind whisper of the graves being dug below.

We'd taken the large cross down from the church and prepared the wood to receive its new flesh. But I didn't savor my revenge. I had a choice; one I wasn't looking forward to making. One I hoped I had the stone to make.

Sadie sat on a rock, her rifle slung over her shoulder, waiting patiently. Her grave eyes met mine. She knew what was to come, what I had promised. She'd meet it fearless, that was the trick of Lorelei's working. All she could feel was the hate left for the man we would consign to the grave. No desires left for her but mine.

Jake and Amaya stood on either side of the cross. In Jake's hand was the Gun, brother to the one held by my daughter, bound to his soul once again. Both of them were restored to true life. As soon as they'd taken the weapons up, Lorelei's bullets had come running out in a glowing orange river of iron. It had scaled them both, the flesh closing when the last drip had fallen.

Granger's corpse was brought by Nahum and Luis. They had taken his fake leg, leaving him with nothing but the stump I'd given him. I fired the last bullet in Lorelei's gun, right into the hollow of his heart.

The working permeated him, and he came back coughing trying to say something as he threw his head from side to side, the stub of his missing hand and leg flailing, trying to find some purchase to haul himself up to breathe. The fight went out of him and he lay, broken, alone, and glaring up at me.

"Figured you would have been scrambling to get back to that."

He nodded his head at the Gun in Amaya's grip, eagerly waiting for its bearer to spill blood, then he chuckled darkly.

Jake stared back cold, looking down at the old man and shaking his head, "Never understood us, Hyde. Had your tail before the shooting even started. Salem had planned the manner of it, our resurrection."

Granger chuckled again, shaking his head. "It's you who doesn't understand, Howe. Past friendship, kin, blood, and black magic, he only cares for one thing . . . and she's holding it."

I clutched the black obsidian knife I'd used to sacrifice Lorelei's life the first time she'd been summoned to this world, the one Virgil and I had killed one hundred pregnant women with on those long-gone days. It had nearly tasted the same in Granger's hands.

Felt its heft and went to Granger, crouching down. "Believe it time your tongue stopped spitting poison."

He screamed as I stabbed the blade into his cheek, sawing with the serrated stone, creating a blasphemous grin of flapping skin and old teeth.

I cut across his gums, listening to him scream, Nahum and Luis holding him steady so I could do my work. I plucked the teeth from him, letting them fall like bloody stones to the floor.

Then I took his tongue.

It came free in a bloody spewing of painful gibberish, and I tossed it away. I didn't need to hear more words, be they truth or lies, come from his lips. I wrapped my hand around the neck of his shirt, dragging him until he lay face up on the wood prepared for him.

It had been a fortunate thing, taking those limbs from him those years back, fewer nails were needed now. He blubbered something I ignored as we angled the old nail over his wrist.

I felt the pressure when I swung the mallet. I saw the spurt of blood and heard the snap of his bones. He spewed a sanguine song from his throat. The second nail went through his foot, affixing him to the old wood that would drink his tears as his wounds wept.

But he hadn't suffered enough, not yet.

Squatted next to him, looking into the marked lead of his left eye. "I thought this would kill you the first time. Does me proud to see what you became. You managed to kill me; none other can make that claim . . . "

I looked at his foot, mangled and bleeding from the nail I'd hammered through it. "Reckon you won't be walking far though."

I'd brought a spoon from the saloon, three bullets sitting easy on it. It wasn't hard to find dead wood to build a fire, and through his agony, he saw the echo of worse punishment.

The bullets bubbled and melted into a steaming grey soup. I brought it carefully to where the old buzzard lay and saw him thrash his head. He snarled through the blood as he tried to speak some curse against me.

Looked to Nahum. "Hold his head."

He wrapped his hands around Granger's skull, fingers peeling his eyelid open. I watched his pupil dance like a black oil spot.

"You've come into my hands, and today I blind you from everything but the sight of me. I'll take your eyes so that all you see is me looking back at you when the sun burns and you choke on the dust. The vultures and coyotes will lick at you, and you won't die."

I tilted the spoon and poured the molten lead into his last eye, and in his ear I whispered to him, "Then you will know, that I am the Black Magpie."

He died as I poured, the small scrap of his soul that I'd maimed flying off to meet the devil. I listened to the last hollow scream drift from his throat, and the fresh blood run from beneath the cooling metal.

I watched the flaps of his mouth flutter like a pennant in the hot breeze, lead eyes dead as the soil, then we affixed the cross in its prepared place. As soon as the wood thumped into the ground, he came back.

I let him die again, listening to his choked gurgling as he struggled for air, only for the magic that pumped life through him to bring him back.

Then I listened to his gibberish prayers and pleadings as he died again, then he returned. Then he died.

The day moved, the sun lowered, and one by one my companions drifted away. Sadie took Nahum and Luis with her down the hill. The three of them lost and hollowed out.

Jake and Amaya stayed longer, my daughter standing at the foot of the cross watching the wheel of rebirth and damnation turn. Then she too went down the hill, leaving me and Jake alone.

"You planning on killing me now?" he asked quietly.

Gooseflesh ran up my arms. Jake knew me well, knew I wouldn't leave without the pistol he carried, or Amaya's . . .

"She's my blood," I said.

He looked me square. "Don't lie to yourself, Salem. You'd kill her too if it was the only way back to one of these damned things." He pointed his Gun at me, and I stared it down. "You might even think you have some murderous purpose now, taking it back from one of us. But either way ends with me putting you in the ground."

He gave me a sad smile, shaking his head. "That's your fate. From the moment you picked it up. You love it, more than your kin, more than death herself, even knowing the ending the Gun has planned for you. And no matter how you change the players, it all ends the same."

My grip tightened around Lorelei's pistol, the pain breaking through the satisfaction of murder that had dwelt in me since I had come back to the world. The truth has a way of carving through a man, deadlier than a bullet, sharper than a knife.

A billow of dust blew west, and we stood between a dead town and the vast and hungry nothing, pitiless and uncaring of what was happening. "If you believe that, Jake, then the whole earth is before us. I'll let you choose the way. If you go left from here, I'll go right, and if you take the right trail, I will go left."

He paused, wrestling with the words, then lowered his Gun. Then he left, drifting down the hill and back to the town.

He was a speck when I looked at Granger one last time, tipping my hat to him. "Be seeing you, Granger." He blubbered some manner of a curse as I left him there to watch over the field of the dead, and I went to make the only choice I really had.

CHAPTER THIRTY-FOUR

I **WHISPERED INTO** the pale gun for Nahum and Luis to prepare horses for Jake, Amaya, and I to leave this place. The clouds were beginning to roll in over the hills. A pyre of black smoke rose high into the overcast sky.

They'd piled those we'd killed, put the flame to them, the flies taking flight as the fire swept over. A few of the bodies were gone, unseen things creeping back from their exile stealing them away to eat, or worse, Granger's hold on the shadows of this place slipping away. I thought I saw the figure of a man standing in the saloon as we passed, his eyes glaring, nothing but a ghost denied.

I went into the cellars beneath the sheriff's office. I knew what was down there and decided that they had done nothing worth starving to death in the dark. The women gathered there reminded me of newborn chicks, naked and making tiny whimpers. The cauterized stumps of their hand waved, like they were trying to fly.

I didn't know how long they had been down here, but by the state of them, I imagined it had been some time. Dirt clung to their skin and hair. From the smell, I would have wagered Granger hadn't seen the bother in cleaning them from their own feces. But from their swollen bellies, it seemed he had seen fit to come calling in a different manner.

I killed them, firing until there was nothing but the smell of gunfire and death. I took them out to a place of sacrifice, an old charred and smoking pit on the edge of the dried lake. And amongst the gore and offal of the dead, we'd brought, Jake and I dug. We didn't speak, didn't look at each other, the rope of past times frayed to hell and back.

Sadie, Luis, and Nahum kept watch over the town, making sure there wasn't some straggler waiting to ambush us.

I retrieved Olivia from the church, feeling the waxen flesh and staring at the grey rot beginning to set in. Maggots crawled along the rims of her hollow eyes and into the ragged wound that had killed her. We wouldn't bury her here; greener places that could see the light of heaven would mark her rest.

Amaya wept over her mother, Jake standing watch above her, his eyes fixed on me. My eyes were only fixed on the Gun on her hip. Nahum came, dragging a coffin from the long disused mortuary.

When her tears had dried, Jake stepped forward and placed Olivia inside the box. He affixed the lid, while Amaya retrieved the hammer and the nails, consigning her mother to the darkness. Her hands quivered when the last nail was driven in, and she turned to look at me. "I'm taking her."

Iron words, certainty there, and unafraid to act on it.

"You'll bury her?" I asked.

Amaya nodded. "She wanted to be buried in El Jardin, I promised her that."

"You made us a promise . . . " The tension cast between Amaya and I broke at the rasping sound of Sadie Faro's voice, she pointed to herself, Nahum, and Luis. "Free us from this, Salem."

Luis pointed to his sewn wounds, to Nahum's, too great to be healed. "Senorita, we are free, free from death."

Nahum's one eye could have burned through the wood as he looked at his friend. "I do not wish to live like this, a ghost in a dead shell."

Amaya stepped forward. "Sadie . . . "

She was within reaching distance of the bounty hunter,

and Sadie's hidden blade in her brace sprang, licking at my daughter's throat, barely tasting her skin. "I don't live, Amaya. Not in full. I barely feel the heat, or the breeze, I can't smell the dead. I do not fear the dark that comes."

She and my daughter stared each other down, testing their wills. And my daughter backed away from her, nodding once.

I raised the pale pistol, but Sadie held up a hand to stop me, looking at Jake.

"Piece of advice, Jake. I see what it has done to you, that Gun."

She lowered her hand with the blade, dropping her rifle and her pistols to the ground. "You're not evil, Jake Howe, but every day the mirror shows less of you . . . and more of him." She nodded toward me, but I didn't feel any joy in it. It wasn't nothing but the truth laid out for him, and I reckoned that this new pain would cut more away from him and replace it with the same sand that drove me.

It was time. I brought the pale revolver to my lips, turning the cylinder until I reached the chamber that had fired the bullet resting in her. I felt the working, and looked into Sadie's eyes. "Wish things had gone different."

Her unafraid eyes blazed mouth curling into a devil's grin that would have ripped my throat had I given her a chance. "You pay for your soul in blood, I thought you could be more, I wanted you to be more. Paid for it in the end."

I blew once over the barrel and watched the life unwind from her, from Luis and Nahum. Their faces went slack, the held off death finding purchase. And then they finally sank to the ground.

I found coffins for them, hitching them by rope to my horse. Luis had prepared it for me, a grey beast that I would ride until I reclaimed the stage I'd found.

We put Olivia's coffin on a cart, letting Amaya drive it. It bore another body on it. I urged the horse over and pointed to my own corpse, the brand still clear as day. "Take this. Split the reward for me between the two of you."

Jake drew close, his hand hugging his holster, and he gestured to the three coffins I would pull behind me. "What will happen to them?"

"I'll take them away to somewhere approaching peace, bury them there," I said.

He looked to the horizon, his weapon no doubt begging him to submit to the all-consuming rage and try his hand, but he made me a promise instead. "I was afraid of you at one time, Salem. Then imagined I had the same grit, even admired you, made myself believe the Good Lord had a purpose for even you."

He turned with eyes of stone. "Reckon I was wrong. But you're my friend, and hell if I don't understand the need for this Gun. So, when that want gets too strong in you when you finally come to try killing one of us, I'll give you that ending you're looking for."

I leaned over from the horse, smelling his scent, his certainty I wanted to kill him festering like an infection, and decided to give him one warning. Least I could do for a friend. I reached into my saddle bag. There were a few things I had collected since this trail had begun, but this had been one of the first, and there were plenty more to be found should I be needing another.

"Take this, Jake. Look at it when you feel that hate for me rising. And remember what happened to those who promised to kill me." I tossed the bloodied crimson mask to him.

I tipped my hat to Amaya, and urged my horse on, heading south, leaving Jake and her behind me. I didn't turn until I was miles distant, and Trail's End was nothing but a rotting carcass on a hostile horizon, and there was no sign of those who had rode, fought, killed, and died with me.

EPILOGUE

WICHITA MOUNTAINS, 1881

BARRIER RIDGE WAS a tiny spit of town before the dry prairie west of these mountains laid their claim. The town fathers had built along the ridge of the mountain, a roaring stream rumbling through the middle that had dried up from the coming winter. And when the well had run dry, the local gin mill was happy to drown the hardscrabble folk in whatever fire or vice they longed for.

There was a cemetery overlooking the endless scrubland that stretched far and away until all of it was swallowed by the fading sun. A good place for a final rest. I dug the graves slowly, letting myself feel the rhythm of the shovel against the dirt, and the dampness of my sweat.

I also felt the eyes of the girl watching me, had seen her peeping through the rows of crosses, a ragged dress frayed with dirt as she kept low to the ground. I called out to her. "You can come close, girl. Have my word you'll leave living."

I saw her startlement. She must've thought the low light of the fading day kept her hidden amongst the field of the dead. I continued digging as she stood tall, hurrying until she stood over me in the hole.

I worked in silence for a moment until she spoke. "Old Mr. Fowler isn't going to like you digging in his graves, mister."

I glanced up at her, arms clasped behind her back, red pigtails draping down off her. She was barely out of her girlhood, with eyes that burned with excitement staring at Lorelei's gun in my holster.

"I'll pay him for the trouble if he comes calling," I replied, digging the shovel into the pliant soil, hearing her whisper of warning in my mind from the weapon at my side. "What's your name, miss?" I asked, wiping the dirt and grime from my hands.

"Elizabeth Hughes. But I go by Liz." Her voice was low, close. I pulled the pale pistol faster than greased lightning and turned, placing the barrel between the girl's eyes, the knife in her right hand clenched tight.

"Going to kill me with that pigsticker, Miss Hughes?"

The girl giggled, dropped the knife, and stared down the pistol barrel. "Killed Davy Bogg's dog when he was sleeping. Ever heard a dog cry? Always wanted to learn what things sound like as they're dying."

I looked into her eyes, seeing what grew in her twisted soul. I imagined she'd be more someday; this little spit of a town on the edge of the mountains couldn't hold something like her.

Decided to offer her some knowledge. "Heard more than just a dog cry, Miss Hughes. Heard the dying of everything that could be killed in this land, even girls who think themselves real killers. Help me bury this woman, and I'd be happy to describe it to you."

Together, we lowered the coffins into the earth, and I told her of death. The sounds folk made as their blood poured out of them like a sweet song. The difference between the lead death of a bullet and a blade slid across soft places. And I spoke of the truth, that the only death worth dealing, was to something that could understand why you were doing it.

"Ending a dog doesn't make you a killer. Stabbing a man in the back doesn't give you sand. If you're going to kill a man, kill his soul."

I shoveled the last bit of dirt over Sadie's coffin, standing for a moment before tipping my hat to the grave.

I turned to Liz Hughes, retrieving her knife from where it lay. I watched her for a moment as she worked the knife back into some unseen sheath in the folds of her dress. "You have a shooting iron?"

The girl frowned, shaking her head. "My Ma thinks it ain't befitting a lady to take up pistols."

I took my horse by the reins, mounting up and looking towards the town. "It's befitting anyone who wants it."

She put her hands on her hips. "I already know that. My Pa's the law around here, and he don't take lip from that fat beast calls itself my mother. I can knock every can off a fence and not miss one! Fastest hand in the whole territory, not that any know it."

I looked down at her, wrestling with the urge to shuffle the girl off, lest she tell her father of the strange man carrying an even stranger pistol.

My hand drifted to my unmarred cheek. It felt peculiar not feeling the devil's mark. Plenty of would-be bounty hunters had known me from it. Didn't expect Liz Hughes to know me by anything other than that, or my name.

The girl must've realized how close she'd come to meeting her maker. Her smile disappeared and she made me an oath. "Don't fret. I'm not telling Pa about it. Besides, he ain't fit to go chasing real shootists no more."

I urged the horse forward with my spurs. There was another reason I'd come to this town, a name given to me months ago by a girl who'd told me a story and then suffered the loss of her beauty to a blade. I looked towards the distant lanterns being lit and wondered under which one my quarry rested.

Liz Hughes trailed behind the horse. I reached into my coat and produced two greenbacks, offering them to her. "For your story, Miss Hughes, and your silence."

She snatched the money with greedy hands. "Have my word, Pa won't know I met you."

Made to leave before I felt the tug at the edges of the pit in me, Hell whispering its temptations. Forbidden fruit that I decided to offer Liz Hughes.

"In a few days, I'm heading west. San Francisco. You remember what we spoke tonight? If you decide to take up killing, come find me."

The girl promised she would and then she left, heading home. And I headed into town.

My horse's hooves made wet footfalls, the mud of the street churned up by the men congregating at the saloon, eager to ease their burdens in the comfort of whiskey and women.

I knew that the man I chased was there; word on the trail was that his intent was to write stories about the Night Tribe. And when I stepped through the swinging doors, I saw him sitting like a bloated tick scribbling away and listening to some farmer speak about his dead dog and missing cows.

The music swelled, card players laughing as they threw their hands down to the beat and won their spoils, women pulling their choices to the stairs and the rooms waiting them. I passed through them like a fleeting shadow.

The sodbuster made his leave at my word and I took his place, staring at the portly man, his eyes wide as I placed the pale pistol on the bar between us.

"I hear you've been telling stories, Mr. Beasley."

ACKNOWEDGEMENTS

Thanks to Steve Wands, and the rest of the Dead Sky Publishing team for taking one more ride with the Black Magpie.

Thanks to my mentors, friends, and peers who believed and helped make this possible: Brian Keene, Stephen Kozeniewski, Wesley and Katie Southard, Kenzie Jennings, Mary SanGiovanni, Bob Ford, Somer Canon, Candace Nola, Bridgett Nelson, John Wayne Comunale, and a long list of others I admire.

Thank you to Christine Morgan, a heck of an editor and friend.

Special thanks to departed friends, Dallas Mayr and Jay Wilburn, for advice, time, and laughter I've never forgotten.

Thanks to my wife, Emily, who has stayed with me through the worst and has ridden with me through the best, has labored over and beta-read everything, and who has helpfully told me when I needed a good kick in the pants.

ABOUT THE AUTHOR

Wile E. Young is from Texas, where he grew up surrounded by stories of ghosts and monsters. During his writing career he has managed to both have a price put on his head and win the 2021 Splatterpunk Award for Best Novel. He obtained his bachelor's degree in History, which provided no advantage or benefit during his years as an aviation specialist and I.T. guru.

His longer works includes *Catfish in the Cradle* (2019), *The Perfectly Fine House* (2020), the *Magpie Coffin* (2020), *Shades of the Black Stone* (2022), *Clickers Never Die* (2022), and *Dust Bowl Children* (2022). His short stories have been featured in various anthologies including the *Clickers Forever* (2018), *Behind the Mask—Tales From the Id* (2018), *Corporate Cthulhu* (2018), *And Hell Followed* (2019), *Splatterpunk Bloodstains* (2020) and *Bludgeon Tools: A Splatterpunk Anthology* (2021).